Roche Harbor Rogue

San Juan Islands Mystery Series

Book Five

**The Writer

**Dark Waters

**Murder on Matia

**Rosario's Revenge

**Roche Harbor Rogue

D.W. ULSTERMAN

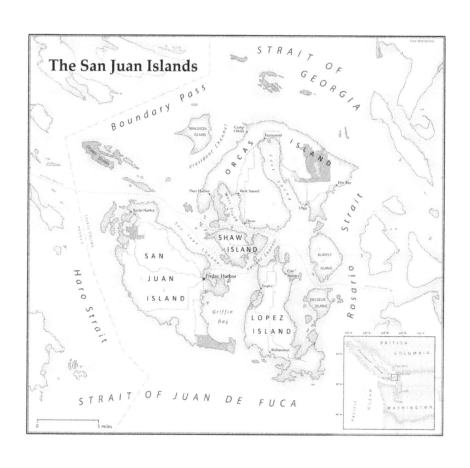

The San Juan Islands

STRAIT OF GEORGIA

Boundary Pass

President Channel

WALDRON ISLAND

Camp Orkila

Eastsound

ORCAS ISLAND

Deer Harbor

West Sound

Deer Bay

Olga

Rosario Strait

Roche Harbor

SAN JUAN ISLAND

SHAW ISLAND

Orcas

BLAKELY ISLAND

Friday Harbor

Port Stanley

Griffin Bay

DECATUR ISLAND

LOPEZ ISLAND

Richardson

Haro Strait

STRAIT OF JUAN DE FUCA

0   5 miles

BRITISH COLUMBIA

PACIFIC OCEAN

WASHINGTON

If you run out of ideas follow the road; you'll get there.

-Edgar Allan Poe

Dedicated to Larry and Judy Gilkerson.

You gave this rogue the most amazing gift ever—your daughter.

I remain forever grateful.

Prologue

"With intensive treatment, best case, you'll have another year, possibly two."

"And without treatment?"

The doctor's mouth tightened. "Six to nine months."

"*That's it*? Are you sure?"

"I'm afraid so. You're welcome to a second opinion, but I've been doing this for some time. Seventeen years in my current position as head of oncology. I know this cancer well. It's a particularly nasty one—highly aggressive."

"What do you recommend? By that I mean, if you were me, what would *you* choose?"

The doctor leaned forward behind his desk. A window overlooking a small garden outside framed his head. It was raining.

"We can initiate treatment immediately. You never know. Sometimes, well, sometimes the cancer is pushed into remission."

"But that's not likely."

"Correct," the doctor said with a nod. "The most probable outcome is what I've already outlined. A year or two with treatment. Six to nine months without."

"You know how I feel about putting poison into my body."

"And you know how I think poison is too strong a term."

The patient's eyes narrowed. "No, it's not. That's *exactly* what chemo is. I'll lose my hair."

"Hair grows back. The side effects are temporary."

"But death is permanent. How long would the treatments take?"

The doctor cleared his throat. "The first round will be two sessions per week for six weeks. Then we'll reevaluate based upon how the cancer reacts. Most often a second round is initiated a few months later. The body requires time to recover."

"From the poison."

"I'm sorry?"

"You want to give my body time to recover from the poison you'll be pumping into it."

The doctor's scowl lasted no more than a few seconds, but the smile that replaced it was forced. He ran a long-fingered hand through the shock of thick white hair atop his head.

"I'm a physician. I consider it treatment. You're the patient. You can call it whatever you like."

"How many patients have you treated for the same kind of cancer that I have?"

"Twelve."

The patient's brows arched. "You answered that quickly."

"I remember nearly every patient I've ever had, and each new case is a new challenge."

"And how many did you manage to save?"

The doctor's jaw clenched. He looked down at his folded hands. "None."

"They're dead? All twelve of them?"

"Yes."

"I'm not ready to die, Doctor."

"Indeed. None of us truly are. I'm very sorry I couldn't give you better news. That said, I *am* confident the treatments will extend your life some."

"But at what cost?" When the doctor didn't reply, the patient continued. "I'll spend a third of that extra time you're promising going to and from the hospital so you can stick a needle into my arm and inject me full of toxic chemo chemicals. And in the end, I still most likely die."

The doctor's tone was cold. "Yes, that's true."

"So, why bother with the treatment at all?"

"It'll give you more time."

"A few months? A year? Most of which I'll spend sicker from the chemo than I would have been with just the cancer."

"We don't know that for sure."

The patient took in a deep breath and then let it out. "Exactly."

The doctor tilted his head. "What do you mean?"

"I mean there's not much upside to going through with the chemo. I don't want to waste a single day cooped up in a hospital with a needle jammed into my arm, or on the floor of a bathroom puking my guts out or looking in the mirror and not recognizing the face staring back at me. I won't do it."

"You're refusing treatment?" the doctor said while blinking rapidly. "Perhaps you should give it another day or two before deciding. This has been a lot to take in. While I understand your reservations regarding treatment, I strongly urge you to give yourself more time to think it over."

"You still haven't answered my question."

"What question was that?"

"If you were me what would *you* do? Take the treatment or not? Don't answer as my doctor. Answer as if you were the patient but with the knowledge a doctor like you has regarding side effects and likely outcomes."

"I'm not sure I can do that."

"Why not?"

"My job is to do everything in my power to heal my patients."

"But you've already told me I won't get better. The cancer *will* kill me. It's inevitable."

"Yes, but the treatment will give you more time. And you never know. Miracles do happen."

"But not to any of your patients. Not the ones who had the same cancer then as I do now."

"There's a first time for everything."

"Did any of those patients refuse the treatment you suggested?"

The doctor shook his head. "No."

"Okay," the patient said with a shrug. "This will be a first time then. I'm going to take my chances without the treatment. No offense but I'd rather be in full control of whatever time I have left."

"Even if it's just six months?"

"Yeah. If that's it then that's it."

"You won't reconsider?"

The patient stood. "Thank you, Doctor. I'm sorry to have been the cause of the news you had to deliver today. It can't get any easier having to tell someone they're going to die. I don't envy this job of yours."

"I'm the one who's supposed to be comforting *you*," the doctor said while getting up. He shook the patient's hand. "Where will you go?"

"Wherever I want," the patient said with a wide smile. "I have the means and I always feel better after a decision has been made."

"There'll be times when you won't feel better. You do understand that, right? Some days, and they may come sooner than you think, some days will be very difficult. The pain will be intense to the point of debilitation. It'll consume you. At the very least let me write you a prescription for morphine. It'll help to take the edge off."

"No need. I'll manage. I want to keep my head clear. I don't wish to waste a single day lost in the fog of medication."

"You should also consider the likelihood of facing the fog of considerable physical pain. Without treatment the tumors will continue to spread unchecked, particularly the ones in your abdomen."

"Fine. So be it."

The doctor stared directly into the patient's eyes. "I'm not sure if I should admire your remarkable resilience in the face of such a grim prognosis or question your mental competence."

"Perhaps it would be easier to do both. Either way, I've made up my mind while it's still mine to do so."

"That you have. Will I be seeing you again?"

"No, I don't think you will. My time might be small but that doesn't mean I have to live like it is. In fact, I intend to live bigger than I ever have. Don't worry about me, Doctor. I'm good."

"Yeah?"

The patient nodded. "Yeah."

The doctor rapped the desk with his knuckles. "Okay. I guess it's good luck to you then. Please do me a favor though. Regardless of where you go, if you ever need anything, or change your mind about receiving treatment or medication, or any questions you might have, don't hesitate to contact me."

"I will. Thanks again." The patient turned around and reached for the door.

"Wait," the doctor said. "Can you at least give me an idea as to where it is you intend to go?"

The patient answered without looking back. "To the place of all our beginnings."

"Where is that?"

"The water."

And with that final reply, the patient was gone.

1.

"**G**od, how I hate having to look at that thing staring back at me. It's a monstrosity of arrogance. Why of all places did he have to build it *there*?"

Adele wished to avoid delving too deeply into Tilda's dissatisfaction over the location of Roland's new home so attempted indifference with a quick shrug. "I guess he likes the views."

"Oh, does he? How nice for him that those views include looking down onto *my* hotel. Had I known the property up on the hill behind the resort was for sale I would have bought it myself to prevent the very thing that's happening to it now. Shame on him. The size of it alone leads me to believe it's nothing more than a desperate attempt at overcompensation. I mean *really*? What single man requires a home with *seven* bedrooms? All that ridiculous copper and that gothic tower—it's absurd."

"I think it looks amazing." Adele regretted the words as soon as they sped past her lips.

The sound of hammering from the construction of Roland's hillside home filtered into Tilda's private quarters on the top floor of the Victorian-themed Roche Harbor Hotel. She put her teacup down. "Amazing? No. That certainly isn't the word that comes to *my* mind. Then again, you're much closer to Roland Soros than I'll ever be. It's only natural your tolerance for his showing off is far greater than my own."

Adele rolled her eyes. "Oh, Tilda, it's just a house on a hill."

"Hah! There it is."

"What?"

Tilda smirked. "There's the loyalty you've come to be so well known for, particularly in matters concerning Roland Soros and Sheriff Lucas Pine. Ah, to be young again and in your position. Decisions, decisions . . ."

"I came here for afternoon tea not to be teased."

"It wasn't so long ago you were far too afraid of me to take such a tone."

Adele raised her cup. "Here's to realizing Tilda Ashland is a woman with more bark than bite."

"Oh, you really *are* in a feisty mood. Could it be all that success with the newspaper is finally going to your head?"

"No, I'm just far less patient than I once was. It's most likely you rubbing off on me."

Tilda grinned. "Touché." She took a sip of tea and a nibble from her cucumber sandwich. "Not that I wish to pry, but have you spoken with Roland recently? I haven't seen him around."

"He's still in New York."

"Really? What for?"

Adele shrugged. "He didn't say. I believe he's supposed to be back tomorrow. Why do you ask?"

It was Tilda's turn to shrug. "Oh, no reason."

Adele scowled. "Tilda, what's going on? Did you hear something?"

"Why would you think I heard something?"

"Because you just shrugged. You *never* shrug."

"That's silly. Everyone shrugs."

Adele shook her head and pointed to her friend. "Not you. I remember when you told me once how shrugging made one appear indifferent or clueless, neither of which was acceptable for a person who wanted to be taken seriously by others."

"I said that?"

"Yes, you most certainly did. Now, tell me what's going on with Roland."

"It was a rumor, nothing more."

"Okay, what's the rumor?"

"Never mind."

"No," Adele said. "You don't get to do that. You brought it up and you're not one to say something on accident, which means you really do want to tell me. Now I've twisted your arm enough, so you don't have to feel guilty. Go ahead. Spill it."

"This is off the record. You didn't hear it from me."

"Off the record? You think this is something that's newsworthy?"

"Yes, most definitely but promise me this stays between us. I mean it, Adele."

"Now you *really* have my attention. Okay, I promise."

Tilda crossed her legs and straightened her long skirt so that the bottom of the fabric brushed up against the tops of her shoes. "It has to do with the bank. It's just a rumor and I really have no idea how much truth is behind it."

Adele waited. After pausing for a moment Tilda continued.

"I was in Bellingham last week meeting with my financial adviser, getting some things in order and whatnot. Toward the end of our meeting he asked me what I thought about Mr. Soros accepting an offer to sell the bank in Friday Harbor. I told him that was the first I'd heard of it. Now you tell me Roland went to New York for reasons he didn't wish to share with you and I can't help but think the two things are very much related."

"Roland selling the bank? I don't know if I can see him doing something like that. It's his family's legacy."

Tilda arched a brow. "Hmm. Yes, but it would also be a great deal of money and we both know how Roland favors cash. He's certainly spending plenty of it on the construction of that eyesore on the hill. Do you intend to ask him about it when he gets back?"

"Definitely. Say, why were you getting some things in order with your financial adviser? Is everything okay?"

"Oh, yes, everything's fine. Just a bit of planning is all. I'm not getting any younger you know."

Though she would never say it out loud, Adele agreed that Tilda was finally starting to show the wear and tear of time. "But you *are* okay, right? No health issues?"

Tilda stood and shook her long, silver-streaked red hair so that it fell behind her shoulders and covered much of her back. "I assure you I'm fine, but I also know that as sharp-eyed as you are these lines on my face haven't gone unnoticed. I really don't fret about old age but would rather not have to feel it. Would you mind if we finish our tea outside on the balcony?"

Adele got up and smiled. "That sounds good. I think the sun is trying to crack through all the clouds. It's just a few more weeks until spring and I'm more than done with all this cold rain."

The two women stood next to each other on the balcony holding their teacups and staring down at the marina below. In another month it would be scurrying with pre-summer activity but on this day, nobody moved on the docks. Even the typical early afternoon wind was taking a break.

"You're looking as fit as ever," Tilda said. "Are you still taking karate lessons in Bellingham?"

"It's taekwondo," Adele answered. "And yes, I earned my green belt just last week."

"Green, is that good?"

Adele smiled. "For me it is."

"Could you give someone a thrashing?"

"I suppose. Maybe. I don't know. That's not really why I'm doing it."

Tilda leaned against the white railing. "Oh?"

"All the stress, the mind racing, it just melts away when I'm training. It's become sort of an addiction, but the kind that doesn't mess you up but rather makes you stronger. I've never felt better."

Tilda's voice lowered to a near whisper. "And if the Russian mafia returns, you could defend yourself?"

"Lucas hasn't heard anything new regarding the Russians. He's been in regular contact with the Canadian authorities and is almost certain that we've seen the last of them."

"As much as I appreciate the protective instincts of our beloved Sheriff Pine, I don't think the Russians are in the business of announcing their intentions beforehand. You sent one of theirs to his death on the cliffs of Rosario, remember?"

Adele's eyes flashed her annoyance. "Of course. That's not something I'll ever forget."

Tilda put a hand on Adele's arm. "I didn't mean to bring up a bad memory. I apologize. It's just . . ."

"Just *what*?"

"I worry about you. You're the closest thing I'll ever have to a daughter."

"I never thought of you as the mothering type."

Tilda's thin smile complemented the playful gleam in her eyes. "Don't make me send you to bed without your supper."

Adele put her tea down and her fists up. "Hah! I'd like to see you try, old woman."

"Old woman?" Tilda's features tightened. "How could you?"

Adele's eyes got big. "Oh, I'm so sorry. I didn't mean it."

Tilda threw her head back and laughed. "I was kidding," she said. "I may be old, but I'm not without a sense of humor. My goodness. Do you really think me to be so thin-skinned? C'mon, let's go back inside. This air is chilling me to the bone."

The two sat down and enjoyed a second cup of tea and some more idle chatter until eventually Tilda's tone grew serious again. "Roland isn't the only one I haven't seen around here in some time. How is Lucas doing?"

"He's fine. Fully recovered from his injuries and happy to have the re-election campaign behind him."

"Are you two still close?"

Adele could feel her cheeks turning red. She hated that she blushed so easily. "We're good."

The gleam in Tilda's eyes returned. "Good as in friends or good as in something more?"

"Good as in it's none of your business thank you very much."

"Ah, I'll take that as a yes."

Adele knew she was being toyed with but didn't mind. She enjoyed the back and forth that almost always accompanied a conversation with Tilda. "Yes, that we're friends or yes that we're something more?"

"I'm still waiting for you to tell me."

"Then sit back and relax because you'll be waiting for a while. Fact is I'm not really sure of the answer to that myself. Neither of us wants to do something that hurts our friendship."

"So, you're both scared?"

"No, we're both being careful."

"Is there a difference?"

Adele nodded. "Yes, there most certainly is. Now please change the subject."

"Assuming the rumors about Roland selling the bank are true, could the two things be related?"

"What two things?"

"You choosing Lucas over Roland and his decision to cash out the family business."

Adele struggled to keep her composure. "I haven't chosen anyone, and nobody has chosen me. Lucas and I are currently just friends. That's it."

"And what about Roland?"

"What about him? Same thing—just friends."

"So, you've managed to stick the two most eligible bachelors on these islands into the friend room? Why, Adele, I never knew you could be so cruel. Well done, young woman. Well done."

Tilda got up and went to the window while sipping the last of her tea. Something she saw outside made her frown.

"What is it?" Adele asked her.

"There's a man on the docks standing next to your sailboat. Come here and have a look for yourself."

Adele put her face close enough to the glass she nearly touched it with her nose. The man was tall, lean, and wore a tweed ivy cap. His dark pea coat was buttoned tightly around wide shoulders and a slim waist. He kept glancing at something in his hand and then looking at the sailboat.

"Do you recognize him?"

Adele shook her head. "I've never seen him before."

"Well, he certainly appears very interested in your little home. You know, there's something vaguely familiar about him, but I can't quite put my finger on it—like a faint reflection of a memory just beyond my ability to recall."

"He doesn't look too dangerous."

Tilda squinted at the glass. "Dangerous? No, not dangerous and certainly not a Russian. He does have a roguish quality about him though."

Adele whirled around and headed for the door. Tilda started to follow. "What are you doing?"

"I'm going to go down there and ask this mysterious Roche Harbor rogue why he's hanging out in front of my boat."

"By yourself?"

"Yes, by myself, though you're welcome to come with me if you want."

Tilda appeared startled by the invite. "Oh, well, I think I probably should. Just let me get my coat." She scurried into the adjoining bedroom.

Adele folded her arms and tapped her foot. "Hurry up old woman. I don't have all day."

When Tilda returned wearing a dark wool trench coat, she gave Adele a hard look that was difficult to tell how serious she was. "There'll be no more of *that*, young lady. Green belt or not, don't think for second I still can't break the likes of you in half."

Adele wasn't sure how true that was, and she had no intention of ever finding out.

2.

"Excuse me. Can I help you?"

The clean-shaved face that turned around to greet Adele was handsome in a uniquely unconventional way. Like the body it was attached to it was also long and lean. The deep-set blue-green eyes were similar in color to the waters that surrounded the San Juan Islands. His warm smile revealed slightly crooked white teeth. When he removed his cap, the light brown hair underneath was a disheveled mess. The entirety of his features reminded Adele of geometry—a mix of sharp angles that bordered on awkward but that collectively somehow managed to make sense.

"You're the owner of this sailboat, yeah?"

Adele glanced at Tilda and then nodded. "I am."

The man's smile widened. "Oh, that's lovely. I can't believe I found it so quickly. Just about walked right up to it. The picture seemed the same, but you never know. One boat can look so much like another."

That voice, Adele thought. *I know that voice.*

It was deep, playful, and thickly accented. Adele felt something and looked down to see Tilda nudging her.

"Are you thinking what I'm thinking?" she whispered.

"Huh?"

Tilda leaned in closer. "He sounds just like him. It's remarkable."

"What do you mean?"

"The accent—it's Irish." Tilda rolled her eyes. "Oh, for heaven's sake. You're supposed to be the investigative reporter here. He sounds exactly like Delroy."

Delroy Hicks was the man largely responsible for Adele's permanent residence on the islands. It was his sailboat she called home in the Roche Harbor marina. He had meant it as a graduation gift—one that would allow her some time to find herself without having to deal with the burden of paying rent. Adele still felt Delroy's playful presence inside the boat's cozy cocoon.

The man put his cap back on and cleared his throat. "Uh, the sailboat was my father's. It's my understanding he called it home for quite some time."

Adele looked up at Tilda who in turn arched her brows. "See," she said. "That's what I was trying to tell you. As you well know, Delroy's manner of speaking, that voice, it was unmistakably his own." Tilda looked the man up and down. "What's your name, young man?"

"I'm really not so young. I'm 36."

Tilda's smile resembled a grimace. "From where I'm standing 36 is still plenty young. Now tell us your name."

"Of course. My given name is Finnian Kearns, but for as long as I can recall everyone just called me Fin."

Adele recovered quickly from the shock of hearing Delroy's voice again as her investigative instincts took over. "Why are you here, Mr. Kearns? Is it about the boat? Because if it is—"

Fin shook his head. "No, that's not it. I wouldn't travel all the way from Ireland for a boat. Goodness no. Time is far too precious to be wasted on something so material as that. It's what the boat represents."

Adele cocked her head. "What do you mean by *represents*?"

A sudden gust of wind nearly blew his cap off before Fin pulled it tighter over his head. "Is your name Adele?" he asked. "Adele Plank?"

"How do you know my name?"

Fin smiled. Adele didn't. "Your newspaper," he replied. "I read it online all the time."

"Is that right?"

"Yes. I assure you my motive for being here is in no way a threat to you, Ms. Plank. I'm a huge fan of your work. The stories of your adventures, well, they're quite remarkable."

"I've never included a photo of my sailboat in any of my articles, Mr. Kearns. How did you know to find it, and me, here?"

"Again, from your articles. Oh, and this picture as well." Fin removed a photograph from his pocket and handed it to Adele. It was of her sailboat. On the back written in ink it said, *My home, Roche Harbor.*

"It was sent to my mother in Ireland."

Adele stared at the words and then looked up. "I recognize Delroy's writing." She handed the photo back to Fin. "How did he know your mother?"

"Ah," Fin said as he put the picture back into his coat pocket. "I was told by her that they were friends, then for a brief time they were lovers. I was the result of that . . . experiment."

"Experiment?"

Fin nodded. "Yes, that was my mother's word for it. Back then, my father apparently had an undeniably adventurous spirit when it came to matters of the heart. He traveled a great deal with his work as a professor and author of anthropology, met many different people, and had quite a lust for life. He was neither heterosexual nor homosexual but rather an opportunist."

"That's a long-winded way of saying the younger version of Delroy was a shameless slut." Tilda chuckled. "No offense intended."

"None taken. My mother would have agreed."

"Would have?" Adele said.

Fin shoved both hands into his pockets and shrugged. "Yes, she passed away last year. Told me about my father just days before it happened. The photo of the sailboat came from a box of letters he used to send to her after the relationship ended. Mother never replied. Not even once. She kept her relationship with Delroy a secret for all those years. After some time passed, I decided I'd journey here to try to learn more about him."

Tilda's eyes widened. "So, Delroy never knew he had a son?"

"No. Mother made that quite clear. He never knew about me."

Tilda clicked her tongue. "My goodness, there's more than a bit of tragedy in that. I don't care for people generally, but even I tolerated Delroy while many more on these islands loved him dearly."

Fin's face brightened. "Yes, like his friend the famous author." He looked at Adele. "I know of him from your articles as well. I had to march right on out and find a copy of his book, *Manitoba*. Didn't like it. Not even a little. Rather long-winded for my taste."

The sound of Tilda's laughter was carried on the wind as it skipped across the marina waters. Adele couldn't recall ever hearing her laugh so hard. Tilda extended her hand and stepped forward.

"I'm so pleased to finally meet someone who'll admit to *not* liking Decklan's oh-so-famous opus. My name is Tilda, Tilda Ashland."

"That's right," Fin said while shaking hands. "You own the beautiful old hotel over there. It's wonderful to now see it in person." His gaze continued up to the top of the hill behind the resort and then his brows drew together. "What is *that* supposed to be? It almost looks like a castle."

Tilda's lips pressed together as she shook her head. "*That* is a big waste of money by a man with far too much of it while also having an equal deficit of common sense. Funny how those two qualities so often go together."

Fin snapped his fingers. "Roland Soros. Am I right? That's his building."

"You seem to know an awful lot about us, Mr. Kearns," Adele said, "but we know so little about you."

"That only makes sense. It's from your wonderful stories. Every article is like another thrilling chapter in your lives. I felt as if we were already friends before I even arrived here. So, I take it I guessed correctly? That is Roland Soros's house? *The* Roland Soros? Oh! And what about the sheriff? Lucas Pine? Is he here as well? I would love to meet him. The writer, Decklan Stone, his wife Calista, Roland Soros, and Lucas Pine, I'd love to meet *all* of them."

"I'm afraid you'll have to settle for just Tilda and me for now. Both the sheriff and Roland are out of town and Decklan and Calista are traveling abroad again. They won't be back until the summer."

"Ah, that's fine, that's fine," Fin replied. "You're the real reason I'm here, Ms. Plank. It's having access to you that's most important."

Tilda stepped forward, putting herself between Fin and Adele. "Why do have such a strong interest in her? And don't lie to me. I'll be able tell."

Fin's smile dissipated like fog bombarded by the heat of Tilda's sun. "I merely meant that it was her stories that made my coming here such a necessity, namely her friendship with a father I never knew. In fact, I was hoping it might be possible for me to see inside his sailboat. I'm just looking for a bit of closure—the chance to understand who Delroy really was."

"It's *my* sailboat," Adele answered. "And it's really not worth much if that's what you're after."

Fin glared at Adele. It was just a moment, but she saw it. The accusation annoyed him. "This isn't about money," he said.

"You understand our suspicions, right?" Tilda remained in protector mode. "A stranger shows up unannounced poking around and then announces he's the biological son of a man everyone here knew as being a happily devoted homosexual. I admit to being intrigued by your story, Mr. Kearns, perhaps even charmed by it, but we're a close-knit group on these islands and don't easily suffer those who would attempt to take advantage. And if you feel I'm being overprotective of Ms. Plank, wait until you meet Sheriff

Pine. If he has any suspicion of wrongdoing on your part that involves Adele, he's likely to break you in half first and ask questions later. This young woman means a great deal to a great many of us. Am I making myself clear?"

Fin took off his cap, held it in both hands, and nodded. "I apologize. Perhaps my coming was a mistake. At the very least I should have been more considerate of the backstory and its impact on those here who knew my father."

"You can see inside the boat," Adele said.

Tilda's head snapped around. "*What*?"

Adele moved past her. "It's okay. You've done nothing wrong coming here, Fin. I should be the one to apologize. I'm being rude. The memory of your father and all that I owe him deserves better."

Fin's voice cracked. "Thank you. It really would mean a lot to see his home. To sit where he sat and look out at this wonderous place as he once did."

"Have a look around. It won't take long. There's hardly room to move in there, really. We can talk. I'll do my best to answer your questions about Delroy, and then, if it's okay with Tilda, we'll walk up to the hotel and enjoy a drink by the fire."

Tilda pointed to Fin. "If you do one little thing out of line, Mr. Kearns, you'll be the next log I burn on that fire. I promise you that."

"I'll be on my very best behavior, Lady Ashland."

"Cut the 'lady' crap. Men who attempt to play cute don't work with me. I have my eyes on you, Mr. Kearns, and I don't blink."

Adele looked at Fin and then tilted her head toward the sailboat. "C'mon, we better get going before Tilda convinces herself she really doesn't like you. She's getting that look about her."

"What look is that?" Fin asked.

"Believe me," Adele said with mock seriousness, "you don't want to find out." She smiled at Tilda. "We'll be done here soon. Couple hours at most. See you at the hotel?"

The wind whipped Tilda's long hair around her head and shoulders as she stared at Fin and nodded. "I'll be waiting."

3.

The tour of the sailboat's cramped quarters was brief. Fin sat at the small pull-out dining table adjacent to the galley and looked around. "Hard to imagine that a man who I'm told had such a big personality lived in such a small space for so long."

Adele joined Fin at the table. "When it came to resting his head, I don't think Delroy required much. He was a big personality but appreciated the simple things. I knew him as a much older man than your mother did. He'd get tired easily due to age and illness, but he still enjoyed a good time and a bit of adventure."

Fin leaned forward, his eyes as wide as his smile. "Go on. Tell me more about him. That is, if you don't mind."

"I won't ever mind remembering Delroy Hicks. He truly was one of a kind. The fact is I wouldn't have been able to save Calista Stone if it wasn't for your father's help. He was right there with me, ignoring the danger, offering advice, and pushing forward. I know Decklan and Calista will be forever grateful to him for that."

"Yes, that trouble with the old sheriff and that remarkable mystery of Calista's disappearance that played out on these islands for decades. I read every word of your article about it and then all the other media reports that followed. I still find it hard to believe I'm sitting here talking to you in person. It's a bit of a mind bender, yeah? You're so famous yet . . . here we are."

Adele scrunched her face up. "Famous? No. Hardly. I'm just me. Especially around here."

"Ah, you're far too humble, Ms. Plank. You *are* famous. I'd wager that where I come from that little paper of yours is read by more people online than the *Dublin Daily*."

"Oh," Adele said while suddenly getting up. "I almost forgot. I have something I know you'll want to see." She went into the stateroom and came back holding a framed photograph of Delroy and her sitting together and laughing while hanging their legs over the bow of the sailboat. She handed it to Fin. "It was taken just a few weeks before he passed."

Fin looked down at the image and then blinked back tears. "He looks so small. My mother said he was a wisp of a man but surprisingly strong. Like a reed that bends but never breaks."

"What Delroy lacked in physical stature he more than made up for in character and intelligence. The world would be a far better place with more like him."

A seagull cried out as it flew over the boat. "This was my father's place," Fin said. "And now it's yours. I'm glad to know he passed it on to you just as I'm also pleased that you were able to provide him one final adventure before the cancer took him." He traced Delroy's image with the tip of a finger. "Too many die alone. You made certain he wasn't one of those." Fin handed the photograph back. "Thank you."

"How did your parents meet? I assume it was in Ireland."

Fin nodded. "Yes. Mother explained how Delroy was there studying the gypsies. He took to their world like a fish to water and they in turn welcomed him just as warmly."

"Gypsies?"

'Yes, gypsies, travelers, or the more derogative term, pikies. It's a wandering community of some 30,000 throughout Ireland with roots dating back to the Middle Ages along with their Romani cousins in Europe."

"You sound a lot like Delroy right now. He loved talking about such things."

The comment clearly pleased Fin. He folded his hands together and leaned forward. "I don't have a formal education beyond my basic schooling but have always had a natural inclination toward such things. I suppose you could say I'm self-taught."

"Your mother was a traveler?"

"Partly on her father's side. She did regular business with them—horse business."

"Horses?"

'Yes, she raised them just like her father and grandfather did before her. Given her gypsy blood, they trusted her. Horses are a major part of the traveler lifestyle. A good horse is valued more than gold. Delroy was living among the gypsies for his research and the gypsies eventually introduced him to my mother as they bartered with her for a mare she was selling. They were inseparable for weeks after that and then he left to return to the university here in America."

"And you arrived into the world not long after."

Fin's faint smile was distant with a touch of pain. "Indeed, I did."

Adele reached across the table and lightly squeezed his hand. "Thank you for making the trip. I'm happy you're here."

"As am I, Ms. Plank."

"Call me Adele."

The twinkle in Fin's eyes was so much like his father's it both delighted Adele and also made her a little sad. "Adele it is," he said with a wink and another crooked grin.

The two continued to talk like old friends. Adele found Fin to be a mixture of easy charm and curiosity that she soon felt completely at ease with. He described his home village of 1200 in the middle of Ireland's interior located an hour's drive north of Waterford and how his mother had sold the old family property prior to her death and then left the proceeds to him with instructions that he was to go off and see a bit of the world. "That was one of her great regrets," he said. "She was always working and never took the time to properly get away from the drudgery of everyday life and didn't want me making that same mistake. So, I took that money and came here to walk in my father's footsteps. I think that would have made her very happy. I don't think she necessarily loved Delroy, but she made clear she adored their time together."

"And without him there wouldn't have been you and it's clear your mother was especially grateful to have had you in her life."

"Yeah," Fin said with a nod. "Pitiful consolation prize that I am."

At Fin's urging, Adele described some of the mysteries she had published in the newspaper, including the conflict with the Russians. "Do you think it's really over between you and them?" he asked.

"It's impossible to know for certain, but I sure hope so. They're a nasty bunch who have no business infecting a place as beautiful as this." When Fin grew quiet, Adele looked at him with narrowed eyes. "What is it?"

"Nah, my thinking is out of line. Never mind."

"Go on, say whatever it is you want to say. You didn't travel all this way to go mute on me."

"I was just wondering, well, what was it like killing that big Russian fellow? Does such a thing haunt you? I imagine it couldn't have been easy to take a life regardless of how much he deserved it."

Adele sat back and bit down on her lip as Fin began to fidget. "Ah, geez. I went and did it. Me and my big mouth. I don't know when to keep it shut. I apologize. It was a terribly rude question."

"No need to apologize," Adele said. "I'm the one who told you to say what was on your mind. Do I regret having to kill someone? Yes. Am I glad I did it? Absolutely. It was either him or me. I chose him."

Fin scratched under his chin as he stared at Adele. "Good on you for putting up such a powerful fight that day. Many wouldn't have regardless of whether they were a man or a woman. You've the heart of a warrior, Adele Plank. I can see that clearly and I'm certain my father saw the same. I wonder though."

"You wonder what?"

Fin's smile was full of playful mischief. "I wonder if you were more concerned with saving the lives of Lucas Pine and Roland Soros than your own. And then I can't help but further wonder which of them you'd wish to save first. Those two names are on the tongues of the women in my village often and many an argument has been the result."

"What in the world are you talking about?"

"Why, team Lucas versus team Roland of course."

Adele started to laugh and then suddenly stopped. "Wait. You're actually serious?"

"Oh, yes. Where I come from, on some days, it's all anyone wishes to talk about."

"They talk about Roland and Lucas?"

"Indeed, they do—*and you*. More specifically, which one you'll end up choosing."

Adele dropped her head and sighed. "Oh, now I understand."

Fin wagged his finger at her. "Methinks this isn't the first time someone has had a bit of fun with this subject."

"No, it isn't." Adele decided to turn the tables on Fin. "So, you seem like an intelligent man capable of forming a reasonable opinion. Tell me. Which one should I choose?"

"Eh?"

"Yeah, go ahead. Is it Lucas or Roland?"

When Fin's confusion caused him to start stammering, Adele slapped the table. "Hurry up. I don't have all day, you nosey potato-eater."

Fin's deep-throated laugh was almost exactly like his father's. "Ah, you got me. I thought you were being serious. Lucas or Roland—I haven't yet met either of the two lads yet. Until then I'll just have to wait before forming a proper opinion on the matter."

"Stick around and you'll get to. They're bound to show up here sooner or later."

"That would be grand. I'd like that. Say, I have a question. I suppose it's a bit out of left field, but I read about it in a travel journal years ago and thought I'd see if you knew anything about it."

Adele was instantly intrigued. "Sure, go ahead."

"I was wondering if you'd ever heard anything regarding the supposed healing powers to be found on Orcas Island. Apparently, Oprah bought a place there for that very reason."

"Oprah? As in Winfrey?"

Fin's eyes were dancing again. "Yeah, is there any other? She's into all that power of the earth stuff, health and long life, right?"

"I suppose we all are to some degree. I mean, who doesn't want to live longer and healthier? I've never been much of an Oprah fan, though you can't deny she's created a lot of success for herself."

"You didn't know she bought a place somewhere on the island?"

Adele shrugged. "We get a lot of celebrities here. The locals don't pay them much mind, which I assume is a big draw to people in the public eye who want to get away for some peace and quiet."

"Like your friend the writer."

"Decklan? Yeah, he's definitely a 'just leave me be' kind of man. You really think there's something to the article you read?"

"Oh, I don't know. That's why I was asking. It fascinated me is all. I recall it mentioning something about an ancient magnetic vortex that runs through much of the island and the waters surrounding it. Apparently, there's only a handful of places in all the world with a similar phenomenon. People seek them out for their alleged healing powers."

"That's news to me. I'll ask around. Now that you brought it up, I won't be able to help myself. I have to find out more."

"That's likely what makes you such a successful investigative reporter. You're among those who suffer from insatiable curiosity."

Adele grunted. "I suffer all right. You ready to head to the hotel?"

Fin stood and smiled. "After you."

Once outside he paused to admire the Chris Craft Lancer that shared the sailboat slip. "That's yours as well?"

Adele didn't hide the pride she felt toward the little diesel-powered cruiser that she had purchased last year from one of the island's longtime locals. Since then, she and the boat were inseparable as she used it to further explore the endless nooks and crannies of the San Juan Islands. "That," she said, "is my ticket to ride."

"You think I might join you on the water sometime soon?"

"Sure. If you can handle it. Chop or no chop, I like to go fast. You might get a little wet—or seasick."

"With you behind the wheel I'm sure I'll be in good hands."

Adele nodded. "Better than most." She looked up at the hotel. "We best get going. It's never a good idea to keep Tilda waiting."

"Indeed. That woman scares the hell out of me."

"Yeah," Adele said, chuckling. "She tends to have that effect on people. Trust me, though, when your back is against the wall, Tilda Ashland is who you want fighting by your side."

Fin stood on the dock with his arms crossed while looking up at the hotel and the resort's other white with green trim buildings, most of which were more than a century old. "I see now why my father chose to live here," he said. "It reminds me so much of home. Yet, it's different. It's better." He glanced back at Adele. "There really is some sort of magic to this place."

Adele closed her eyes, lifted her head, and enjoyed the contrast of cold wind and warm memories. Her brief reply was a whisper of her own accumulated experience since coming to the islands—a change in course that undeniably altered her life for the better. Another seagull's strident wail seemed to urge her to hurry up and say the words.

"I know."

4.

ADele stopped walking toward the hotel when she realized she was being closely watched by an attractive, dark-haired woman standing at the top of the marina entrance. It was Marianne Rocha, the Seattle-based television news reporter who, it was rumored, had taken a keen interest in Roland since first getting to know him while she investigated all the related trouble with the Russian mafia for a news story last year.

"Nice to see you again, Ms. Plank," Marianne said with a wave.

"Who's that?" Fin murmured.

"Potential trouble."

"She's very attractive."

"Yeah," Adele growled between clenched teeth.

Marianne looked like she had just walked off a television studio. A dark skirt hugged her thighs while the tight white sweater she wore struggled to contain the generous swells of her breasts that also happened to be announcing how cold it was outside for all the world to see. "I was just on my way down to your boat," she said.

Adele continued walking up the marina ramp. "Why?"

Marianne gave Fin a long look and then stuck out her hand. "Hello. My name is Marianne Rocha, Action Five News."

"I'm Fin Kearns." The two shook hands. "Nice to meet you. You're in the news business, eh? Just like Adele."

Marianne flashed her perfect, brilliant white smile. "Yes, I suppose we do share an interest in getting to the bottom of a story. Your accent—is it British?"

"God no," Fin said with a grimace. "I'm from Ireland."

"What brings you all the way to the islands, Mr. Kearns?"

Before Fin could respond, Adele intervened. "I was about to ask you the same thing, Marianne. What are you doing here?"

"Perhaps we could go inside to talk? It's chilly out here."

"Yeah," Adele said. "I noticed. We're on our way to the hotel. You're welcome to tag along. Is this about a story you're working on?"

"I'd rather not say until we're inside."

Adele looked back at her. "Suit yourself."

Tilda sat by herself in front of the fire inside the hotel lobby. She glanced at Adele and Fin and then did a double-take and got up when she noticed Marianne coming in with them. "Hello. Would you like a room?" she asked.

"No," Marianne answered. "I'm just here to see Ms. Plank."

Tilda arched a brow. "I remember you. You're the news woman who made all those false accusations against Sheriff Pine last summer. You've once again crawled out from under your big city rock I see."

Marianne wilted under Tilda's hard gaze. "It's okay," Adele said. "This won't take long. We'll sit down at that table over there." She looked at Marianne. "You have ten minutes."

Fin appeared nervous at being left alone with Tilda until she poured them each a shot of whiskey. He dropped into a comfortable leather chair, held up the glass, grinned at Adele, and then drank it down. "I'll be fine," he said. "You go have your talk. Me and old iron britches will hold down the fort here."

"Iron *what*?" Tilda hissed.

Fin's mouth dropped open. "Oh, uh, I assure you I said it with affection."

"And you won't be saying it again. *Understood*?"

"Yes ma'am."

Adele walked across the lobby's wood floor and sat down at a small circular table as Marianne scurried to join her. "How do you know Mr. Kearns?" she asked while taking the seat across from Adele.

"That's none of your business. Just focus on why you're here. Your ten minutes start now."

"There's no need to be like that."

"Like what?"

"Like such a . . ."

"Go on," Adele said. "Say it. You know you want to."

Marianne folded her hands in front of her and took a deep breath. "We might never be the best of friends, Ms. Plank, but I believe my intentions for coming here are good. It concerns someone we both care for."

Adele waited to hear more.

Marianne continued. "It involves Roland."

"What about him?"

"Do you know where he is? Have you spoken with him recently?"

"I'll give you a yes on the first question and a no on the second. Hurry up and get to the specific reason why you're here."

"I'm worried about him."

"Roland? Why?"

Marianne cleared her throat. "I'm not sure if you know but we've had a few dates. They seemed to go well at first. And then . . ."

"And then what?"

"He became different. Tired. Irritable. Distracted. Like something was really bothering him—something he refused to share with me."

"Maybe he lost interest but didn't want to hurt your feelings."

When Marianne scowled, it made her appear even more beautiful, like a forlorn, dark-haired Ingrid Bergman. "I don't think that was it. Just like I don't think Roland is the kind of man who would string someone along. If he didn't want to see me anymore, as unlikely as that is, he'd tell me."

"Look, Roland is a complicated man. There are a lot of layers there. Even I don't know all there is to know about him. I don't think anyone does—including Roland."

Marianne shook her head. "I've been around plenty of complicated men. This is different. You said you know where he is. Could you please tell me?"

"If he didn't tell you that himself, I'm guessing he had a reason. I don't wish to violate his trust."

"Or perhaps you think you might be able to keep him all to yourself."

Adele rolled her eyes. "Really? What's next? We gonna go fight behind the gym after school?"

"Do you know when he'll be back?"

"I do."

"*Well?*"

"Well what? It's none of your business. Besides, you're supposed to be a reporter, right? Figure it out yourself."

"You're ridiculous. You know that? A jealous, ridiculous child of a woman. Fine, act that way. I'll wait until he comes back. Is that what you really want? Having me on your precious island day after day until Roland returns?"

"Look, Marianne, it's no secret I don't like you and I'm pretty sure you feel the same about me. If Roland chose to go out with you a few times that's his business. I'm not his keeper. That said, if he's avoiding you then he has his reasons and that's between you and him. Keep me out of it. I don't run a relationship repair shop."

"To think I once hoped we might work together."

"I'm sure it's for the best that we don't. Now, if you don't mind, I have friends I'd like to get back to and you should have somewhere else to go because you're not welcome here."

"Friends? You mean the mystery man from Ireland? Does Roland know about him?"

"Why would he?"

"Oh, please," Marianne said, smirking. "Don't play innocent with me. You and I both know there's been plenty of your water under the Roland bridge."

"That's disgusting."

"You're right. The thought of you two together makes me sick."

A spark from the fire popped loudly on the other side of the lobby. Adele could feel Tilda and Fin watching her. "I'm not going to ask you again," she said. "It's time for you to leave."

"I don't believe for a second you're half as tough as you think you are. In fact, I'm pretty sure I could throw you out of here if I wanted to."

Adele glanced down at Marianne's four-inch stiletto heels. "In those shoes? I doubt it. You're not meant for these islands. Go back to Seattle where you belong and leave us alone."

"You need to stop torturing Roland. Let him go. Let him be with someone who cares for him. Who wants the best for him. *Who loves him.*"

Adele's eyes widened. "You love Roland?"

Marianne sat up straight and stuck her chin out. "Maybe. I'd like a chance to find out, but it's a lot more difficult with you in the way."

"What are you talking about? I'm not in your way."

"Whatever. Keep hiding behind the false deniability you've spent so much time constructing. Sooner or later, Roland will finally move on from you, and when he does, I intend to be there for him in a way that you never could."

"Lady, you're crazy. I'm serious. You should really think about getting some help. If you're having problems with Roland, I assure you I'm not the cause. If you came all the way here to convince me otherwise it was a wasted trip." Adele stood and extended her hand toward the door. "We're done here."

Marianne got up slowly with her hands gripping the edge of the table. She leaned forward close enough that Adele could feel her breath against her face. "We're done when I say we're done."

"Hey, here's a newsflash for you. Marianne Rocha is an idiot."

Adele was stunned by the speed and power of the slap that followed that remark. The blow spun her face to the side and caused her eyes to tear up. Before she could recover, both of Marianne's hands were around her throat and squeezing—hard. She heard Tilda warning Marianne to let her go and Fin yelling for them to break it up.

What followed was instinct. Adele didn't think about her fist launching into the bottom of Marianne's chin or her knee smashing into the side of her hip at the very same time.

It just happened.

Marianne's head rocked backwards as her legs buckled. Adele shoved against the newswoman's shoulders with both hands, sending her crashing against the wall behind her.

Marianne grunted, gasped for breath, and then slid down sideways onto the floor.

Adele jumped forward like a jungle cat moving in for the kill, hardly making a sound as her eyes locked onto the side of Marianne's exposed cheek. She clenched her fists, flexed her leg, and prepared to kick the newswoman into oblivion.

"What the hell is going on here?" a familiar voice bellowed.

Adele instantly recognized the tone. She had been on the receiving end of it more times than she cared to recall.

Sheriff Lucas Pine had arrived.

5.

"Adele was defending herself," Tilda said. "The other one started it."

Lucas stepped in front of Adele, gently pushed her back, and then turned around to look down at Marianne. "Ms. Rocha?"

"Help me up, you idiot," Marianne seethed.

Lucas pulled her onto her feet. "What happened?"

"What happened?" Marianne pointed at Adele. "What happened is she assaulted me, and I want her arrested—*now*."

"No-no," Fin said. "That one there attacked Adele. She started it just like Ms. Ashland described."

Lucas turned around and stood face-to-face with Fin. "And who are you?"

"I'm Fin," he said with a toothy grin.

"Fin who?"

"Fin Kearns."

"Are you a guest at this hotel?"

Fin shook his head. "Nah, I'm here for Adele."

"Excuse me?" Lucas said as he tucked his thumbs into the front of his gun belt.

"Yeah, we just met today, but it's like we've been lifelong friends. Two peas from the same pod we are. Isn't that right, Adele?"

Lucas's head swiveled slowly toward Adele. "*Really*?"

"Uh, hello, Mr. Sheriff. Did you forget something? Like arresting the little pony-tailed animal that attacked me."

"I didn't forget you, Ms. Rocha," Lucas replied. "I also didn't forget there are two other witnesses who state it was you who attacked Ms. Plank first." He glanced back at Marianne. "Which means I would likely have to arrest you before I arrest her. Is that really what you want?"

"Sheriff Pine, those two aren't credible witnesses. They're friends of the accused. Do your job and put her under arrest."

Lucas turned all the way around and looked down at Marianne. "There are scratches on Ms. Plank's neck. Did you put them there?"

Marianne avoided the sheriff's eyes. "I have no idea."

Lucas sighed. "Ms. Rocha, I don't wish to call you a liar, but I'm also pretty certain you do know how she got those scratches. I think it's best you leave the hotel."

When Marianne went to say something, Lucas wagged his finger in front of her face. "No. Keep quiet and get out before I change my mind and give you a ride to the station in Friday Harbor."

"Fine," Marianne said with a nod. "You are a ridiculous man, and this is a ridiculous place. I'm happy to leave. I never should have come here to begin with."

"Now that you mention it, why *are* you here, Ms. Rocha?"

"I was attempting to locate Roland."

Lucas turned his head and coughed loudly into his hand. When he looked up, his forehead was covered in a thick layer of greasy sweat. "I apologize. I can't seem to shake this cold. Anyways, I think it best that you be on your way."

Marianne's gaze lingered on Lucas's broad-shouldered form for several seconds and then she smiled. "I agree. Until next time, Sheriff."

"That will be the last time that woman steps foot inside of here," Tilda said as soon as Marianne was gone.

Fin scratched his chin. "Oh, I don't know. She wasn't *all* bad. In fact, there were a few parts to her I found friendly enough."

Adele caught Lucas trying not to smile as he watched Tilda roll her eyes and walk away. "Come upstairs with me, Mr. Kearns," she ordered. "I sense the sheriff would like to have a conversation with Adele in private. And besides, I assume you need a place to stay the night. I'll let you curl up in the corner at the end of the hall. Might even throw a blanket over you. What do you say?"

Fin cocked his head and looked at Adele. "Eh? You want me to go upstairs?"

Adele nodded. "Yeah, pick a room to stay in—my treat. I'll be up soon to have a look."

"You sure?" Fin said. His eyes narrowed as he looked Lucas up and down.

"I'll be fine. Really. And don't mind Tilda. She's mostly bark with just a bit of bite."

"I heard that," Tilda called out. "Hurry up, Mr. Kearns. I don't think you'll wish to try the sheriff's patience. He's already not feeling well."

Fin's mad grin returned as he continued to size up Lucas. "Ah, patience isn't one of your virtues then, is that it?"

Adele, sensing that Fin was getting under Lucas's skin, quickly intervened before Lucas decided to twist her new Irish friend into a human pretzel. "Time to go, Fin. Wait for me up there. Thank you."

"I'll be waiting," Fin said while walking slowly up the stairs. He stopped and pointed at Lucas. "Don't you dare try anything with her, Sheriff, or you'll have to answer to me."

Adele knew that if Lucas's eyes were bullets it would have been a massacre. "Let me give you a bit of advice," he told Fin. "I don't know you well enough yet to miss you when you're gone."

Fin gave Lucas a thumbs up. "That's a good one, Sheriff. Who would have thought such a manly mouth could also be so smart."

Tilda yelled down from the second floor. "Mr. Kearns, I'm sure you're familiar with the saying about not poking a bear? I strongly suggest you take that advice now and *stop poking the bear*. Especially one who also happens to have a gun hanging off his hip."

Another coughing fit made Lucas double over. "Is it okay if we sit in front of the fire? I'm freezing."

"Sure," Adele replied. After they sat down Lucas put his head back against the chair and closed his eyes. "Ah," he said. "That's better."

"You should be home resting. You look awful."

Lucas chuckled as he wiped his eyes. "Gee, thanks." He took a deep breath. "There's work to be done. That's why I'm here. It couldn't wait and I didn't want to talk about it over the phone."

Adele leaned forward. "What's going on?"

Lucas's eyes moved from side to side as he looked out at the early evening gloom that had fallen over the resort. "I had a conversation this afternoon with my law enforcement contact in Vancouver. They received an Interpol alert regarding Liya Vasa. They're certain she's alive and on the move."

Hearing the name made Adele's stomach tighten. It had been Liya's brother Visili who had very nearly killed both Lucas and her last year.

"On the move where?"

Lucas was sweating again. He wiped his brow with the back of his hand. "They pinged a cell phone linked to her in Mongolia last week."

"*Mongolia*?"

"Yeah, apparently her father has long-standing connections with some of the more criminally inclined tribal leaders there. Poppy fields, human trafficking, that sort of thing."

Liya's father was Vlad Vasa, a Moscow-based crime lord considered to be one of the most ruthless and dangerous men in the world.

"Well, if Liya is hiding out in Mongolia isn't that a good thing? It means she isn't here, right?"

Lucas continued to stare outside. "That's the problem. They no longer believe she's in Mongolia. That's why I was notified."

"Then where is she?"

"They don't know."

The tightening in Adele's stomach was getting worse. She forced herself to remain calm. "Do you think she would actually try to come here?"

"She might. Especially if her father gave her his approval to do so."

"Approval for *what*?"

"Get revenge for Visili's death? Send a message? Who knows?"

"And you think that means coming after me?"

"Most likely all of us. You, me, Roland. Now that I think about it, where is Roland?"

"New York. He's due back tomorrow."

"What's he doing in New York?"

"I don't know."

"Roland Soros leaves for New York and doesn't tell anyone the reason why?"

"I didn't say he didn't tell anyone. He just didn't tell me."

"Huh," Lucas grunted.

"Spit it out. What are you thinking?"

"I don't know. It seems kind of odd that Roland leaves town around the same time I get word Liya Vasa might be making a move against us."

"Don't go there, Lucas. There's no way Roland would leave us behind if he thought we might be in trouble. Besides, how would he find out something like that before you?"

"It's Roland we're talking about. He has ways. I wouldn't put it past him."

Adele shook her head. "No. Roland would never do that. After everything we've been through? He's our friend. He's been your friend since you were both kids."

"Speaking of friends, what's the deal with Mr. Kearns? He makes quite a first impression and I'm not sure I cared for it."

"Doesn't he remind you of someone?"

Lucas frowned. "Should he?"

"C'mon, *think*. The accent, the voice . . ."

"He's English? That's not too uncommon around here."

"Not English—Irish."

"Okay, he's Irish. So?"

"Delroy Hicks. You remember him?"

"Sure," Lucas said, shrugging. "He passed away right before I became sheriff. You two broke open the Calista Stone case."

"That's right."

"Mr. Hicks was Irish."

"Uh-huh."

Lucas arched his brows. "And?"

"Geez, Sheriff. I really hope Liya isn't actually on her way here because you are definitely off your detective game."

"They're both from Ireland. Got it. So, what's the connection to you?"

"The connection to me is Delroy Hicks."

Raindrops started to hit the windows. The fire had nearly gone out. Lucas slumped in his chair and sighed.

"I'm sorry, Adele. I have no idea what you're on about. You know me though. I'll be looking into who this Fin Kearns is. Where your safety is concerned, I'll leave no stone unturned."

"That's what I'm trying to tell you. Fin and Delroy—that's the connection."

Lucas's eyes widened. "Wait. Are you saying—?"

"That's *exactly* what I'm saying. They sound so much alike, don't they?"

"Maybe. I wasn't around Mr. Hicks all that much even though he was friends with my father. I knew of him, of course. Just about everyone on the island knew of Delroy Hicks. In fact, now that I think of it, wasn't he gay?"

"He was. Well, sort of. Gay, straight, everything in between, it seems that was Delroy. At least the younger version of him."

"Okay, just to be clear. You're telling me the man upstairs with Tilda is the son of Delroy Hicks?"

Adele smiled and nodded. "That's right."

"What's he doing here?"

"He said he wanted to learn more about his father."

"And how'd he know to look you up?"

"The newspaper. He's read all my articles."

Lucas stretched his long legs out in front of him. "They read your stuff over in Ireland?"

"It's a great big new world out there, Lucas. You should think of joining it some time."

"Did you just call me ignorant, Ms. Plank?"

"I'd never dream of doing so, Sheriff Pine."

Lucas's grin was interrupted by more coughing. "God, I hate being sick," he said after catching his breath. "I forget how popular the online version of your newspaper has become beyond the islands. You've really managed to generate a lot of success, haven't you?"

"The paper is doing well, yes. I'm very lucky."

"Luck has nothing to do with it. You're good at what you do."

"You mean getting into trouble?"

"Into trouble, out of trouble," Lucas said. "You manage to do both better than most."

"I'll take that as a compliment."

"Good, that's what I intended it to be." Lucas got up and then coughed again. "I should get going. For now, I don't see any immediate threat from Liya. She'd have to pull off a miracle to get back into Vancouver in order to make her way here. She's on every law enforcement watch list in the world right now. I wanted to let you know and I wanted to tell you in person. You and me—it's been a while."

Adele stood, looked up at Lucas, and then realized how exhausted he really was. "It's always nice to see you, Lucas. I know I'm repeating myself, but you really do need to get some rest." She stood on her toes and pecked his cheek. "But don't be a stranger. I'll always make time for you."

"How long will Mr. Kearns be visiting?"

"I don't know. He didn't say. Oh, and thanks again for the help with Marianne Rocha."

"You didn't need my help. If anyone knows how tough you are it's me. That woman didn't stand a chance against you."

"Tough enough to make you go home and get into bed?"

"Sure, if you're the one tucking me in." Lucas leaned forward and kissed the top of Adele's head. "But leave the Irishman here. I don't play well with others."

Adele laughed. "That's exactly the kind of thing Roland would say."

Lucas scowled, stepped back, and turned to leave. "If I hear anything more regarding Liya I'll let you know."

The door closed. Adele watched Lucas walk beneath the resort's outdoor lights with his hands stuffed into his pockets. The rain was getting worse. His head was down, his back bent, and his shoulders hunched. Adele hated seeing him that way.

He looked small.

He looked weak.

Worst of all, he looked sick.

6.

He's easy like Sunday morning.

That's the line Adele kept repeating in her head as she watched Roland casually amble along the dock toward her sailboat. It wasn't morning though. It wasn't even Sunday. That didn't matter. Every inch of him reflected a man without a care in the world. Adele was a little surprised by how much it annoyed her to see him like that.

Even his hair appeared more relaxed. It was longer these days, hanging down to his neck and covering the tops of his ears while his face was hidden underneath a light-brown beard. Gone were the custom-fit clothes and fashionable footwear, replaced by a denim jacket, white T-shirt, worn jeans with a hole in the knee, and a pair of torn and frayed dark canvas sneakers. In a matter of a few months Roland Soros had gone from island prep chic to borderline bohemian. Adele hadn't decided yet if she liked the change or not. For now, it was just different.

"There you are," Roland said when he spotted her leaning against the bow of her boat. "How's your day going? It's warm. I think we might be in for an early summer. What say you?"

"What say me about what?"

Roland stopped, lowered his chin toward his chest, and smiled. "You're in a mood. Don't deny it. I know you too well. What did I do this time?"

"Maybe I just don't feel like talking about the weather. How was New York?"

"Same as the last time I saw it: big, loud, and it always makes me happy to be back home."

"You never did tell me what you were doing there."

"No? Huh. Did you ask?"

"I'm asking now."

"Geez, what's with the interrogation? I just flew into Friday Harbor no more than an hour ago and you're the first one I made a point of coming to see. Would you care to know why?"

Adele shrugged. Roland scratched his head. "Because I wanted to," he said.

"Must be nice to do whatever you want whenever you want."

Roland's easy-going shell started to crack as his features tightened. "Hey, I can turn around and go."

"Sure, run away. Keep all your secrets to yourself while the rest of us who care about you are kept in the dark."

"C'mon, Adele, what's going on?"

"How's business?"

Roland looked up at the sky, closed his eyes, and sighed. "Ah, now I get it. You heard."

Adele played dumb. "Heard what?"

"Yeah, you heard. I suppose it won't matter now if I tell you I planned on mentioning it when I returned from New York. That's the truth."

"Tell me what, Roland?"

"That's enough. I don't care for the negative energy you're giving off right now. We can sit down and talk, or I can leave. Just tell me what you want."

"Gee, you're so generous."

"Fine, be that way. Call me when you want to see me again. Or not. It's up to you."

"Wait. We do need to talk."

Roland nodded. "Good. Let's walk to the end of the dock. I'm expecting a delivery."

The two sat with their feet dangling over the water. There was still enough chill in the air to put goosebumps on Adele's arms. If Roland was cold, he didn't show it.

"What delivery?" Adele asked.

"It's a surprise. A big one."

"You sound excited."

"I am. It's been a long time coming, but today is the day."

"Does it have anything to do with New York?"

"No. Well, sort of. Who told you about the purpose of my trip?"

Adele stared at the watery reflection of Roland and her sitting together. "Tilda heard something through the financial grapevine."

"And you're upset I didn't tell you first?"

"Is it true? Are you selling the bank?"

Roland didn't answer right away. From somewhere in the distance an unseen ship blasted its horn. "It's looking that way," he finally said. "We hammered out most of the details at the meeting in New York."

"Why? Why give up something that's so tied to your family's history and the history of these islands?"

"I'm tired, Adele. I know that probably sounds like the comment of a spoiled rich kid, but it's true. I've been working nonstop for a long time to make something bigger and better of myself. To outgrow my family's shadow. Over the years, I've lost thousands and thousands of hours analyzing data, numbers, and financial statements. All that time sitting at a desk in front of a computer monitor cooped up in my office. Recently I decided I was done with all that. None of us really know how long we have. We're all living and dying in our own personal versions of hospice care. I don't want to waste any more time trying to prove anything. I don't want to waste any more time period. I've done it. I grew the business. I nearly lost it to the Russians. Then I put it back on solid financial footing, and now the time feels right to step away and do something else. Owning that bank isn't who I am. It never was. I won't ever be happy pretending that it is."

"Do you understand why I'm upset that you didn't tell me any of this before?"

"Sure. I do now. And I also admit that I shouldn't need you to have to remind me. I apologize. I get it. You run the local newspaper. This is a big story and you don't want to see it scooped by a Bellingham or Seattle news source. That said, I didn't want anyone to know about it until I was sure it was going to happen. Now I'm sure and now you know. If you want to run a story on it, you have my blessing. I'll even give you an interview if that'll help you to forgive me."

"I'm not just talking about the sale of the bank, Roland. You never told me anything about you being so tired and wanting to do something else. I thought by now we were close enough to have those kinds of conversations. Sometimes getting to the truth with you is like pulling teeth."

Roland put his arm around Adele and squeezed her shoulders. "I know. I'll work on that. I plan to work on a lot of things. You'll see."

"You've always been such a strong advocate for maintaining local control of the islands. A lot of people around here are going to be upset seeing your family's legacy gobbled up by some big bank conglomerate."

"The world keeps spinning. Time moves on. They'll get over it."

"You sure about that?"

Roland shrugged. "They will or they won't. Either way I don't care. I don't owe them my destiny and I damn sure don't owe them my happiness."

"The purchase price—it must be a lot of money."

"It *is* a lot of money. Likely more money than my grandfather would have ever thought possible the day he took his first deposit. It's the kind of money I can do a lot of good with."

Adele turned her head to look up at the construction site behind the resort. "You mean like the new home you're building on the top of the hill?"

"Fact is that home is partly the reason I'm selling the business. I paid extra for the lot to keep the transaction quiet and the construction costs are already close to 30% over budget. It's getting obscene. If I'm not careful everyone is going to start calling it Roland's folly."

"You're hurting for money? I thought you said the bank was back on strong financial footing?"

"It is—which makes it a very good time to sell."

The same horn blast from earlier repeated itself but this time sounded closer. "Let's go have a look at the house," Roland said. He stood and then helped Adele up. "Do you have time?"

Adele nodded. "Sure."

When they walked past the hotel Adele knew Tilda was somewhere inside watching them. "You-know-who isn't too happy about your new house," she said.

"Tilda Ashland isn't too happy about a lot of things."

"You don't worry about making an enemy of her?"

"She'll come around." Roland looked down at Adele and grinned. "They always do."

The construction crew had already left. Roland took Adele by the hand, walked her up to the unfinished top floor, and pointed to a floor-to-ceiling opening in the wall. "That space there is for a custom-designed window I'm having imported all the way from London. It's the same craftsman who does glass repairs for the properties of the Royal Family, including Buckingham Palace."

"All that for a window?" Adele said.

"It deserves nothing less. Come here and check out the view. It's why I bought the property. Be careful though. Don't get too close to the edge. It's a long way down."

Adele could see the rooftop of Tilda's hotel, the marina docks, all the boats both great and small, including her own, and beyond that the deep waters of Spieden Channel and the brown-scarred northern tip of Spieden Island. A pair of bald eagles soared overhead not more than a hundred yards from where Adele stood.

It was all undeniably beautiful.

"See what I mean?"

"It's something, Roland. It really is. When do you think you'll be moving in?"

Roland grimaced. "Not soon enough. I'm really hoping before the end of the summer, but with all the delays already who knows? I have a contingency plan though."

"What's that?"

The same horn Adele had heard twice before sounded for a third time. Roland, his eyes gleaming, pointed through the opening in the wall.

"There she is."

Adele leaned forward and blinked several times, not believing what she saw. A glistening white Burger yacht slowly made its way into the harbor. "That's your boat," she exclaimed. "The one that burned down. How's that possible?"

"Not quite the same. The one coming into the marina now was delivered here from Florida. It's a 1957. Same builder. Same floorplan—75 feet. I won't even tell you how much I spent having it restored to better than original condition. Thankfully the proceeds from the sale of the sailboat I purchased last year covered most of the cost. I'll be living on it full time until the house is completed. You and me—we're going to be dock neighbors. You're welcome to stop by and borrow some eggs any time you want. And I wouldn't say no to a sleepover should you be so inclined. I could cook you up those eggs in the morning. I make a mean scramble."

"A new home. A new yacht. Selling your family business. That's a lot of change, Roland. I don't know if I can keep up."

"And I haven't even told you about the trip I'm planning."

"Trip?"

"Yeah, that's partly why I purchased *Scaparre*. That's Italian for escape, which I thought was appropriate given how I intend to use her. I plan to take her up the Inside Passage next month and then, hopefully, by the time I get back, the construction on the house will be just about finished. Oh, and there's one other thing. More of a favor really. You don't have to decide now. In fact, I'd rather you didn't. Instead, take a few days to think it over."

"I'm afraid to ask."

"Well, I was hoping for some company on the trip. Someone I could share the experience with. What do you say?"

"Me? Oh, Roland, thank you, but I can't just up and leave like that. I have work. The newspaper doesn't write itself."

Roland crossed his arms and frowned. "That's not entirely true. Jose handles layout, the ads, most of the repeatable content like the community calendar, and the all-important web page. You could send him the content from the boat. I had an entire state room converted into an office with high speed satellite internet. I was thinking you could use the trip as a travelogue for the paper. Your readers would love it."

Roland was right about Jose. In just a few years he had gone from delivering the paper to overseeing its day-to-day operations. It's why Adele had made him a part owner. He worked hard, he worked well, and the paper likely wouldn't exist without him.

"Huh. It seems you know as much about my business as I do."

When Roland's face took on the look of dejected Basset Hound Adele immediately felt bad. "Hey, I'm grateful that you considered including me. I'm sure it would be a wonderful trip. It's a very nice gesture."

Roland held his hands up in front of him. "Don't give me an answer yet. Think it over. I'll be around." He smiled as he again pointed at the arriving Burger yacht. "As in I'll literally be about a thirty-second walk from your slip."

Once again Adele had to secretly admit to herself that she could never manage to stay mad at Roland for long. No matter how much she thought he deserved that anger, despite his secrecy and his bouts of inconsiderate selfishness, there was something warm, inviting, and intelligent that was always there just beneath his I-don't-give-a-damn exterior. It both infuriated and fascinated her.

He's complicated sexy. There, I said it.

"Penny for your thoughts?"

Adele flinched. "What?"

Roland was still smiling. "You looked like you were thinking pretty hard about something."

"I was."

"Yeah? Want to tell me about it?"

"No."

Roland chuckled. "Fair enough."

Adele heard a noise outside and looked down. An overweight old man dressed in a dark blue track suit was shuffling along the concrete walkway.

Don't look up. Don't look up.

The old man looked up.

Adele felt her heart skip a fearful beat. "Oh no," she said as she drew back from the opening.

Roland reached out and touched Adele's shoulder. "What's wrong?"

"It's him," Adele whispered.

"Who?"

"He's right outside. I think he saw me."

Adele inched forward and looked down again. The old man waved. His sausage-like fingers were covered in gold rings. "Hello again, little girl," he gurgled. The sound of his voice made Adele feel sick. "And I see you as well, Roland. Come down here. There are matters we must discuss."

Yuri Popov had returned to Roche Harbor.

7.

By the time Adele and Roland reached Yuri at the bottom of the hill Tilda was already there. Adele had to jog to keep up with Roland who was nearly running toward the Vancouver mob boss.

"What the hell are *you* doing here?" Roland barked.

Yuri ran a hand over the thin strands of oil-slick hair that was combed back over his age-spotted scalp. "Roland-Roland-Roland," he said in his thick Russian accent. "Is that any way to greet an old friend? Although I must admit I nearly didn't recognize you with all of that fur on your face."

"I've already called the sheriff," Tilda declared.

Roland stood directly in front of Yuri with his fists clenched. Adele worried he was about to throw a punch at the much older man. Yuri tilted his head and smiled at her. "There is the newspaper girl with all of her remarkable stories. I never miss a new edition." He turned toward Tilda. "You called the sheriff, yes?"

"That's right," Tilda answered. "He'll be here any minute."

Yuri nodded. "Good. It will save time. I'll be able to speak with all of you together."

"I asked what you're doing here," Roland said. "You better tell me now or I swear to God I'm going to throw you into the water and let the crabs have at you until there's nothing left."

Yuri laughed and then pointed at Adele. "Just like your story a couple years ago, yes? The poor young woman who was murdered and put into the crab pot near Ripple Island. How remarkable that one so young as you repeatedly finds herself in such trouble. You must truly have a nose for it."

When Roland reached out and grabbed a handful of Yuri's tracksuit, the Russian's lips drew back like a dog issuing a warning to a potential intruder. "It is not wise for you to touch me like that, Mr. Soros. See?"

Yuri pointed at Adele. Roland turned and then gasped. A red laser dot marked an area directly below Adele's chin.

"I come in peace," Yuri said. "But I didn't come alone. Now take your hand off me while we wait for the sheriff to arrive."

As soon as Roland let go and stepped back the laser on Adele's chest vanished and Yuri's smile returned. "That is better, yes? We can all be friends again now that we understand each other."

"Hey now, what's all this about?"

Tilda rolled her eyes. "Mr. Kearns, I told you to stay inside the hotel."

Fin kept walking until he stood next to Adele. "Everything okay? You all look like someone just pissed in your soup." He stared at Yuri. "That is except for you, old timer. You're all smiles."

"Who is this?" Yuri said.

"I'm Fin. Who are you?"

"Fin? Like fish?"

"No, like *me*, Fin Kearns. And you are?"

"I have business with them not with you. Please shut up."

"*Shut up*? That's not nice and it's no way to greet someone you just met. How about we start over? My name's Fin. Who are you?"

Yuri nodded at Roland. "Tell this strange man who I am so he knows that when I tell someone to shut up, they shut up."

"Tell him yourself," Roland replied.

"Yeah," Fin said, grinning. "Now go on. Tell me yourself."

Yuri's mouth moved like he was trying to grind his molars into dust. "I am Yuri Popov and I am not someone you would wish to make angry. So, I will tell you again to shut up."

Fin wagged his finger. "You forgot to say please."

Adele pulled him behind her. "He's a mob boss," she whispered into his ear.

Fin's eyes got big as he put a hand on each cheek which made him look like he was trying out for a *Home Alone* reboot. "Oh nooooo!" Then he started laughing. "I know all about Yuri Popov. I read about him in your articles. And now here he is in the flesh. And boy oh boy is there a *lot* of flesh."

"I asked you to shut up," Yuri snarled. "I asked you nice. And yet you talk, and you talk, and you talk."

Adele took note of two things at that moment. The first was that, despite his age and poor health, Yuri Popov could still pull a weapon on someone quicker than most. The second was how Fin didn't appear bothered by having a gun pointed at his face. Then she noted something else; the laser dot was on her chest again.

Roland stepped between Yuri and Fin. "Everyone calm down. Yuri, you need to put that away or Sheriff Pine is going to haul your ass off as soon as he gets here. Is that what you want?"

"I am not afraid of your island sheriff. Let him come. I am tired of waiting. And he will wish to know what I have to say. All of you will."

Roland put his hand on Yuri's gun and gently pushed it down. "I don't think you want the first thing Lucas sees when he arrives to be you threatening someone. He's taken out one of your men before. I have no doubt he'd do the same to you."

"There you are," a female voice cried out. "I've been looking all over for you."

All heads turned toward Marianne Rocha as she somehow managed to maintain her balance while scampering across the paved parking lot in her heels.

"Crap," Roland murmured.

Yuri licked his lips. "Oh, very pretty lady, Mr. Soros. She is yours?"

"No, she's not *mine*. She's . . . I don't really know what she is."

Marianne called out again as she frantically waved like a lost child being reunited with their parents. "Roland, it's me."

"What are you doing here?" Roland asked.

"I travel all the way from Seattle and that's the greeting I get? Come on. Let me have a hug."

The awkward hug turned into an even more awkward kiss as Marianne took Roland's face and drew him toward her. When he pushed her away, it looked like she might slap him. Then she smiled, pulled her sweater down tight, stuck out her chest, and shook her head.

"Stop being so shy. We're all adults here."

Roland was caught shooting a glance at Adele. "Hey," Marianne hissed. "I'm talking to you. *Me*. Not her. Isn't there someplace we can go to be alone?"

"Marianne, this isn't a good time. You should have let me know you were coming."

"Let you know? You don't think I tried? You wouldn't return my texts, my calls. I was worried, Roland."

"I've been busy, and I don't have time to talk right now. Perhaps tomorrow?"

"Busy with who?" she said, pointing at Adele. "With her? Why does it always have to be about *her*, Roland? I'm sick of it. There are plenty of men I know who would die to have my attention."

Yuri's laugh was like thick mucus dripping down a hot radiator. "Oh, what do we have here? The kitties will fight, yes? And such attractive kitties they are."

Marianne's head snapped toward Yuri. "Wait, I know who you are—Yuri Popov, the Vancouver crime boss. I did an expose' on you and your associates last summer." She looked around at all the faces staring back at her. "What's going on here?"

"I am sorry." Yuri shrugged. "I did not see your report. Like Mr. Soros today, I was busy then. Also, I do not watch much television. I prefer to read. Like Ms. Plank's newspaper on the computer. I read that all the time. It is very good. You should read it. It manages to be informative yet entertaining. Not at all like the regular news."

Adele wondered if it was scientifically possible for a woman's head to literally explode because Marianne

Rocha's appeared close to doing just that. The newswoman's chest heaved as she leaned toward Yuri.

"If you didn't watch my report how did you know it was on the television?"

Yuri's smile was dark chocolate laced with arsenic— sweet and deadly. "I did not see your report, but I heard about it. You know of me and I know of you, Ms. Rocha. I know where you work. I know where you live. And yes, I have associates in Seattle who know the same. I would be much more careful about who you discuss on your program if I were you."

"Is that a *threat*, Mr. Popov?" Marianne tried to sound tough, but Adele heard the fear in her voice.

Yuri waved his hand dismissively. "There is no need for accusations. We are all friends today. As for tomorrow? We shall see."

"We're *not* friends you fat, sweating pile of garbage."

Yuri glared at Tilda. "What did you say to me?"

Unlike Marianne, there was no fear in Tilda's reply. "You heard me."

"Put the gun away, Yuri," Roland said. "A vehicle is coming. It's likely Sheriff Pine."

Yuri put the gun into his pocket. "See? I listen. I did not come here for trouble, Mr. Soros. I came to warn you." He looked Adele up and down. "I came to warn all of you."

Roland was right. It was Lucas who exited the San Juan County SUV that had parked directly behind Tilda's hotel. When he saw Yuri, he froze for a second and then drew his weapon.

"Don't move, Mr. Popov, and keep your hands where I can see them."

"I would take your own advice as well, Mr. Sheriff."

When Lucas saw the red dot on his chest, he slowly lifted his head, locked eyes with Yuri, and then responded with surprising calm. "Everyone please step away from Mr. Popov."

Even Tilda moved quickly and silently to comply. It was the cold business side of Lucas Pine few on the islands knew existed. Adele had witnessed the sheriff's protective power and determination first-hand in Rosario last summer. It had saved her life.

"Sheriff Pine," Yuri growled. "Is this really necessary? I am an old man. My arms grow tired."

"He has a gun in his pocket," Adele said.

Yuri's head withdrew further down in between his broad shoulders, giving him the appearance of a badly perspiring turtle. "It is just a toy, Sheriff. I know better than to bring a weapon here."

"Don't move. Not an inch." Lucas stepped forward, reached into Yuri's pocket, and took out the gun. "It doesn't feel like a toy."

Yuri grinned. "There are no bullets. It's empty—like a toy."

Lucas kicked the gun away and then scanned the marina. "Is that a real shooter out there targeting my chest or just another toy as well?"

"Shooter? I have come alone. My passport is valid. I am here legally and am breaking no laws."

Tilda shook her head. "That's a lie. He told us he came in peace but that he didn't come alone."

"Mr. Popov," Lucas said, "you get on your phone and tell whoever you have out there that if I see another laser mark on anyone here, I'm arresting you on the spot. Then I'm calling the FBI. Do it. Now."

Yuri made the call, spoke a few sentences in Russian, and then put his phone away. "There. It is done. Now can we talk?"

"I have nothing to say to you, Mr. Popov. I do intend to make sure you turn around and get the hell out of here. Either that or I'm cuffing you and taking you in. It's one or the other."

"Sheriff, please, just a moment of your time. Travel is not an easy thing for a man in my condition and yet I came all this way to warn you in person of what is coming."

Lucas's eyes narrowed. "What do you mean? What's coming?"

"Evil, Sheriff—uncontrollable, twisted, hateful evil. At this very moment Liya Vasa creeps toward these islands like some terrible, insatiable beast, demanding that her brother Visili's death be avenged. She will not rest until everything that you cherish most, everything that you love or would ever love, is taken from each of you and destroyed forever."

8.

After Yuri left, following the closed-door meeting inside Tilda's hotel, Roland was the first to pose a question. "What do you think?" he asked the others.

Tilda held a glass of wine between her elegant, long-fingered hands. "I think it's insanity to believe anything that comes out of that man's mouth. He'll remain a criminal until his last breath, which I sincerely hope comes sooner rather than later."

"He's right about the threat from Liya," Lucas replied. "International authorities believe she's on the move."

Tilda set her glass down. "But how do we know if she truly intends to come *here* as Mr. Popov would have us believe?"

Lucas shrugged. "We don't. At least not yet."

"We might not know until it's too late," Adele added. "Not until she's staring us in the face."

Roland adjusted the gold Rolex on his wrist. "Why would Popov lie? I'm not saying he isn't, but what would be his motivation? I know him well enough to know he rarely does anything without an angle—namely one that benefits him."

Tilda nodded. "*Exactly.* He came here to manipulate us. I'm certain of it."

"Okay," Roland said, "but why?"

Everyone looked at Lucas. He shifted in his chair and shrugged again. "Believe me, I already have my ear to the ground. My law enforcement contacts in Vancouver know to update me if anything new develops on the Liya Vasa front. Beyond that it's up to us to remain vigilant, but I'd also suggest we go on living our lives. Tilda could be right. Perhaps Mr. Popov came here just to scare us."

"Or distract us," Adele said. "There's the motivation you're looking for, Roland. Popov has us looking around every corner for Liya while he's doing something to line his own pockets. Possibly drugs, stolen goods, human trafficking, it could be anything. When it comes to crime, I've learned first-hand the Russian mafia is pretty much an anything goes operation."

Roland didn't appear entirely convinced. "Sure, that *could be* what he's up to."

"Or not," Lucas countered. "It could also be exactly what he says it is—an attempt to warn us about Liya. Yuri Popov is a dangerous criminal but Liya Vasa? She's psychotic. If she does show up here there'll be no reasoning with her. I know my saying that makes me sound like I'm the one scaring you, but that's not it. Just be careful but live your lives. My deputies have already been alerted to the potential threat as well as every other government agency in the area. We're going to be fine."

They were interrupted by a knock at the door. Fin called out from the other side. "Mind if I come in?" Tilda went to the door and unlocked it. Fin stepped inside, looked around, and then whistled.

"Some serious business this, yeah? Hopefully it's been sorted. That Russian fella, he's really in the mob?"

"He is," Tilda said as she returned to her seat at the table. Fin remained standing. "There gonna be trouble?"

When no one else replied, Adele broke the silence, sensing Fin's desire to be part of the group. "There could be. We're here for each other though. We always are."

Fin smiled. "Ah, it must be nice to live with people you can count on."

Tilda motioned for Fin to join them. "It is. Pull up a chair, Mr. Kearns. Can I offer you a drink?"

"You have tea?"

"That I do," Tilda said with a nod as she got up and then returned with a cup.

Fin took a sip. "Mm," he said. "That'll do. Thank you. So, is this a meeting of the Roche Harbor Round Table?"

Adele noticed both Roland and Lucas staring at Fin. Roland cleared his throat. "Mr. Kearns, what part of Ireland did you say you're from?"

"The Irish part," Fin answered with a lopsided grin.

Roland arched a brow. "That answer makes you sound like a man trying to hide something. I'm sorry if I'm a little behind the others, but I'd like to know what you're doing here."

Adele leaned forward in her chair. "He's Delroy's son."

"Delroy Hicks?"

"That's right."

"Delroy didn't have any children."

Fin chuckled and spread his arms out. "And yet here I am."

"It's true," Adele said. "Delroy didn't know. Only Fin's mother did."

Roland frowned. "Okay, but that still doesn't answer my question. Why are you here?"

When Fin started to answer Adele cut him off. "I got this." She turned and faced Roland. "After he learned about Delroy he looked up the islands, read my articles, and decided to come here and see them for himself. If I was him, I probably would have done the same thing."

"I thought Delroy was gay."

"Really, Roland? This day and age and you're stuck on *that*?"

"It's not a matter of being stuck so much as it is a matter of biology. Right?"

Tilda shook her head. "Don't look at me. You're on your own with that one."

"Ah," Roland said. "You're just upset my new home will allow me to look down on you."

Tilda sipped her wine. "You'll never look down on *me*, Mr. Soros."

Roland smiled. "Nor would I ever dare to, Ms. Ashland."

"This is *brilliant*," Fin declared. "The banter, the back and forth, the good-natured tension, all of us here now inside this wonderful hotel, surrounded by the beautiful waters outside. Do you realize how truly blessed you are to live in such a place?"

Tilda raised her glass high. "To the islands."

"And to a new friend who also happens to be the son of a dearly departed one," Adele added.

The toast was made. The room went quiet. Then Lucas turned to the side, doubled over, and coughed. "Sorry about that," he wheezed. His hands were trembling.

"Hey, you don't look so good," Roland said. Adele detected the worry in his voice. He was genuinely concerned for his childhood friend.

Lucas used a napkin to wipe his brow and then grimaced. "I'll be fine. Just tired is all. Give me a few minutes to sit here and drink my water and I'll be good to go."

Roland touched Lucas on the shoulder. "You sure?"

Lucas pushed the hand away. "Yeah, I'm fine. Really." He looked at Fin. "So, Mr. Kearns, what's on your agenda? Do you intend to stay on the islands for a while?"

"I do," Fin answered. "If everyone here will have me. I was hoping Adele could help me check out something over on Orcas Island."

Lucas set down his just-finished glass of water. "Yeah? What do you want to see over there?"

"It's a phenomenon I read about—a magnetic field that's said to have healing powers, give people long life, that sort of thing. It's likely rumor, perhaps based on old Native American legend, but it intrigues me and since I'm here I'm hoping to have a look around for myself."

"I heard about that," Tilda said. "Healers come from all over the world to study the crystals on the island. I had always assumed it was nothing more than some new-age tourist marketing campaign or whatnot, but you actually think there's something to it?"

Fin shrugged. "I'm open to the possibility, yes. Ireland is itself an island, a very old one, steeped in mythology. I believe my natural curiosity about such things is deeply imbedded in my people's DNA. We have long had a fascination with the unexplainable and those things that go bump in the night." He turned to Adele. "What do you think? Are you and that gem of a Chris Craft available to take me to Orcas for a day or two?"

Adele hadn't been back to Orcas since Liya Vasa's brother Visili had tried to rape and kill her there. Visili was dead. She was very much alive. It was time to move on from that horrific encounter. "Absolutely," she replied, smiling. "I'll be finishing up the next edition of the paper all day tomorrow but should be free the day after. We can leave first thing in the morning. I'll do some research beforehand to help us decide where on the island we should go first."

Fin tipped his cap. "Brilliant. Thank you."

Lucas stood then teetered to one side. He braced himself on the chair as Roland got up and grabbed hold of him. "Easy, Sheriff. It appears your mind is writing a check your legs can't cash."

"I said I'm fine," Lucas grumbled. "Get your hands off me." He took two long strides toward the door, grabbed hold of the knob, and then stood there silent and unmoving until he let out a low groan while glancing behind him at the others. "No doctors," he gasped. "I mean it. Don't piss me off with that nonsense. I just need to rest."

Those were the last words Lucas spoke before his eyes rolled up into the back of his skull and he crashed onto the floor.

9.

"**S**heriff, you're not going anywhere. The room is yours for the night. Rest up."

Lucas didn't appear pleased by Tilda's demand that he stay in bed, but he didn't refuse the offer. Adele put a damp cloth over his forehead and squeezed his hand. "You gave us quite a scare. You're running a high fever—104."

"Rectal or oral?" Lucas asked.

Adele scowled. "*What?*"

Roland, who was standing near the door, tilted his head back and laughed. "Nice to see you can joke about doing a face-plant, Sheriff. And let me tell you, dragging you into that bed was no easy thing, you big lard."

Lucas raised his hand high, looked at Roland, and extended his middle finger.

Roland, smiling ear-to-ear, held up both hands and repeated the gesture. "Right back at you, Sheriff Face-Plant."

"Okay, that's more than enough macho nonsense for one day," Tilda said. "Everyone out. He needs sleep." She looked back at Lucas. "I'll check in on you in a couple hours. Are you sure you don't want to see a doctor?"

Lucas closed his eyes and shook his head. "Not necessary. I'm feeling better already. I'll be out of your hair in no time."

"There's no rush, Sheriff. You're welcome to stay here for as long as you need." Tilda turned out the light and shut the door while Adele and Roland waited for her in the hallway. Fin had already excused himself and gone to bed for the night.

"Should we see about bringing someone here to have a look at him?" Roland asked.

"No," Tilda replied. "He does seem better. I'd guess he's been fighting the flu. Was probably badly dehydrated. Lucas is a strong man. He's also a proud one. Having a doctor come here when he asked us not to would likely do more harm than good at this point. Don't worry. I'll keep an eye on him. Are you two still going to Friday Harbor?"

Adele nodded. "Yeah, we need to speak with Marianne Rocha before she catches the late-night ferry back to the mainland."

"I don't care for that woman," Tilda said. "She's trouble. The sooner she's gone the better."

Roland was already heading downstairs. Adele moved to catch up to him. "Call me if anything changes with Lucas."

"I will," Tilda answered. "Be careful."

***

The first half of the trip to Friday Harbor was a quiet one. Adele drove the Mini while Roland sat in the passenger seat with his head resting against the window. She looked over at him. He smiled at her.

"Something funny?"

"No," Roland said. "I was just thinking how so much is different since you came to the islands. It's been quite a ride. A lot of changes."

"Any regrets?"

"Not really."

"That doesn't sound like a very sure answer."

Roland sat up and rolled his head from side to side. "I'm not complaining."

"Do you know what you're going to say to Marianne?"

"Nope."

"Really? Do you think we can trust her not to do a story on Yuri?"

"I don't know her well enough to vouch for anything she may or may not do."

Adele downshifted as she neared a curve in the road. "Did you two sleep together?"

Roland reached down and turned the radio on. Tom Petty was singing about free fallin'. "I love this song."

"Uh-huh," Adele said with a smirk. She turned the volume down. "Smooth change of subject. I'll take that to mean yes."

"Take it however you want. That's your prerogative."

The Mini's front tires chirped as Adele took another corner nearly twenty miles over the posted speed limit. "Marianne could become a problem for us, Roland. Yuri won't like seeing his face plastered all over the local news channels."

"Since when are our actions dictated by what Yuri Popov wants?"

"Oh, I don't know. Maybe since you started doing business with him a few years ago, which led to all the mess that followed, including having to deal with Liya Vasa."

"That's not fair."

"Life's not fair. You weren't there, remember?"

"What the hell are you talking about?"

Adele braked, turned hard into the bend, and then accelerated. "That time at Rosario when Visili Vasa nearly killed Lucas and me. You weren't there in the room. You don't know what it was like—how horrible it was."

Roland stared straight ahead. Adele turned her head to look at him. "What? Now you have nothing to say?"

"Just keep your eyes on the road. And you might want to slow down."

"Don't tell me how to drive."

"Fine. I'll just sit here and shut up."

"Don't act like this is my fault, Roland. Don't you get it? Don't you care? I'm scared."

"Of what?"

"Of Liya Vasa and what she's capable of. Doesn't it bother you that she might be coming back? Or are you too busy thinking about all the money you're going to make when you sell the bank? Maybe people are right about you. I've defended you more times than I can remember, but I guess I need to consider the possibility I was wrong. That when it comes down to it, all Roland Soros *really* cares about is money—and himself."

"I'm not going to argue with you, Adele. As much as it seems like you want to, I won't do it. I need to speak with Marianne to try to make sure she holds off on any reporting about Yuri so that you and Lucas and everyone else can be safe. I can't do that if I'm angry. And I know you don't really believe what you just said about me."

Adele pulled into a parking space near the ferry terminal. "We're here."

Roland sighed. "Yeah. We're here. I think it's best that I speak to her alone, but I'll need a ride back to Roche."

"I'll wait."

"You don't have to. I can find another way."

"Roland, I said I'll wait. Go find Marianne. Talk with her. I'll be here when you get back."

Adele watched Roland walking up and down the rows of vehicles as he looked for Marianne. Eventually she lost sight of him. The ferry sat at the terminal, its many lights and hulking mass of metal making it appear like a giant beast waiting for its next meal.

A few minutes later, the ferry workers began motioning for the vehicles to load. One row, then another, and then another, until all the vehicles were gone. The ferry's horn blasted as it began to pull away from the dock. Soon it was fully enveloped by the dark, watery horizon.

Where is he?

Adele got out of the car. She could hear the water lapping up against the pebble-strewn beach that ran the length of the dock pilings. The terminal lights blinked out for the night, leaving Adele to stand in inky blackness.

"Roland?"

No answer.

"Roland? Where are you?"

Adele cursed under her breath and then continued to call Roland's name. She heard her phone chime, took it out, and read the text message.

Spoke with Marianne. All good. I'll find a ride back to Roche. Drive safe.

Adele shook her head and then texted back.

Stop acting like a child. Get over here. I'm waiting.

Roland didn't respond. Adele put her phone away and started walking around the ferry terminal parking lot. "I'm not leaving," she shouted. "I'll stay out here all night if I have to. Don't think I won't. Is that what you want?"

Adele heard a faint splash and then another. She followed the sound until she reached a set of concrete stairs that led down to the beach. The sound stopped. She peered into the gloom trying to locate the source then took one step down and then another.

"Roland? Is that you?"

The stairs smelled of seagulls, saltwater, and sand. Adele took out her phone and used it as a flashlight. The last few steps before she reached the beach were still slick from when the tide had come in earlier.

"You don't act scared."

The sound of Roland's voice made Adele jump. "Where are you?"

"Over here. Just keep walking."

Adele found him standing in the dark skipping rocks across the water. "Not cool, Roland. You don't just leave like that. I was waiting for you."

"I do what I want. All I care about is myself. Isn't that what you just said?"

"You want me to worry? Is that it? Because if it is then congratulations. Mission accomplished."

Roland skipped another rock, turned around, and put his hands on his hips. "What do you want from me, Adele? Tell me and I'll do it. Do you want me to go away? Do you want me to stay? Are we just friends? Are we something more? I'm asking because right now I don't have a damn clue. You don't want me to sell the bank? Fine. I won't sell it. You don't want me building a new house? Okay, I'll tear it down. You don't want my boat in the same marina as yours? Just say the word and it's gone. You want me to give you my blessing to be with Lucas? Go for it. JUST TELL ME WHAT THE HELL YOU WANT."

The clouds parted, allowing the beach to be illuminated by the light of a nearly full moon. Adele stared into Roland's eyes and saw his frustration, his confusion, and his pain.

"I want the same for you that I want for everyone I care about, Roland. I want you to be happy."

Roland shook his head. "That's not an answer and you know it. Do you regret when we were together on the yacht? Remember? Is that what's come between us? That we had sex that one time?"

"No, Roland, I don't regret what happened that day. Regret has nothing to do with this."

"Then what is it?"

"I don't really know. All this Russian stuff, Liya Vasa, Yuri, what happened with Visili, it started with *you*, Roland. You and your greed, your desire to always make more money. That's what brought this trouble to the islands. Why don't you get that? Why can't you take responsibility for it? You made this mess and all of us have been left fighting to clean it up."

"So, you're saying your life would be better if I wasn't a part of it. Is that it?"

When Adele tried to reply, Roland interrupted. "No, don't deny it. That *is* what you're saying. You can't move past the fact I did some business with Yuri. Even after I took your advice and terminated the casino project and then gave my entire Cattle Point property to the county so they could build a drug treatment center, you have this need to continue holding it over my head. I don't understand why, but it's clear you do. Fine. You keep holding on to your resentment, Adele, but don't expect me to keep putting up with it. I'm moving on—without you. Life is too short to be constantly beaten down by people who claim to care. I don't need that."

"Roland, stop it. You're taking this too far. It's late. We're both tired and stressed and saying things we're going to later regret."

"I'm saying exactly how I feel. Isn't that what you're always telling me to do?"

"Not like this. C'mon. We'll talk more about it tomorrow."

Roland shook his head. "No, we won't."

Adele realized then how serious Roland was. She felt her throat tighten and her heart pound. "You don't mean that."

For a second Adele thought she saw in Roland's eyes a desire to finally relent and give in to reason, put aside his hurt feelings, and return with her to the car. Then those eyes hardened, his head lifted, and he retreated to some place deep inside of himself where Adele knew he wouldn't allow anyone to follow—not even her. The two words that came next cut as much as any blade ever could.

"Goodbye, Adele."

10.

Adele woke up feeling nearly as tired as when she went to bed. Most of the night was spent lying on her back in the dark wondering if she owed Roland an apology.

They had argued before, but this was different. The way Roland sounded, the way he looked at her when he said goodbye, it felt permanent. Adele wouldn't accept that. She couldn't. The thought of life without Roland Soros in it didn't compute. They had shared too much, come too far, for it to suddenly end.

The wind blew the rain sideways as it pummeled the outside of the sailboat. It was going to be a cold, wet day in the San Juans. Adele pushed herself out of bed and put on a pot of coffee. She looked through the porthole over the sink. The docks were empty.

Adele hoped a quick shower would help her to wake up. It didn't. The coffee didn't do much either. She brushed her teeth, put on a rain jacket, pulled its hood tight over her head, and stepped outside.

Even the normally vocal seagulls were hiding out from the weather. White caps slapped against boat hulls as the dock gently swayed from side to side. Adele zipped the jacket up to her neck and leaned into the wind with her head down, trying to keep the rain from hitting her in the face.

She decided to pay Roland an early morning visit on his yacht. They would sit down, talk it out like they had always done before, and things would go back to whatever passed for normal between them.

The Burger remained tied up at the end of the dock. Adele had worried Roland might have moved the yacht before morning. She wondered where he might have gone if he had actually done so. Friday Harbor? Anacortes? Bellingham? It didn't matter. He was still in Roche and soon their most recent argument would be another story to laugh about later.

Adele walked up the boarding ramp, stepped onto the yacht, and pressed her face against one of the windows. It was dark inside. She tried one of the side doors and found it locked. She went to the back of the boat and tried the aft entrance. It too was locked. Adelle knocked on the door. When Roland didn't answer, she returned to the side door and knocked there. Still no answer.

The wind was getting stronger. Adele knocked again, waited, and then walked back down the boarding ramp. Her shoes were getting soaked by the rain. She wondered if Roland might still be sleeping inside the yacht or if he had possibly stayed the night somewhere in Friday Harbor. She took out her phone and texted him.

Let's talk. Are you on the yacht?

The message was immediately kicked back. Roland had blocked her number.

C'mon, Roland? Really?

Adele knew Tilda would be up already. Few woke earlier than her. She also made excellent coffee. Adele put her phone away, put her head down, and headed toward the hotel.

"You're soaked," Tilda remarked as Adele stepped into the lobby. "Go sit down by the fire. Would you like some coffee?"

Adele took off her jacket and hung it on the rack just inside the door. "Yes," she replied. "Thank you. My first cup didn't take. I hardly slept a wink last night."

The fire felt good as Adele rubbed her hands in front of it. Tilda arrived with the coffee and then took the chair next to her. "Okay, I know that look," she said. "What's bothering you?"

Adele sipped from her cup and wondered why Tilda's coffee was so much better than her own and then realized she hadn't given her an answer. "It's Roland. We had an argument. A bad one."

"You two have argued before. Why is this any different?"

Adele watched the fire's flames dancing in the century-old stone hearth. "He was really upset this time. I'm not exactly sure why though."

"Were you able to speak with the newswoman before she left?"

"Yes, Roland did. I stayed in the car. He said she agreed not to broadcast a story on Yuri."

"And you fought after that?"

"We were fighting before, during, and after. He even blocked me on his phone. He's never done that. He actually told me goodbye. I think he really meant it, Tilda."

"Oh, I doubt that. So, what did you say to him?"

Adele frowned. "You think this is my fault?"

"No, I'm just trying to better understand what might have started it. You're being defensive. That usually means you're aware on some level that you might have contributed to whatever caused the argument. I say this as someone who has been the primary cause of many an argument. We often don't realize how hurtful the things we say can be."

"I told him I was scared about Liya Vasa."

"And did you blame Roland for that?"

"I suppose. I mean, he *is* to blame."

"Will blaming Roland for what he did or didn't do *before* make you any safer *now*?"

"I want him to understand how his actions have consequences."

"Why?"

"What do you mean *why*?"

"Adele, you can't make him into the version of Roland Soros you want him to be any more than he could force that change onto you. He is who he is."

"So, none of us should work to be better versions of ourselves?"

"I didn't say that. You're being defensive again."

"Stop saying that. I heard you the first time."

"Then stop being defensive."

"I didn't come here for a lecture."

"No, you came for a sympathetic ear, but I'm more concerned with telling you what you *need* to hear, not what you *want* to hear."

Adele put her coffee down and folded her arms across her chest. "You know what I need? Well then, by all means do tell."

"I don't think you realize how intimidating your success is to both Roland and Lucas and how much they want to prove themselves to you and everyone else on these islands."

"My success?"

"Yes, Adele, your success. You came here with nothing and created something remarkable. People from all over the world read your newspaper. Do you know why?"

"Go ahead. Explain it to me."

"The stories in your paper, they avoid the snark and bias that dominates other news sources. You write about people in a way that many find almost impossible to ignore. I used to read the *Island Gazette* with nothing more than mild curiosity. Now? I never miss an issue. For me it's a must-read and clearly, given how your readership has grown, I'm not the only one who feels that way. Your stories are so compelling because they are honest, they're real, and they allow us to share in your own journey of self-discovery."

"Okay, I appreciate the compliment, I really do, but what does any of that have to do with Roland and Lucas?"

Tilda put a hand on Adele's knee and smiled. "Roland is the only surviving link to one of the most powerful and influential men to live on these islands. His life has been spent in the long shadow of that legacy. He was given a business that he had nothing to do with creating. Everyone knows that, especially Roland.

"Lucas is the son of a beloved physician. Like Roland, he too was born into a name that awarded him privilege he didn't have to earn. When he went off to make something of himself beyond this place, he failed. He returned a former golden boy, a broken athlete, a might-have-been. So, he becomes sheriff in the hope of making himself into something more than merely the son of Dr. Edmund Pine.

"And then you come along with hardly more than two pennies to rub together, alone, defiant, far braver and more intelligent than most, who then ultimately, undeniably, becomes this great success—all on your own.

"This isn't the first time you've shared with me your frustration with either Roland or Lucas. What I think you possibly fail to recognize is that frustration is largely coming from their desire to prove themselves worthy of your respect. I'm not saying that should always excuse their actions but rather that those actions most likely come from a well-intentioned place."

Adele had been watching the flames as she listened. She turned and looked at Tilda. "I'm not going to apologize for succeeding with the newspaper."

"I'm not talking about apologies. This is about understanding. Do you know how wonderful it is to have two men like Roland Soros and Lucas Pine in your life? They both care for you so much. Don't abuse that caring by trying to turn them into something you think you would find more acceptable. Allow them to be the men they are. If you can't do that then perhaps Roland was right last night. Goodbye might very well be the proper road to take at this point."

"No," Adele said with a shake of her head. "That's not an option. Not for me. I *want* Roland in my life."

Tilda sat back in her chair, straightened her ankle-length skirt, and crossed her legs. "Okay, then you go find him and straighten this out. Tell him how much he means to you. Be honest—as honest and real as the stories in your paper. I believe that's what most men want."

"Speaking of which, where's Brixton? I haven't seen him in a while."

Brixton Bannister was the former Hollywood actor who had faked his own death years ago and then took up residence inside a hidden cave on Ripple Island on the northern edge of the San Juans. Following his return to the world of the living, he had spent an increasing amount of time with Tilda at the hotel. So much time, in fact, that most Roche Harbor regulars assumed the two were a couple. Adele had never seen Tilda so happy as she was when Brixton was around.

Tilda sighed. "I was wondering when you would bring his absence up. Where is he? I'm not sure. Perhaps back at his place on Ripple Island. We might very well have had our own goodbye moment."

"Really? I thought you two were doing so well."

"I fear Brixton couldn't accept that the world had happily moved on without him. He was certain his return from the dead would have created more interest. When it didn't, he became increasingly frustrated about what his purpose in this new-to-him world was to be. He would leave on that little skiff of his for days at a time, often without letting me know. When I complained, he informed me he would always be his own man and that a life constantly inside the walls of a hotel was not for him. After that I said nothing. He would leave and then return looking more gaunt, wild-eyed, and less civilized than before. The last time he left was nearly a month ago. I haven't seen him since."

"I'm so sorry, Tilda. Here I was going on and on about Roland. I had no idea."

"It is what it is. I miss him, but I also refuse to allow a man to dictate my moods. There is so much life yet to be lived and so little time in which to do it."

"But if you think I should seek out Roland why don't you feel the same about Brixton?"

Tilda arched a brow. "All due respect to Brixton, but he is no Roland Soros. Now, if I were thirty years younger . . ."

"Huh. And here I was thinking Roland always rubbed you the wrong way."

"Oh, Roland annoys the hell out of me to be sure. He's arrogant, impulsive, self-involved, but those qualities often come with those people we find most interesting. Besides, my instincts for such things tell me he's well versed in how to rub a woman the *right* way. Then again, you'd know far more about that than I."

Tilda laughed when she saw Adele's cheeks go red. "It feels good knowing that despite all your success I can still make you blush."

Adele got up. "And on *that* note, I think it's time to get going. I'll be busy most of the day finalizing the next issue and then I'm stopping by the bookstore to do some research for the Orcas Island trip with Fin tomorrow."

"When do you plan on seeing Roland?"

"Sometime after I get back from Orcas. I figure it's a good idea to give us both a day or two to mull things over. But if you see him let him know I want to talk."

Tilda stood and smiled. "I will."

The two women hugged. "Thank you for listening and for the advice," Adele said. "It really did help me to see things more clearly."

"I'm sure you'll get it all worked out soon. Be careful driving in this rain. Stop by later for some evening wine if you have time. I'll let Fin know you're coming."

Adele stopped at the bottom of the stairs. "How's Lucas doing?"

"Oh," Tilda exclaimed. "I can't believe I forgot to tell you. He was already gone by the time I got up, so I assume he's doing much better. As for Fin, he's still in his room sleeping the morning away. He doesn't appear to be the early to rise kind. For now, he's the only guest I have in the entire hotel. Won't be that way in a couple more months. I figure I should enjoy the slow time while I still can. Soon it'll be wall-to-wall visitors around here."

"I hear that. See you tonight."

The howling wind nearly yanked the hotel door from Adele's grasp. She had to use both hands to push it shut. The trees on the hill behind the resort were bent sideways as their branches whipped about like the arms and legs of a panicked army in retreat.

Adele heard the thump of a car door closing behind her and turned around. A black sedan idled on the other side of the nearly empty parking lot. Its windshield was covered by rain and its wipers were off, so it was impossible to clearly see who was behind the wheel. A gust of wind blew Adele against the side of the Mini. She grimaced, put her head down, and began walking toward the other car.

The sedan's motor revved once, twice, and then a third time. Adele stopped halfway between her car and the other.

Who the hell is it?

She took another step toward the vehicle. "Hello? Can I help you?"

The sedan's motor revved again.

The hair on the back of Adele's neck stood up.

Get in your car. Get in your car now.

Adele walked slowly backwards so she could keep her eyes on the sedan. One careful step, then another, and then another, until finally her hand brushed the Mini's door handle.

The other car crept forward. Adele dropped into the driver seat and locked the doors. She turned her head to look out the window when the sedan's rear tires spun on the wet pavement as it suddenly lunged toward the Mini.

Adele cried out, jammed the key into the ignition, slammed the shifter into gear, and popped the clutch. The Mini shot forward, pushing her back into her seat. She glanced into the rearview mirror and saw the sedan skidding through the space she had been parked in just a second earlier. Adele turned the wheel hard. The other driver did the same until both vehicles sat facing each other with no more than forty yards between them.

The sedan's engine roared as it catapulted across the parking lot. Adele gripped the wheel tightly and waited.

You want to do this? Fine. Here I am.

The car came within a few feet of Adele's bumper and then lurched to the right, missing the Mini's by inches. The rainwater hissed under its tires as it sped past. Adele still couldn't see for certain who was driving. She thought she saw a flash of blonde hair but wasn't sure.

Is it Liya?

The sedan spun around and then took off onto the road leading away from Roche Harbor. Adele considered going after it but then decided against it, thinking that might be exactly what the driver of the other car wanted.

B97684W

It was the sedan's license plate number. Adele would drive into Friday Harbor, stop at the sheriff's office, and give it to Lucas for him to look up. That would have to do.

For now.

11.

Lucas was still sick which made Adele felt guilty about burdening him with what happened to her in the Roche Harbor parking lot. His cheeks were flushed, his eyes glazed, and the cough sounded even worse than the night before.

"You need to get out from behind that desk and go to the doctor," she said. "Have one of your deputies cover for you."

"As you well know, this is a three-person department and a county with nearly a dozen major islands," Lucas replied. "They're busy. I'm here. And despite how I look I assure you I'm still doing my job. I'll run the plate numbers and see what comes back. Is there anything else you can tell me about the driver? Something you might have forgotten when you first told me?"

"No, I couldn't see inside the car. I thought it might be Liya for a second, but then again she's already in my head since Yuri's visit yesterday so I might have been seeing something that wasn't actually there."

"Do you feel they intended to hurt you?"

"I don't think so. This was more an attempt at intimidation rather than a direct confrontation."

"You sure about that?"

Adele nodded. "Unfortunately, and as you know, this isn't the first time I've had to deal with something like this. Whoever it was I'm almost positive they were trying to scare me."

Lucas looked down at his computer screen. "Huh."

"What is it?"

"That license plate number you gave me—it's local."

"Really? Who does it belong to?"

Lucas wrote something down on a stickie note, tore it off, then got up. "You're not coming with me."

"I didn't say I was. I have work to do, but I'd like to know who the owner of the car is."

Lucas pressed his lips together. "I mean it. I can't have you turning this into one of your personal mysteries to solve. I need to be allowed the time to question her properly without any interruption or influence from you."

"It's a woman?"

"Yes."

"C'mon, Lucas, tell me who it is and then I'll step back and let you do your job while I go to the newspaper office and do mine."

"I'll tell you after I'm done questioning her. Do we have a deal?"

"Sure, but eventually I'd like to talk to her myself."

Lucas wagged his finger. "See, that's what I'm worried about—*interference*. At this point we have a name of the car's owner. That doesn't mean she was the one driving it this morning."

"It also doesn't mean she wasn't."

"Adele, give me your word you'll let me handle this."

"I won't get in your way. I promise."

"Good. Thank you."

"I do expect to get an update as soon as you're done interviewing her though."

Lucas coughed, cleared his throat, and nodded. "That's fair." He wiped his forehead with the back of his hand.

"One other thing," Adele said. "If you're still this sick after tomorrow I'm taking you in to see the doctor. That's not open to negotiation."

Lucas straightened to his full height and gave Adele a tired smile. "Lucky for me I'm already feeling better. I'll turn in early tonight and be right as rain by morning."

"I never cared for that saying. There's nothing right about rain. And I'm not kidding. If you're not better, I'll tie you to my bumper and drag you to the clinic if that's what's required to make you take better care of yourself."

Lucas patted Adele on the head as he stepped by her. "You're so cute when you try to act tough. I'll be in touch."

He opened the door and then turned around. "You still going out to Orcas tomorrow with that Fin fella?"

"Yeah. Have you looked into him yet like you said you would?"

"Yup. Already left a message with someone from Interpol. I don't expect to hear back from them any time soon though. Inquiries from a county sheriff like me are likely to be on the very bottom of their priority list."

"You contacted Interpol? For Fin? Don't you think that's a bit excessive?"

"His name didn't come up in our system, so I figured I had to throw a wider net given he comes from Ireland."

"Yeah, Fin Kearns, international man of mystery. Geez, Lucas."

"It's my job, Adele. Some guy shows up out of the blue, claims to be the son of Delroy Hicks, and now has you running around with him in search of healers and crystals?"

"He's a nice guy. I also think he's a little lonely. And he's Delroy's son. I owe his father a lot, which in a way means I owe Fin as well."

"Nice or not, I'm gonna make sure he checks out. You ever stop to consider what happened to you at Roche this morning could be related to Mr. Kearns showing up here?"

"No, because it's far more likely to have something to do with Liya Vasa and we both know who's to blame for that mess."

Lucas cocked his head. "What do you mean? The only one who's to blame for Liya is Liya."

"Never mind. Go do your interview."

"Wait, are you upset with Roland? You think it's his fault?"

"I think any time Yuri Popov shows up to these islands Roland is at least partly to blame, yes."

Lucas shut the door. "Hold on a second, Adele. Look, I don't recall ever being the one to jump in first to defend Roland Soros, but you can't drop Liya Vasa at his feet. That's not fair. I know what happened to us at Rosario, what happened to you, it was a horrible thing, but we got through it. We survived. Did you two argue about this last night?"

Adele realized her close friendship with Lucas made her sometimes forget something important—he was a cop with a knack for noticing things quicker than most. "I don't want to talk about Roland right now," she said.

"Yeah, I see that. The fight you two had must have been a doozy. I also know you and I have had our share of disagreements as well, but we always manage to patch things up eventually. That's what friends do. You and Roland are no different."

Well, besides the fact I slept with Roland and never slept with you.

Lucas checked his watch. "I really should get going."

"Of course. Go ahead."

"And you're off to work on the paper?"

"No, I'm going to secretly follow you, so you'll lead me to the owner of the car."

"Very funny."

Adele wasn't joking. That was exactly what she intended to do. She smiled. "I guess we both better get going. I'll be waiting to hear what you find out."

"And I'll be sure to tell you first thing."

The two left the sheriff station together. Adele got into her car and waited as the rain continued to fall. She watched Lucas walk up to his vehicle, cough, and then get behind the wheel. When he drove off, Adele paused to make sure he would be at least half a block ahead and then she pulled onto the street and followed. It was just three blocks later when Lucas parked in front of Roland's bank and went inside.

Adele stopped on the side of the road behind a pickup truck and waited. Her eyes widened as she gripped the steering wheel tightly. The same black sedan that had been in Roche Harbor pulled into the spot next to Lucas's SUV. The driver got out.

"What the hell?" Adele whispered to herself.

It was Sandra Penny, Roland's vice president of operations. Adele had spoken with her last year inside of her second-floor office. Sandra appeared exactly as Adele remembered: tall, thin, and blonde. She also recalled her being as intelligent as she was attractive.

Lucas met Sandra just outside the entrance. The two stood under the roof's overhang talking. Lucas motioned toward the sedan. Sandra shook her head. Lucas went to the back of the car and took a picture of the license plate. Sandra opened the driver door and then Lucas leaned down and looked inside. The rain had almost stopped. Lucas spoke with Sandra briefly then walked her to the bank entrance and opened the door for her. After she was inside, he turned around and stared at the black sedan for a few seconds before getting into his vehicle.

Adele continued to watch and wait. Her phone rang. She glanced quickly at the number, not wanting to take her eyes off the bank.

It was Lucas. She took the call. "You get all that?" he asked.

Adele grimaced as she kept the phone to her ear.

"I saw you following me," Lucas continued. "At least you kept your distance. I suppose that means you kept your promise so thanks for that."

"The vehicle belongs to Sandra Penny?"

"Correct. She was late to work today because she said she was having car trouble."

"Or she was the one at Roche."

"Far too early to be jumping to that conclusion, Adele. I'm investigating. I'll ask you again to stay out of it and allow me do my job."

"Or I could march into her office now and demand that she tell me what's going on."

"Don't you dare. I mean it."

"No worries, Sheriff. I'll give you a little more time."

"Gee, thanks."

"Did Sandra mention if Roland was at the bank?"

"Sorry, it didn't come up."

"Did she seem nervous?"

"I'm not going to discuss the case with you. Here's my advice, not that you would ever take it. Go work on your paper. Then enjoy the trip to Orcas tomorrow. When you get back, we'll sit down and have another talk about what happened in Roche. I should know far more by then and I promise I'll keep you in the loop. Until then, stay away from Sandra Penny."

"Should I be concerned?"

Lucas didn't reply right away.

"Lucas?"

"I'm looking into it, Adele. At this point I really don't know what's going on. It's like I said. I'll have more to share when you get back from Orcas. The weather is supposed to improve. Should make for a nice trip."

"I'll let you know as soon as I'm back." Adele watched Lucas roll his window down, stick his hand out, and give her a thumbs up.

"Good," he replied. "I'll be waiting."

Lucas drove away while Adele remained parked across from the bank. She again wondered if Roland was inside and had to fight the urge to go in and find out. Instead, she attempted to text him again, but the message was blocked the same as last time. It was getting late and there was newspaper work to be done. After one last look at the black sedan, Adele started the Mini and sped off.

12.

"**G**et over here, you!"

Suze Blatt, the 60-year-old owner of Island Books, spread her arms wide as she walked out from behind the counter to greet Adele.

"I was wondering when I'd see you again. It's been much too long."

"I know," Adele replied. "Things just keep coming up."

"Well, here you are now and not a moment too soon. I was actually thinking of closing early. It's been so slow. In the summer I'm always saying how much I look forward to the off season and then in the off season I'm complaining about the lack of business. I guess that makes me hard to please. Is this a newspaper or a pleasure visit?"

Adele breathed in the scent of aged paper that always permeated the old bookstore. Unlike a phone or computer screen, each book that lined the shelves had character, personality, a story waiting to be told. "Both," she said.

"Ah, business *and* pleasure. Say no more. That means it's coffee time."

Suze scurried off into the hallway behind the counter and then returned a few minutes later. "It'll be ready in a jiffy. So, what brings you by?"

"I'm going to Orcas Island tomorrow to learn more about the rumors of a magnetic field there that's supposed to heal people, or give power to crystals, or something like that. I'm not exactly sure what yet. I was hoping you could help enlighten me."

Suze pushed her glasses further up onto her nose. "Are you talking about the hippie commune stuff from the 1970s?"

"Perhaps. I have no idea what you're talking about but I'm here to learn."

"And what has you chasing this information? Is it for a story?"

"Partly, yes. It's also for a visitor to the islands who's come here seeking the same information."

"*Really*? Sounds mysterious. Who's the visitor?"

"It's really kind of remarkable."

Suze propped her elbows onto the counter and leaned forward. "Okay, you have my full attention, young lady. Who is it?"

"His name is Fin Kearns."

"I'm sorry, I don't know who that is."

"He's the son of Delroy Hicks."

Suze's mouth fell open. "*What*?"

Adele chuckled. "I know, right? I had pretty much the same reaction as you just did. But it's true. As soon as I heard him speak, it was Delroy's voice, his tone, his mannerisms. Fin is his son."

"But Delroy, he was—"

"Gay, I know. Well, apparently, he was more of an equal opportunity dabbler than we knew. Especially as a younger man."

"My goodness. Old Delroy is long gone but he's still managing to surprise us. Well, with that bit of unexpected information out there, what does this have to do with a visit to Orcas Island in search of healers, crystals, and magnets?"

"Not magnets. A magnetic field. Fin said he'd read about it and wanted to find out if it was true. That got me thinking about it and now I think I might be as intrigued as he is. So, here I am hoping to learn more before heading out tomorrow."

"With this Fin Kearns?"

"That's right. I'm taking him there on my Chris Craft."

Suze held up a finger. "Hold on. Coffee is ready. Be right back." She returned with two cups on saucers and gave one to Adele. "Okay, let's see. Orcas Island. Magnetic field. Healing power. Crystals. Let's try the local history section first."

Suze looked up and started to silently mouth the titles of the books on the shelves. She stopped to take a sip of coffee and then continued. This process was repeated several times until she stopped and shook her head.

"I'm certain we have something on that very subject. I just know it. Think Suze, think. Ah! That's it—right over here. And how ironic."

Suze moved to a different row and pointed to the top shelf. "There, on the left side. Four textbooks with a name very familiar to you, providing information you likely won't find on the Internet."

Adele saw the books and then saw the name of the author on the spine—Professor Delroy Hicks.

"It's our Delroy section. I haven't taken one of those books down since he died, but I'm almost positive you'll find what you're looking for. It's the one with the black-and-white photo of that healer fella on the cover, guru what's-his-name who was all over the news that one summer. I was no more than ten or eleven at the time, but I remember my mother complaining about him. It was all anyone around here was talking about for a while. The Anacortes newspaper called it the war of the crystals or the crystal wars. Well, it was crystal-something anyways."

Adele spotted the book and took it down. It was a large paperback titled *The Mystery of the Lekwiltok Crystal.* A photograph of an older, stern-faced man stared back at her. He had shoulder-length white hair, a wide brow, and especially prominent cheekbones that jutted out like a pair of sharp glaciers that threatened to break through the skin of his face. A large crystal hung around his neck. Adele tapped the book cover.

"This is guru what's-his-name?"

"That's him," Suze answered with a nod. "Scary looking, isn't he?"

"I'd say more serious than scary. Was he Native American?"

"Not sure. Might be. I haven't actually read that one. Rumor is the use of the past tense doesn't yet apply to him though."

Adele looked up. "People think he's still alive?" She opened the book. "This was published in 1981. That's nearly forty years ago."

"I know," Suze said. "That's the last word I heard on him. Granted, it's been, oh, five or six years since he's come up, but there are still people around here who remain convinced he's still alive."

Adele put her coffee down on another shelf, held the book in both hands, and stared at the cover again. "He appears to be at least 60 years old in this photo, perhaps even 70."

Suze smiled. "Indeed."

"That would make him a very old man. Likely one of the oldest human beings on the planet."

"Definitely."

"Impossible."

Suze clicked her tongue. "When did you become such a pessimist? Not probable? Yes. Impossible? No. These are the San Juans. Live here long enough and you'll come to learn almost anything is possible."

Adele turned the book over and found a photo of Delroy wearing his fedora and smiling into the camera. He looked so young, so confident, a man who appeared to have the whole world eating from his hand. The resemblance between him and Fin was striking. She read the book's back cover description.

In 1905, former Seattle mayor and wealthy shipbuilding magnate, Robert Moran, his health in precipitous decline, was given a death sentence via his personal physician. He had but one year to live.

Moran moved to Orcas Island in 1906 hoping to get a few more years but also fully expecting and prepared to die.

Death did come to Mr. Moran—in 1943 at the age of 86. He had outlived his wife, most of his friends and family, and the doctor who had declared him not long for this world some four decades earlier.

Rumors long swirled around Moran's miraculous recovery and subsequent long life, most of which was spent in unusually robust health. Some claimed it to be by God's grace. Others whispered he obtained this seeming miracle through darker means.

Enter the remarkable figure of Karl Bloodbone, said to be a direct descendent of the fierce Lekwiltok tribe of British Columbia that centuries earlier regularly raided the San Juan lands occupied by their gentler southern Salish Indian cousins. Bloodbone is a self-described shaman, healer, mystic, and warrior. His many detractors call him a fraud whose only interest is emptying the pockets of those desperate enough to seek his help.

Bloodbone also claims he was the one who healed Robert Moran in 1906, an event which would have taken place 73 years before this writing. He explains his own impossible longevity as being the result of metaphysical transmutation whereby his physical form is periodically reborn while his spiritual form remains constant.

Eternal life.

The Mystery of the Lekwiltok Crystal is the result of six months of study in and around the equally fascinating and incriminating human riddle that is Karl Bloodbone. It may not be the story he wishes to be told, but it is the one that I am now required to share with the world because, quite simply, it is the truth.

-Delroy Hicks: Professor of Anthropology

"Wow," Adele said. "This is incredible."

Suze appeared disappointed. "Gosh darn it. I should have taken the time to read it myself. Is it really that good?"

"It could be. Delroy sure knew how to sell a story. Now I'm more excited than ever to be making the trip to Orcas tomorrow. Still, this is an old accounting of stuff that took place there years ago. I'm not sure where I should start or who might still be around who knew this Karl Bloodbone personally."

Suze rubbed her chin. "I think I might have an idea."

"Really? Who?"

"You met her last summer—Mother Mary Ophelia."

"The nun on Shaw Island?"

"That's the one."

"And you think Mother Mary knew Karl Bloodbone?"

Suze nodded. "I do. My mother said so. Apparently, there was some kind of protest years ago involving Bloodbone and his followers and Mother Mary was part of it."

"Bloodbone had followers?"

"The word most people around here used was cult. The community leaders on Orcas, including the local pastor, wanted him gone. I believe Mother Mary represented the Catholic Church's support of the pastor and his fight against Bloodbone. It was quite a happening. I'm guessing at least some of Delroy's book is about that conflict. It went on for two or three years. Got so bad even the governor issued a press release telling everyone to knock it off."

Adele held Delroy's book against her chest. "This has the makings of quite a story for the newspaper. Jose has been worried the online readership is showing some weakness in recent months. This might be exactly what we need to rejuvenate people's interest."

Suze smiled. "I was thinking the exact same thing."

"How much for the book?"

"No charge. I'm glad I was able to help. Just don't lose it. I intend to read it when you're done. You can do me one favor though."

"Name it."

"Bring Fin Kearns by when you have chance. I'd love to meet him."

Adele gave Suze a quick hug. "Deal. Maybe next week?"

"I'll be here. Until then you be safe out there."

Adele waved as she headed out the door. "Will do. Thanks again, Suze."

Only a few clouds remained in the sky. Adele breathed in the cool, dry, late-afternoon air. She looked down at the book cover and found herself locking eyes with Karl Bloodbone. A chill ran through her body. She went to reach for her car door, heard a scratching noise, looked up, and then gasped.

A giant raven sat perched atop the Mini's roof. Adele saw her own face reflected within the great bird's glistening black eyes. She stepped back from the car and raised the book over her head.

"Go away. Shoo. Get out of here."

The raven leaned forward, adjusted its wings, and let out an angry croak. Not knowing what else to do, Adele hissed at it like a cat. The sound made the raven hop backwards, flap its wings, and then take off toward a nearby tree line.

That was creepy.

A departing ferry's horn bellowed across the streets of Friday Harbor. Adele ran her hand along the Mini's roof feeling for scratches that the bird might have left. Finding

131

none, she opened the door and got behind the wheel. As soon as she turned the ignition a pair of midnight wings nearly covered the entire windshield. The raven landed on the hood and then began pecking at the glass with enough force Adele worried it might crack. She turned on the wipers. The raven jumped back but kept its eyes on Adele. When she leaned to the side, the raven's head followed.

Adele backed the car up slowly onto the street while the raven remained perched on the hood. She worried that if she took off too fast the bird could be injured. Part of her was okay with that. Another part of her didn't wish to see any animal suffer even if it was one that appeared intent on trying out for a remake of Alfred Hitchcock's *The Birds*. She turned off the wipers and sped up. The raven partially spread its wings to keep its balance as it hopped forward and resumed pecking at the windshield.

"Get off my car," Adele yelled while continuing to accelerate. As she neared a stop sign, she waited until the very last moment to hit the brakes. The tires chirped as the Mini came to a sudden stop. The raven croaked loudly as it rolled backwards down the hood. Adele heard a soft thump from the front of the car.

She waited.

Oh no, she thought, fearing the bird was injured or dead but also too afraid to open the door to check. Instead, she backed up a few feet. Seeing nothing, she backed up a few more feet and then a few more feet.

The raven was gone.

I would have seen it fly away. Where is it?

Instinct made Adele glance to her left. The raven was flying straight for the driver side window. She mashed the accelerator, forgetting the car was still in reverse. Her body lurched forward until the seatbelt tightened and held her in place. She could hear the raven's wings slicing through the air as it passed over the car's hood right before it circled back for a second bombing mission.

Not this time.

Adele threw the shifter into first and accelerated. The car lunged forward. She turned right and hit second gear. The Mini's turbo growl filled the interior. Stop signs were ignored in favor of more speed. Adele didn't slow down until she was three miles outside of Friday Harbor. She looked in the rearview mirror and then up through the sunroof. The sky was clear. No mad raven followed.

In the passenger seat Karl Bloodbone glowered back at her. Adele grabbed the book and flipped it over so that it was young Delroy's smiling face she saw.

"That's better," she whispered as the Mini raced down San Juan Island's interior roads. Driving at night had never bothered Adele before but this time she wanted to be back to Roche before dark.

The sun had nearly set. Shadowy fingers appeared to be reaching out and choking the paved path ahead. Adele's eyes narrowed as she gripped the steering wheel more tightly and drove on.

She'd make it.

But just barely.

13.

Adele was disappointed.

No matter how fast she pushed the little Chris Craft Lancer, even when she nearly buried the bow into an oncoming wave and sea spray washed over the windshield, Fin's relaxed smile never left him as he sat in the passenger seat enjoying the ride.

"You sure you haven't spent more time on the water?" she yelled over the wind.

"Not even a little," Fin replied. "A few times as a kid but this is the first time I've been on a boat like this in years. It handles wonderfully by the way and you clearly know what you're doing behind the wheel."

Adele lowered the speed to improve the smoothness of the ride. The Lancer's sharp bow sliced through the early morning chop of Wasp Passage. She pointed to the right. "That's Shaw Island there." Then she pointed to the left. "And that's Crane Island. We'll follow Shaw's shoreline until we reach the ferry terminal on the northeast side. Shouldn't be more than another 10 or 15 minutes."

Fin's smile grew wider. "It's so beautiful." He zipped his jacket up to nearly the bottom of his chin. "Despite the cold."

"It'll warm up soon."

"Look at that." Fin pointed to a pair of Canadian geese flying just a few feet over the water. One of them honked at the Chris Craft as it sped by them. "How marvelous." He turned in his seat and faced Adele. "This nun you plan to speak with before we continue on to Orcas, she's the same one I read of in your newspaper?"

"That's right—Mother Mary Ophelia."

"And you believe she knows something about the rumored magnetic field on Orcas Island?"

"She might. She's been a part of these islands for a long time."

Fin nodded. "Sounds good." He stuck his arm out over the side so the tips of his fingers skimmed over the water.

Adele leaned back in her seat and looked up into the clear sky. The combination of the droning rumble of the Chris Craft's diesel engine and the hiss of the water as it parted along both sides of the hull was among the most pleasant sounds she had ever known.

The boat traffic was minimal. They passed a few sailboats and then a fisherman on a small aluminum skiff who had hooked into a winter blackmouth salmon. As the fish was being brought aboard Fin stood up and applauded. "Well done, mate!" he shouted. The fisherman gave him a quick wave and then proceeded to club the salmon in the head. "Ah, that was rather brutal," Fin said, scowling.

"That's fishing," Adele replied. "He'll be eating well tonight."

"You fish much yourself?"

"A little. I love ling cod."

"Yeah? What's that?"

"That," Adele said, "is one of the ugliest but most delicious things in these waters. You like fish and chips?"

Fin's expression became very serious. "My dear girl, I'm Irish. Fish, chips, and a pint . . . it's the earthly equivalent of the Father, Son, and the Holy Ghost."

"Then you'll definitely enjoy some deep-fried ling. Maybe someday I can take you out fishing some time."

"I'm not big on making plans. God's laughter has taught me more than a few lessons on that, but I'll keep the invite in mind. Especially if there's a bit of garlic mayo to dip it all in."

Adele casually turned the wheel to avoid a floating log. "You mean tartar sauce?"

"No, where I come from garlic mayo rules the day. We do have tartar of course, but it isn't nearly so popular as a bit of vinegar and some garlic mayo."

"Huh," Adele said. She was a dedicated foody always on the lookout for new ways to enjoy old favorites. "Garlic mayo. I'll have to give it a try."

Fin smiled. "You'll love it. I promise."

Adele pointed straight ahead. "There's the ferry terminal."

The terminal and the small dock adjacent to it were both empty. Adele pulled alongside the dock, tied up, and shut the motor off. Fin hopped out, stretched, and then looked back at her. "What now?"

Adele grabbed her backpack and headed toward the dock ramp that connected to the narrow road that disappeared into the tree-lined hillside. "Now we walk."

Soon they were deep in the woods. Fin kept looking up. "So many trees," he said. "I've never seen so many big trees in all my life."

After twenty more minutes of walking Adele stopped next to a dilapidated wood fence that ran alongside the road. "We're almost there. I just remembered something though." She took off her backpack, unzipped it, and reached inside. "I picked this up in Friday Harbor yesterday. Your father wrote it. I spent about four hours last night reading through nearly all of it."

Fin took the book, looked at the cover, and then turned it over and stared at Delroy's photo. "He's not much older there than I am now."

"You two look a lot alike. You're taller but the face, especially the eyes, they're almost exactly the same."

"Who's the scary looking fella on the cover?"

"That is, or was, Karl Bloodbone. He's the one I'm here to inquire about."

"With the nun?"

"That's right. Apparently, she knew him."

"You said he *is* or *was* Karl Bloodbone. Obviously, he's dead by now. This book was written a long time ago."

"Well, there's a bit of uncertainty about that."

Fin looked at the book cover again. "He's already an old man in this photo. He can't possibly still be alive."

"I agree it's not likely. I was told this Bloodbone has become something of a whispered legend around here."

"Can I read it when you're done?"

Adele took the book and returned it into her backpack. "Of course. C'mon, let's go."

They went no more than a hundred yards further when a familiar voice called out to Adele. "Ah, is that my young newspaper friend coming this way? And such perfect timing. I'm enjoying a walk on this beautiful island morning."

Mother Mary Ophelia looked exactly as Adele remembered her. Old and bent, yet strong like the gnarled branches of an ancient tree. She even wore the same knee-high rubber boots as when she and Adele had first met.

"Hello again, Ophelia. You're looking well."

"Ha!" Ophelia barked. "I'm looking old and don't you try to deny it." Her eyes narrowed as she noted Fin. "And who is this?"

"This is my new friend, Fin Kearns. He's the son of Delroy Hicks and has come here all the way from Ireland."

"Delroy's son you say?"

"That's right."

Ophelia stood directly in front of Fin and peered up at him. "Yes, I see the resemblance. I knew Mr. Hicks. There was a time I knew him well. An interesting man. What some might call a free spirit. Tell me, Mr. Kearns, do you share your father's views on God?"

Fin arched a brow and cocked his head. "I'm afraid I can't answer that."

Ophelia scowled. "And why is that?"

"Because I don't know what my father's views on God were. We never met. He didn't even know I existed."

Ophelia's eyes softened almost immediately. She reached out and held one of Fin's hands. "I apologize for my rudeness."

"It's quite all right," Fin said. "There's no way you could have known. It is what it is."

When Ophelia smiled, the lines around her eyes deepened and spread across her cheeks. "What we think and what truly is are often two very different things, Mr.

Kearns. I know the pain of that disconnect all too well. I know it but I don't suppose I'll ever truly understand. Not entirely anyways."

Fin appeared as confused as Adele was by Ophelia's words. He cleared his throat. "Perhaps *you* could tell me what my father's views on God were."

Ophelia let go of Fin's hands and tilted her head upward. "He believed the modern version of God to be far too cartoonish and commercialized to be taken seriously. He was never intentionally cruel in his assessment, at least not around me, though was clearly amused by what he called the fabrications of organized religion. And though Delroy might not have been religious I'm certain he was a deeply spiritual man."

"I see," Fin said.

"I didn't ask about what you *see*, Mr. Kearns. I asked about what you *believe*."

"From what you've just told me I believe my father and I would have shared a great deal in common regarding our views on God and organized religion."

Ophelia nodded. "Very well. You may be wrong, but at least you're interesting. That's more than most can say." She turned toward Adele. "So, what brings you back here?"

"I have some questions I was hoping you could answer."

"Questions? Regarding what?"

Adele took the book out and handed it to Ophelia. "Regarding this."

Ophelia's hands trembled as she stared at the cover. She immediately gave the book back to Adele and shook her head. "No. I'm very happy to see you again. We can visit. We can reminisce. And you're both welcome to stay at the convent for as long as you like, but I won't spend my time discussing that creature. Not now. Not ever."

"I don't understand," Adele said.

Ophelia sighed. "All the better that you never will. Trust me. No good will come of it. There are things in this world you don't disturb, Adele. The monster on that book cover is among them."

Fin adjusted the cap on his head. "That man, or monster, or whatever, is long gone by now. We're just hoping to learn more about what he was involved in. Namely the rumors of healing that are said to be part of the island's history."

"And why do you wish to know about any of *that*, Mr. Kearns?"

"It fascinates me."

"And that's it?"

Fin shrugged. "Sure. I came here to learn more about my father. I also came to learn more about the healing stuff some say can be found on Orcas. And now, just today, I'm told that my father went in search of the very same thing.

That feels more than a little bit like destiny, don't you think? It wouldn't be right for me to have come this far only to then ignore such a thing."

Ophelia straightened. Though she was physically much smaller than Fin the powerful confidence of her personality made her appear greater than the sum of her aged parts. "For a man who likens God to a cartoon you express a remarkable amount of faith in the unknown."

"Not faith so much as curiosity."

"Curiosity killed the cat, Mr. Kearns." Ophelia nodded at Adele. "I care a great deal about this one and I don't wish to see her hurt."

"Ophelia," Adele replied, "you know I can take care of myself. And you also know I'm going to Orcas to investigate these rumors about Karl Bloodbone with or without your help."

The mention of Bloodbone made Ophelia visibly wince. She covered her eyes with her hand. "Lord forgive them," she whispered.

Adele and Fin shared a quick look. "My father survived his time with Bloodbone just fine," Fin said.

Ophelia's hand dropped slowly away from her eyes. "Did he?"

"Did he what?" Adele questioned.

"Did Delroy Hicks survive *just fine* as your new friend seems to think?"

Adele was alarmed by what she heard in the old nun's voice. Mother Mary Ophelia was afraid.

"Ophelia, what's wrong? Why does this have you so upset?"

"Please," Ophelia replied. "I'm begging you not to take this path. Go back to Roche Harbor. Return to Ireland. Think of this no more." She looked at Fin. "Your father came to me then just as you are doing now. He knew of my prior history with Bloodbone. And like you he wanted to know more. I was so much younger then. Confused by things I didn't fully understand but also equally naïve and vain and not wanting to appear too much like a stupid and frightened woman. So, my warnings to Delroy were too quiet, too accommodating, too easily dispatched by his natural charm and curiosity. I watched him leave the dock here at Shaw on his way across the water to Orcas and then watched him return months later. Outwardly he was the same man who had left. Beneath the confident exterior, though, he was different. Changed. Haunted. Something within him was missing. I knew who had taken it and that its taking had been the price Delroy was forced to pay for having dared investigate the thing that goes by the name of Karl Bloodbone."

Adele stood stunned and silent, not knowing what to say. Then she heard a sound that made her throat tighten and her eyes widen. In a tree above her head came the gurgling croak of a raven.

Ophelia glared up at the great black bird and made the sign of the cross. "You are not welcome here," she shouted.

The raven let out a shrill cry, leapt from the tree, and fell toward the group below. Both Adele and Fin jumped to the side. Ophelia stood her ground with her arms spread wide. Her eyes were lit by a righteous fire, her hands curled inward like claws, and her lips pulled back in a feral snarl.

"Come on then. I'm right here. Try to finish what was so long ago started."

The raven swooped low, barely missing the nun's head. When it attempted to pull up with a powerful flap of its wings, Ophelia's hand closed tightly around its tail feathers. The bird screamed as it was flung to the ground and its body skidded into the tall grass that grew alongside the road. Ophelia lost her balance and fell backwards, hitting the dirt and gravel road with a loud grunt. The raven immediately regained its footing and bounded toward Ophelia with its head low.

"Bloody hell," Fin cried out as he threw a rock that bounced off the road directly in front of the bird, momentarily halting its progress. Adele began whirling her backpack around her head. The raven squawked, backed up, and then took off into the trees. Adele turned around to help Ophelia up. "Did you hurt anything?" she asked.

"Just an old woman's pride."

Fin stared into the trees, clearly shaken by the attack. "I would never believe it if I hadn't seen it with my own eyes. That was absolutely insane. Do birds get rabies?"

Ophelia brushed the dirt off her jeans. "Quick thinking throwing that rock. Another second or two and that thing would have been on me."

"Apologies for missing so badly," Fin said. "I was actually trying to hit it."

Adele slung her backpack over her shoulder. "Birds don't get rabies. I saw that same raven in Friday Harbor yesterday outside the bookstore. It attacked my car."

Fin's mouth fell open. "Are you serious?"

"I am."

"You mean to say that thing followed you all the way here? That's impossible."

"And yet," Adele said with a shrug, "that's exactly what happened."

Ophelia took a step and then grimaced. "I think I did manage to hurt something—my ankle."

When Adele went to help, Ophelia waved her away. "I'm fine. Just a bit tender. I'll walk it off. Can I interest you two in a snack?"

Fin nodded. "I can eat."

"Thank you," Adele said. "But we can't stay long."

Ophelia turned around. "You're still going to Orcas, aren't you?"

"Yes," Adele answered. "I plan to be there within the hour."

"Before you go, and against my better judgement, I have something you'll want to hear."

Fin stepped forward. "My father's story, what he shared with you when he returned from his time with Karl Bloodbone. That's it, isn't it?"

Ophelia nodded. "It is. There is much that wasn't part of that book. Things he kept hidden from the public likely for fear of being called crazy. But he told me and until now I have told no one else. Do you wish to know of it?"

Both Adele and Fin said yes. Ophelia closed her eyes and sighed. "Very well. Let us return to the convent. It'll be far safer to speak of such things there."

The old nun limped her way back home as Adele and Fin followed close behind.

14.

"Careful, it's hot," Ophelia said as she filled Adele's and Fin's teacups and then pointed to the plate in front of Fin. "The cheese and the crackers were made here as well. Enjoy."

Fin bit into some cheese. "Mm, it's wonderful. Thank you."

Ophelia sat on the wooden bench on the other side of the table and then filled her own cup. The convent's main hall was as Adele remembered it: the scuffed wood floor, the high exposed wood ceiling, and the massive chandelier that had been a gift from St. James Cathedral in Seattle. Though austere it was also a warm place full of history and the accumulated devotion of the nuns who had long called it home.

"We can speak freely," Ophelia remarked. "No one will overhear what is said. The other two sisters are visiting friends and family out of state. They aren't due to return for another week."

Adele nibbled on a corner of cheese. "Remember, we can't stay long."

Ophelia nodded as she kept her eyes fixed on Adele. "So, shall I begin?"

"Please," Adele replied.

"You've read the book in your backpack?"

"Yes, most of it."

"And?"

"And what?"

Ophelia sipped her tea. "What did you think of it? Namely, what did you think of its assessment of Karl Bloodbone?"

"Delroy considered him a fraud."

"That's right," Ophelia said. "But it was Delroy Hicks who was the fraud because his book was a lie and he knew it."

Fin pushed the plate of cheese and crackers away. "I don't understand."

"I met Bloodbone before your father. As I already told you, that's why Delroy came to me before going to Orcas. He wanted help in understanding what made Bloodbone tick. I knew what Bloodbone was, but I didn't share it with Delroy. I should have, but I didn't."

"Why not?" Adele asked.

Ophelia folded her hands together and bowed her head. "I feared I would sound crazy. I had no proof of anything. It was all just a feeling—instinct. Something in his eyes, how he looked at others. How he looked at me. I sensed the darkness in him. I should have been more forthcoming. Truth is truth no matter how unlikely it might seem to some. Instead I just told Mr. Hicks to be careful. To not trust anything Bloodbone said. He left here intrigued but not fearful. I failed to adequately prepare him for what he would later discover—a discovery that confirmed what I knew even though I had not seen it for myself."

It seemed to Adele as if the entire convent had gone silent in anticipation of what Mother Mary Ophelia would say next. She reached across the table and squeezed the old nun's hand. "What happened?"

Ophelia shut her eyes tight and shook her head. Only after her eyes opened did she continue. "Delroy was gone for months and then he suddenly returned. He was the same but different—very different. He spent three days here at the convent before going on to Roche Harbor. For the first two days he said little about Orcas Island and Karl Bloodbone. It was the morning of the third day as we walked alone on the road leading to the ferry terminal when he finally spoke of the experience.

"Bloodbone never slept. Never ate. Never drank. Delroy wondered why he would hide those things from him. Day after day, week after week, month after month, he couldn't understand Bloodbone's dedication toward upholding the ruse of not needing drink, food, or rest. In fact, he remarked there was an almost total absence of anything of note happening throughout the encampment. There were nearly forty followers the first month Delroy had arrived there. Three months later that number was half. Soon after, it was only Delroy and Bloodbone.

Everyone else had gone without warning or explanation. One day they were there and the next they were not. Delroy had assumed they had left out of the same boredom he had been suffering from while there.

"It was the night before Delroy was scheduled to leave Orcas that he awoke to find Bloodbone standing over him inside the little shack that was just big enough to fit the cot he had slept on during those long six months. Startled, he propped himself up onto his elbows and asked Bloodbone what he wanted. Bloodbone told him he was to lie about what he had seen. When Delroy replied he hadn't really seen anything, Bloodbone grabbed hold of his wrist, pulled him out of bed, and dragged him outside.

"The moon was full, bathing the empty encampment in its light. The clearing was encircled by old growth trees. When Delroy looked into those trees, he found hundreds of eyes staring back at him—eyes of blackest night. On nearly every branch of every tree he saw them—ravens.

"One called out. Then another and then another. The noise they made was so unbearably painful Delroy was forced to cover his ears and drop to his knees. The wailing ravens continued, until just as suddenly as it started, it stopped. Delroy looked up into the eyes of Bloodbone who was smiling back at him.

"Bloodbone yanked Delroy back onto his feet and ordered him to follow. They took a path Delroy had never seen before. He didn't have time to ponder how that was possible as he struggled to keep up as they climbed the side of a hill. Up they went, through brush and bramble that inexplicably appeared to make way for Bloodbone as he approached. At some point Delroy realized they were no longer going up the hill but rather *into* it. He was surrounded by earth above and below and on all sides. And still Bloodbone pressed forward, going deeper and deeper into the darkness. When Delroy stumbled over a root, Bloodbone paused, turned around, and warned that should Delroy fall too far behind he may never return to the outside world. The earth would simply swallow him up as if he had never been."

"Jesus," Fin muttered.

Ophelia slapped the table. "Watch your tongue, young man."

Fin quickly apologized. Ophelia took in a long breath, let it out, and then resumed the story.

"Delroy realized the path forward was being lit by something. That something was the large crystal that hung from Bloodbone's neck. The deeper into the hill they went the more intensely the crystal glowed. There was also a hum, faint at first but growing more powerful. Delroy likened it to the sound of an electric transformer. He could both hear it and feel it below his feet. Bloodbone's pace quickened. He yelled for Delroy to hurry.

"And then all prior darkness ceased. Everything was light upon more light. Delroy told me he cried out, blind, confused, and fearing for his life. Eventually his eyes adjusted, and a new world took shape all around him. It was a massive, glowing wall of multi-colored crystal that extended down into a seemingly bottomless abyss below. Bloodbone stood near the great precipice with his back to Delroy. 'Is this nothing?' he bellowed. And then, very slowly, very deliberately, he turned around. The light of the crystal against Bloodbone's chest pulsated like a heartbeat in rhythm with the strange humming Delroy felt. Thump-thump-thump, it went.

"Bloodbone held Delroy in his eyes, staring for what felt like hours as the crystal continued its incessant beating. Delroy said he attempted to move but couldn't. No matter how hard he tried, his limbs simply wouldn't obey. He wasn't even sure he was blinking. All he heard, all he felt, all he knew was the humming beat of whatever unknown power lay deep inside the earth. Thump-thump-thump.

"Then the humming stopped. The light of the crystals dimmed. 'See me,' Bloodbone ordered. Delroy had no choice but to obey. As much as he wanted to, he couldn't look away. He watched Bloodbone's face collapse into itself. The skin pulled back, broke apart, until only a skull remained. It was then and only then that Delroy was able to cry out, though he still couldn't move. He screamed and he screamed. The thing called Bloodbone spread its arms wide, teetered backwards for a moment, as if pausing between this world and the next, before falling completely into the void below.

"Delroy crept forward inch by inch, until he was able to look down. At first, he saw nothing but unmoving, impenetrable, blackness, like the universe before God turned on the light. Then the darkness took shape and began to rush upward toward him. Delroy crouched low and covered his face as a thousand wings buffeted the air around him. It was the ravens again, emerging from the pit to return to the world outside. Delroy crawled out behind them, sobbing like a child. He made his way down the hill until he finally reached the shed. He scrambled inside and collapsed onto the cot, thinking himself too frightened to sleep.

"But sleep he did, long and deep. He awoke the next morning feeling more rested and alert than he had in years. His mind raced to replay the events of the night before, but already the recollection was fragmented to the point he thought it might have been nothing more than an unusually vivid dream. That is until he rose from his bed and saw the words carved on the inside of the door.

"Be a slave to the truth or know freedom from the lie."

"What could that possibly mean?" Fin asked.

Ophelia's thin smile already hinted at the answer to come. "The world would never believe the truth of what he experienced. Delroy's academic reputation would suffer greatly. So, he chose freedom. *He chose the lie.* His book dismissed Karl Bloodbone as an eccentric—one made more notorious by those desperate to seek out his alleged power to heal. An interesting study but ultimately a fraud like so many others before him. In turn, Bloodbone was given back what he wanted most—the safety of obscurity. He was notorious no longer but merely another passing moment in time, an inconsequential footnote of our local history."

"But you don't believe that," Adele said. "You think Bloodbone was something more."

"Indeed. I know Bloodbone *is* something more."

"C'mon," Fin scoffed. "The story you just shared with us, and it is admittedly one hell of a story, was told to you some forty years ago. Legend or not, Bloodbone is certainly long gone by now."

Ophelia leaned forward. "Tell that to the raven that attacked us outside."

Fin shrugged. "Coincidence or some oddly aggressive version of a raven that is unique to the area. It's hardly proof of the supernatural. I'm certain there is a more rational explanation than the one you appear intent on trying to convince us of."

"Blessed are they that have not seen and yet have believed, Mr. Kearns."

"And it is blind faith that human history has time and time again proven to be the most dangerous," Fin replied.

Ophelia scowled. "You are indeed your father's son."

Fin grinned. "Thank you."

The two stared across the table at each other until Adele broke the silence. "Ophelia, do you really believe Bloodbone could somehow still be alive?"

The old nun's head dropped low as her shoulders slumped. She suddenly appeared every bit as old as her many years indicated. "All I know is that there has been no proof he isn't." When she looked at Adele, she was close to tears. "Please, I beg of you, don't seek him out. Whatever he was, whatever he might still be, leave it alone."

Twenty minutes later, Adele was back on the Chris Craft looking behind her at Ophelia who stood watching their departure from the dock. Despite her sore ankle she had demanded to see them off. Neither Adele nor Fin were willing to leave it alone. If anything, the story Ophelia had shared only made them both even more determined to retrace Delroy's long-ago steps.

"Huh," Fin said.

"What?"

"Well, there she is on that dock watching us make our way to Orcas just like she likely did when it was my father doing the very same thing all those years ago. I guess history really does have a way of repeating itself."

Ophelia waved. Adele waved back, sat down, and gripped the wheel. Across the water, Orcas island loomed. It was nearly noon. Adele was surprised by a sudden desire to turn toward Roche and leave the trip to Orcas behind. It would be so much easier and safer.

Since when do I choose easy and safe?

The Lancer's bow pointed toward Orcas.

The more difficult choice was made.

15.

The trip from Shaw Island to the Eastsound village on Orcas was brief and uneventful. Adele did glance to her right as she passed the cliffs of Rosario on their way there, recalling her violent struggle with Visili Vasa that ended with the Russian falling to his death against the rocks below. The memory remained too vivid, too uncomfortable, to obsess on. Far better to move ahead and leave such things behind. So, that's what Adele did, pushing the Chris Craft's throttle forward and speeding on toward the Eastsound visitor dock.

Soon they were walking the idyllic village streets on their way to the Orcas Island Historical Society building. The destination had been Ophelia's suggestion. "Look up a woman named Prunella Brown," she told Adele. "She was a Bloodbone follower. If anyone there still knows how to get to the old encampment it would be her."

Fin appeared delighted by the old world meets new age vibe that was a hallmark of the Eastsound experience. "It's just like that line from the Don Henley song," he said. "A Deadhead sticker on a Cadillac. You can feel all the money coursing through the veins of this place, yet it also feels equally unpretentious."

"You have it about right," Adele replied. "I've always thought of Eastsound as Friday Harbor's rebellious little cousin. Yes, the people here have money, but they don't care to talk about it. Where Friday Harbor openly promotes and thrives on the commerce it creates, Eastsound comes off somewhat embarrassed by it."

Fin smiled as he continued to gaze into all the shop windows that lined the village's main street. "That's a very Irish sensibility. Be grateful for one's wealth but never prideful. Having more than others should always be a private matter."

"There," Adele said as she pointed to a single-story log cabin that sat atop a small hill a hundred yards off the main road. "That's the museum."

They walked up the hill and then turned around. Eastsound was directly below and beyond that the waters of Fishing Bay. In the distance a ferry made its way toward the village. Adele felt Fin nudge her arm. He was looking at a large, multi-colored totem pole that rose up from the ground near the museum's main entrance. "You see that?" he asked.

At the very top of the totem was carved an oversized head and body of a raven with its wings spread out. Adele walked up to the pole and read the bronze plaque affixed to its base.

Donated to the Orcas Island Historical Society by notable Native artist and healer, Karl Bloodbone: 1987

"Well," Fin said, "I guess that means we've come to the right place, yeah?"

Adele kept staring at the plaque as she nodded. "I guess so. At least we now know for certain Bloodbone was still around here after the time with Delroy."

"And donating artwork no less. Seems he was more civic-minded than the story my father told to your nun friend."

Adele reached for the door. "C'mon, let's see if this Prunella Brown is here."

It was unusually warm inside the museum. Adele heard an electric wall heater blasting away. Shelves and display cabinets were filled with photos and memorabilia depicting the rich San Juan Islands' history, from the Native people of centuries ago, to the slow trickle of white settlers in the 1850s, and the booming logging and fishing eras of the early 1900s that followed. Adele looked around wondering if they were the only ones there. The old wood floor groaned loudly with every step she took.

"I know you," a voice called out from the shadows of a narrow hallway behind the counter near the center of the room. Adele watched the crevice-lined face of an old woman emerge from the darkness. Her silver hair was cut short. She wore a dark turtleneck sweater and loose jeans. An off-white crystal dangled from her bird-thin, wrinkled neck. "You're the newspaper writer. I hoped we might someday meet." She extended a bony hand marked with age spots. "It's an honor. My name is Prunella, but everyone just calls me Prune. It was a cute little nickname back when I was younger. Now my face looks far too much like an actual prune so I'm not nearly so fond of it."

Prune laughed at her own joke as Adele shook her hand. She turned toward Fin. "So, I know her, but who are you?"

Fin flashed his big smile and tipped is cap. "The name is Fin Kearns, ma'am."

Prune cocked her head. "Irish?"

"I am."

"Have we met before?" She leaned forward and squinted up at Fin. "Perhaps in another life?"

"Uh, I don't believe so. This is my first time visiting the islands."

"No," Prune said as she began to slowly stroke the crystal around her neck. "That's not true. You've been here before. I'm certain of it."

Adele cleared her throat. "He's Delroy's son."

Prune's eyes widened. "Delroy Hicks?"

"That's right," Adele answered.

Prune reached up to touch Fin's face. "Do you mind?"

Fin shrugged. "Sure."

The old woman slowly ran her fingers along Fin's cheek, his temple, and his brow. "You *are* his son. That's why I sensed you'd been here before. Part of you was. The same part that stands here now." She stepped back. "What can I do for you two?"

Adele removed Delroy's book from her backpack and handed it to Prune. "I was told you knew the man on the cover," she said.

Prune looked down at the book and scowled. "Oh, how I've always hated that picture. It's so deceptive, only depicting the dark without the light. The yin without the yang. It's such an unbalanced perspective. Karl isn't nearly so ominous as this photo would have people believe. He's like most of us—a perpetual contradiction."

"You're speaking of Mr. Bloodbone in the present tense," Adele noted.

"That's right," Prune replied. "And why wouldn't I? None of us ever truly dies. Mr. Kearns is ample evidence of that. When I see him, I feel his father's presence. And so, in a way, in the most important of ways, Delroy lives."

"Do you believe Karl Bloodbone is still alive?"

Prune handed the book back to Adele. "Is this to be used as a story for your newspaper?"

"It might be. It's also about Fin wanting to learn more about his father."

"We've had our fill of media attention around here over the years. It's been quiet for a while. I've experienced both extremes and am certain I prefer the quiet."

"Mother Mary Ophelia sent us here," Adele said. "She thought you'd be willing to help us."

Prune leaned against the counter. "Now there's a name I haven't heard in a *very* long time. How's Ophelia doing these days?"

"Good," Adele answered. "As tough as ever."

"That she is," Prune said, chuckling. "Like a piece of old leather. It was quite a war between her and Karl. I was so much younger then, but I remember it well. And then came Delroy Hicks and all his notes and questions and pictures. Before long, we grew tired of the attention and scattered to the four corners of the earth. Well, not me of course. I remained here. This island is the only world I care to ever know. I tell you what. I'll happily take a little time to sit and talk with you two if you do something for me first."

"What's that?" Adele asked.

Prune pointed to a box that sat on one side of the counter. "Make a donation to the museum. It's the slow season and we're hurting for funds. Look around. This place is the culmination of years of work and dedication. Unfortunately, people don't always stop and consider how that kind of work requires a certain level of financial support in order to keep it going."

Fin took out a $20 bill and held it up. "This work?" He dropped the money into the donation box.

Prune nodded. "That works just fine, Mr. Kearns. On behalf of the Orcas Island Historical Society, I thank you." She motioned toward the hallway. "Now, if you would both follow me to the office we can sit down there and have us a chat."

The windowless office was a ten-by-ten space with a desk, a few chairs, and a rusty file cabinet. The only source of light was a single bulb that hung down from the middle of the ceiling.

"Have a seat," Prune said as she plopped into the chair behind the desk. She pushed a bowl toward Adele and Fin. "Feel free to have some hard candy if you like. It's made local."

Adele and Fin both declined the offer. Fin then pointed at Prune's crystal necklace. "I've read up on the crystals from around here. Some seem to think they have the power to heal. Given you're wearing one is it safe to assume you think the same?"

"I've come to learn it's never safe to assume *anything*, Mr. Kearns. As for our island crystals, yes, some do believe them to possess a myriad of useful properties, healing being among them."

"You mind my asking how old you are?"

Adele wanted to smack Fin on the back of the head for asking. Prune didn't appear bothered by it though. She took a piece of candy and plopped it into her mouth. "My birth year in this life was 1930."

"You're *89*?" Adele said far louder than she intended.

Fin was looking down counting his fingers. He nodded. "Yeah, that's right. You're 89."

Prune shrugged. "And?"

"And you appear to be in great health," Adele answered. "Good on you."

"On the islands living to a ripe old age is rather common, especially on *this* particular island. You didn't know that?"

"As I mentioned, I read about it," Fin said. "But seeing an example sitting right across from me is quite another thing."

"Then you also likely know that the life expectancy for people living in the San Juans is among the highest in the world. I'll be 90 in two months, yet there are quite a few around here older than that."

Fin nodded. "Sure. What I'd really like to know is why people here are living such long lives."

Prune started to rub the crystal again. "You mean you wish to know if our crystals have anything to do with it?"

"Crystals, magnetic fields, whatever you got I want to hear it."

"And what about you, Ms. Plank?" Prune asked.

"I'm curious as well. I wasn't aware it was normal for people on Orcas to live so long."

"We don't like to boast. It's a blessing we mostly keep to ourselves so as to avoid too many people poking around with their questions and biases wanting something for nothing. Not that it's been a secret. You're not the first to come here looking for answers and you're not likely to be the last."

"Which is it?" Fin said. "The crystals like the one you have there or the magnetic field?"

"There's no simple answer. Like all things it's interconnected."

Adele put the book down on the desk so that Bloodbone's picture faced Prune. "So, you *do* believe there's something different about Orcas?"

"Oh, yes, this is a very special island."

"And what about Karl Bloodbone?"

Prune glanced at the photo, cracked down on the candy with her teeth, and then leaned forward to stare into Adele's eyes. "If he wishes to be found you'll find him. If not there's nothing I or anyone else can do to change that."

Adele didn't blink. "Where do we start?"

Prune looked away. "Locate Raven Creek on the eastern slope of Turtleback Mountain. There are no public trails on that side of the hill. Follow the creek north until you come to the remains of an old logging road. Beyond the road is an even older path hidden by grass and trees. Take it and you may find nothing, or you may find something. In the end, hope that you're allowed to then find your way back."

"You make it sound a little dangerous," Fin said.

Prune shrugged. "It's no more or less dangerous than you, Mr. Kearns."

"Have you been there recently?" Adele asked.

"No," Prune replied. "Not for some time. I'm old. It would be a difficult climb. I like to believe I could do it if I *had* to, but I don't wish to find out that I'm wrong. The last time I was there the shack Delroy slept in was still standing, though the grass around it was several feet tall. If it's still there it'll be even more difficult to spot by now."

Fin's eyes danced with excitement. "When was the last time you saw it?"

"On my 80th birthday. I camped there alone and spent the night looking up at the stars. When I awoke the next morning, I found the most beautiful bouquet of wild purple camas flowers lying next to me."

Adele returned the book into her backpack. "And you think it was Karl Bloodbone who put them there while you slept?"

Prune's face lit up as she recalled the memory. "Yes, of that I have no doubt. Karl adores camas bulbs. He snacked on them often. They're like a sugary-sweet onion but better—much better. I recall Delroy being quite fond of them as well. We all were."

"How far is it from here?" Fin asked. "Too far too walk?"

"If you hope to get back before dark then yes, but I can help with that." Prune stood and walked into the hallway. "Follow me." She went outside to the back of the cabin. "See? These will get you there and back soon enough." She pointed to a pair of antique bicycles. "They were donated to us last year. They're turn of the century. Not this century—the last one. 1905 I believe. All original except the tires have been updated. Everything works. I've ridden them myself."

Fin grabbed one of the bikes and ran his hand along the top of its red-painted steel frame. "Oh, this is brilliant," he exclaimed. He looked at Prune. "May I?"

"Certainly."

Fin walked the bike onto the road, got on, and began peddling around in circles. "C'mon," he yelled out to Adele. "Get to it, woman. Time is wasting."

"Just remember to follow the creek until you find the old logging road. Once you reach the path, you'll have to leave the bikes behind. The only way up the hill is by walking. If you start to see marked public trails that means you've gone too far west. Turn back, relocate the path, and try again. Eventually you should come to a small clearing. If you find the shack, you'll know you've made it."

"Is that all we'll find there?" Fin asked. "The shack?"

Prune watched him as he continued to ride in circles. The hint of a faraway smile crossed her face. "I can't answer that."

"Why not?"

"Because I don't know. Just be careful. I'll be here waiting." She turned her head and looked up at Adele. "You'll be different when you return. Changed in some way great or small. Are you prepared to accept that?"

"Changed how?"

"Again, I don't have the answer. For each person who has ever been up there it's different. Some have said it was nothing. Others have said it was everything. In the end that part of the journey will be yours and yours alone to interpret."

A raven landed atop the totem pole. It squawked once, ruffled its feathers, then flew off toward Turtleback Mountain. "I'm a little embarrassed to admit it," Adele said, "but a part of me is kind of scared."

Prune nodded. "You listen to that part of yourself, young woman. Listen close because you know what? You should be."

16.

Adele and Fin located the logging road where Prune told them it would be. Finding it proved a lot easier than biking over it. The ground was dotted with a multitude of potholes, ruts, and rocks. Adele glanced back to see Fin gritting his teeth as he narrowly avoided crashing. Finally, they reached a large boulder that marked the end of the road.

Fin got off his bike and leaned it against the boulder. "There's supposed to be a path?" he asked.

Adele put her bike next to Fin's and then walked beyond the boulder and looked down. "I think so. It's grown over, but it's still here. See?"

"Can't hardly tell. If that's a trail it's been a mighty long time since anyone's used it." Fin looked up at the hillside. "It's gonna be a climb."

"Yeah. So, let's start climbing."

They walked in silence for nearly twenty minutes until Fin stopped and turned in a complete circle. Adele asked him if something was wrong. He shook his head.

"Not sure. You feel that?"

Adele was about to say no when she noticed a very faint vibration under her feet. She leaned down and put her hand against the ground while recalling Delroy's story that

Ophelia had shared with them, including his description of hearing a strange humming coming from the earth.

Thump-thump-thump, it went.

"It's the same as what my father told your nun friend," Fin said.

Adele stood and then kept walking. "C'mon."

After another ten minutes they came upon the clearing. Fin's eyes lit up as he spotted the top of the shack's roof. "It's still here," he exclaimed right before he took off running toward it. Adele waited and looked around to make sure they were alone. The humming under her feet had gone away. The grass was nearly up to her waist. The tall evergreen trees that encircled the clearing reminded Adele of a wall. She wondered if it was to keep things out or to keep them in.

"Come over here," Fin shouted.

Adele walked toward the shack and found its door hanging open. "Where are you?"

Fin's head popped out. "Right here. You got to see this. I'm serious. You *really* have to see it."

Adele stepped into the shack. A single cot lay against the wall, partially lit by a narrow beam of daylight that shined down through a hole in the roof. Fin closed the door and then used his cell phone to illuminate the inside. He was grinning like a madman as he pointed at the door.

"The words are right there."

Fin was right. Though badly faded, the same message Delroy had shared with Ophelia and that she had then shared with them were carved into the wood.

Be a slave to the truth or know freedom from the lie.

Fin was nearly crying as he traced the words with his fingers. "It's just like the story. I wonder if I'm the first to see it since my father was here? Wouldn't that be something?"

Adele thought it unlikely but didn't want to tell Fin that and ruin the moment for him. "You could be," she said instead.

"Ah, I'm being silly. Of course others have been here. Still, what a thing to be in this place where Delroy had such a remarkable experience. What a thing indeed." He sat down on the cot and looked up at Adele. "Now what?"

"We try to find the trail that leads to the cave. The one Delroy couldn't find himself the day after Bloodbone took him there."

Fin clapped his hands together. "I was hoping you'd say that." He got up and pushed the door open. "Any ideas on where we should start?"

Adele stepped outside and looked around some more as Ophelia's voice whispered inside her head.

They took a path Delroy had never seen before. He didn't have time to ponder how that was possible as he struggled to keep up as they climbed the side of a hill. Up they went, through brush and bramble that inexplicably appeared to make way for Bloodbone as he approached.

Adele turned to the east, to the west, to the north, and to the south. Fin's brows lifted as he watched her. "Well?"

"This way," Adele answered while pointing north. "Where the undergrowth is thickest." She walked directly toward two of the biggest trees that bordered the clearing and then stopped. "There."

Fin squinted at the mass of brush. "Eh?"

"There's an opening between those two trees. It's small but it's there. See?"

Fin shook his head. "No, not really."

Adele kept walking. "Follow me."

"Ah," Fin hissed. "I'm stuck."

Adele turned around and saw Fin trying to remove a thorny branch from his pants leg. "Are you hurt?" she asked.

"No, I'm fine. There, I got it. Okay, let's keep going."

The barely visible path was steep and narrow. Adele stopped to catch her breath while Fin appeared unfazed by the difficult climb.

"You do this kind of thing often?"

"What?" Fin said. "Hiking? Not really."

"Well, you're in good shape."

Fin tipped his cap. "I'll take that as a compliment. You think we're close to the cave?"

"I'm not sure. I guess we just keep going."

It wasn't long before Adele had to stop and rest and again. She took out a bottle of water from her backpack and then noticed Fin was still barely breathing hard. "C'mon, what's the deal? Are you a runner or something?"

"I hate running," Fin replied. "I guess I'm just blessed with good lungs."

Adele glanced up at the sky. "We better find it soon. It'll start getting dark before too long."

"That wouldn't be so bad. We could make a campfire and stay the night in the shack."

"That cot won't sleep two."

Fin shrugged. "No worries. I'll sleep under the stars. You brought water and snacks, right?"

Adele held up the water bottle and gave it a little shake. "Sure."

"Then we'll be good for the night if necessary."

"I'd much rather sleep in a real bed so let's find the cave sooner rather than later."

"Hey, I'm the one following you, remember?"

Adele put her water away and resumed the hike up the hill until she came to the top and looked around. Fin whistled at the spectacular view. "My goodness," he said. "Check out all that green and blue."

Trees stretched out for miles below until they reached the water that extended even further beyond. "That's Mount Baker over there," Adele said.

Fin brought out his phone and took a picture of the great snowcapped giant that rose up into the clouds in the east. "It looks like a place the gods would happily call home. Is that steam coming off it or are my eyes playing tricks?"

"No, you're right. It's a volcano that regularly lets off geothermal steam throughout the year. Most people mistake it for mist. I studied it a little in college. The last major eruption was in 1880. My geology professor was convinced it was due for another one soon."

"Not today I hope."

"No. He said it could be tomorrow or a thousand years from now. I guess that's soon by geological standards."

Fin continued to stare at the mountain. "Yeah, I guess. Thankfully we don't have such monsters in Ireland."

"We must have missed the entrance to the cave," Adele said. I guess we retrace our steps and see if we can find it. You want to lead the way this time? A different set of eyes might help."

"Sure. I'll see what I can see."

Fin moved down the trail with far more speed and confidence than Adele. The first time she slipped Fin looked back, asked if she was okay, and then continued. The second time she slipped he looked back and she wasn't there. "I'm alright," she yelled, not wanting him to worry.

"Where you at?" he called out. She could hear him coming back up the hill toward her. Then his smiling face appeared over the opening. "Ah, there you are. Well done. You've found it."

Adele got up and wiped the dirt off her backside. "Purely by accident I assure you. My butt found it first."

Fin hopped into the cave. They both lit up their phones and looked around. The stone walls were nearly black. Fin cocked his head.

"There it is again—the vibration."

Adele heard and felt it as well. She peered down the dark passage that disappeared into the hillside. "Full disclosure," she said. "I'm a little claustrophobic."

Fin put his arm around her shoulders. "Nothing to worry about. We'll be in and out of here in no time." When he started to move forward, Adele pulled away.

"Wait. Give me a second."

"Take all the time you need," Fin replied. "If you want to wait here that's okay. I can go in alone. It shouldn't take long."

"No, I'm coming with you. We should stick together. Just keep the light on. If it goes dark in here, I might have a serious freak out."

"I doubt that. Don't forget I've read all your articles. You've been in far tougher situations than this. We're just having ourselves a leisurely stroll."

The further they moved into the cave, the lower and narrower it became until Fin had to crouch to avoid hitting his head. The stale air smelled of dirt and rock and something else Adele couldn't yet place. She noticed her hand was shaking and willed it to stop.

Fin paused. "How are you doing?"

Adele scowled as she nodded. "I'm good. Keep going."

Deeper and deeper they went. "You smell that?" Fin said.

"Yeah. Been smelling it since we got in here." The smell was getting stronger, making it hard to breathe.

Fin scrunched his face. "It's sour, like rotting fish. Maybe something crawled in here and died."

That possibility did nothing to calm Adele's nerves. She thought of stopping and turning back but seeing Fin's light moving farther into the black void made her keep going. She didn't want to be left alone.

"Hey." Fin looked back at Adele. "I think we made it."

Adele quickened her pace until she stood next to Fin. The width of the passage was nearly double what it had been, but the smell was even worse. Adele had to focus on not throwing up. Fin held his phone light out in front of him. Covering her nose, Adele did the same.

A massive crystal wall greeted them. It absorbed the light from the phones and reflected it back in a multi-colored wave. The grin on Fin's face suddenly dropped away.

"What the hell is *that*?"

It was a dark pyramid-shaped pile of something that was nearly as tall as Adele. The very top of it appeared to be wet. Fin shined more light on it. "That's where the smell is coming from," he said.

Something stirred. Adele thought she felt a gust of warm air wash over her.

Fin turned around. "You hear that?" he asked.

Adele refused to lift her head. "I don't think we want to know."

Fin chuckled. "It'll be fine." He looked up and then raised his phone.

It wasn't fine.

The cave ceiling was a swirling, leathery mass that shrieked its rage at being disturbed. Adele opened her mouth to scream, but nothing came out. Her phone fell from her hand and hit the ground with a loud crack.

Fin blinked his eyes multiple times as he shuffled backwards. "My God," he whispered.

Adele ran.

It only took a few strides for her to realize how dangerous it was to be running so fast in the dark. She warned herself to slow down. To be more careful. To wait for Fin.

But it was too late.

17.

"Hey, kid," Delroy said. "How's it going?"

"You're not supposed to be here," Adele replied. "You're dead."

"That's right. I wasn't asking about me though."

"Am I dead too?"

Delroy laughed. "No, of course not. It's just a bump to the head, remember?"

"No, not really."

"That's not true. Wanna know how I know?"

"I'm pretty sure you're going to tell me anyway."

"Yeah, I suppose that's true. Anyway, you were running too fast in the dark. Running from all those bats in that cave because you allowed the fear to take over and that's never good. You know better."

"Sorry to disappoint you."

Delroy sat at the end of the cot Adele was lying on. He reached over and poked the golf ball-sized lump on her head. "That hurt?"

"Ouch. Yeah it hurts. Geez."

"Sorry. Just checking. It's good you felt that. Means you're going to be okay. Me? I don't feel anything anymore. You'd think that would be nice, right? No pain, no hunger. Nothing is too hot or too cold. Thing is, I'd give anything to stub my toe and feel something. I miss it. I miss all of it—the good, the bad, and everything in between."

Adele tried to sit up, but her chest felt like it weighed a thousand pounds. "You're dead and I'm dreaming."

"Shh, take it easy. You'll wake up when you're ready."

"Where's Fin?"

"I believe he went back into the cave."

Again, Adele tried to sit up but couldn't. "The cave? Why?"

Delroy cocked an eyebrow. "If I knew that so would you because you're me."

"What? That doesn't make any sense."

"Sure, it does. You said it yourself. I'm dead and you're dreaming. So, whatever I know you know because it's your dream not mine."

"Scoot down so I can get a look at you."

Delroy slid toward Adele and smiled. "How's that?"

"Better. You look good."

"I look how you remember me—old and dying. Could have used a few pounds, but all in all I suppose I was holding my own. Lived a good life. Saw a lot of things. Did a lot of things. I was quite the hedonist for most of that time. Wasn't much I didn't want to experience at least once."

"Including having a child you never knew about."

Delroy's face darkened. "His mother should have told me. I would have done right by him. Even at my very worst I would have been man enough to see him properly supported and loved."

"I know you would have. It's okay. Fin is a lot like you."

"Is he? Be careful then. Don't miss something important."

"All I miss right now is you."

"Oh, my little Adele. All grown up and finding her own way. And look at you now on this cot—*my cot.* It's another adventure that's come full circle by way of your being here."

"Speaking of which, is Karl Bloodbone somehow still alive? Could such a thing really be possible?"

Delroy shrugged. "You tell me. It's your—"

"I know. I know. It's *my* dream."

Delroy pulled his fedora down low over his eyes and smiled. "Life is but a dream, Adele. As for Karl Bloodbone, he was always more of an idea than an actual man. Sure, there was the flesh and bone personification of all that, but it was the spiritual possibilities of what he represented that I found most interesting. It's very much like any great religion. There's this little kernel of truth that over time expanded and enveloped people and events far beyond its original conception. My life was spent trying to understand the spaces between the who, the how, and, most importantly, the why of such transformative human phenomena."

"So, you're saying the rumors that Bloodbone is still alive are false?"

"Not quite. I'm saying it doesn't really matter if he is or isn't. What people believe is what matters because it's those beliefs that will shape and motivate the actions and consequences that follow."

"You're losing me."

"No, you're losing yourself. I'm just a reflection of your own subconscious."

"The Delroy Hicks version of my subconscious."

"Indeed, in all its contradictory glory. I'll say this. You've read my textbooks, you've known me personally, so you have my disposition down pretty good. If there was ever to be a Church of Delroy movement around here, you'd be a more than capable original disciple. Even Christ needed Paul to spread the word after his abrupt departure."

"I don't know if I should be offended or annoyed by that comment."

"You should be amused. It's a joke. Perhaps not a good one but an intended joke nevertheless."

Adele looked at Delroy's long and lean face, making note of every line, crack, and beautiful flaw. She started to cry. "I really do miss you."

Delroy put his hand over hers. "I know. This isn't only to be a sentimental visit though. You have work to do.

Mysteries to solve. People to be made more whole—including yourself."

"I don't understand."

"Yes, you do, or you wouldn't have had me say it."

"We came here because Fin wanted to retrace some of your steps."

"That's only part of it. You came here for more than that. You came here because it's what you do. If there's an unknown, you can't let it be. Something in you demands to discover the answer. You sense connections yet to be revealed."

"You sure that's me talking and not just you?"

Delroy's eyes reflected Adele's image back to her as he squeezed her hand. "I wish that were so. Still, in a way, yes, I'm speaking to you. The mind is a very powerful thing. All that you know of me, everything we experienced together and that you have since experienced on your own are part of this conversation with yourself."

"That's deep."

"You're being sarcastic."

Adele closed her eyes and smiled. "I know."

"Do you remember the day you found Calista Stone in that horrible black pit below the old sheriff's house?"

Adele's eyes opened. "Of course." She would never forget the day Martin Speaks took the life of his son, Will, before turning the gun on himself.

"Think back to the moment Calista crept up those stairs. How filthy she was, how weak, and yet somehow still so strong. All those many years forced to live in that hole. How does one survive such an experience and then manage to recover from it so quickly?"

"She's a strong woman and wanted to be with Decklan again. You say the mind is a powerful thing. So is the heart."

"Yes, that's certainly part of it, but could it also have been something more? Think about it, Adele. You found Calista on this island, a prisoner held captive deep down in the earth in a place not far from this shack. She should have died in that pit. She should have but she didn't. Why not?"

"I don't know. She wasn't meant to. She didn't allow it. She was too strong a woman to let death have her."

"You're merely reciting easy explanations. That's not who you are. That's not how you think. You're a seeker of truth. A solver of riddles. I would have done it myself, but unlike Calista death took me. It's now up to you. Go there and see for yourself. I know you've thought of it. Now's the time."

"You mean the place where Calista was kept prisoner? You want me to go down into that hole? Why in the world would I do that?"

"This place and that place may have something very important in common."

"I'm not going back there. No way. I was lucky to leave that house alive. I just knocked myself silly running out of a bat-infested cave. That's enough adventure for a while."

"For most people that's likely true. You're not like most people, Adele. You're different. You're better. And you're certainly far braver."

"Wasn't it you who told me there's a fine line between bravery and stupidity?"

Delroy looked upward with narrowed eyes. "Did I? Admittedly it does sound like something I could have said. Regardless, you have little to fear. These islands like you. They always have. Go to the old sheriff's home. See if there is a connection between there and here."

"What does this have to do with Bloodbone?"

"Perhaps everything. Possibly nothing. You won't know until you know. And that's the thing, isn't it? People like us, if there's a path that might lead to an answer, we take it. We take it even if there's a chance that in the end it takes us. That's what I did when we first met. Even though I was an old man being eaten from the inside out by the cancer, your desire to solve the riddle that was Calista's disappearance was that path and I had no choice but to take it with you. And I enjoyed every step for it allowed my final days to be spent doing something worthwhile. But now I wonder if that particular path was left unfinished. If there is not still more of the riddle yet to be solved."

Adele could hardly hear the last few words Delroy spoke. She watched his face retreat into shadow even as he whispered her name over and over. Then the same face moved back into the light.

No, it's not the same. That's a face that knows how to lie.

"Adele," Fin said. "Are you awake?" He looked concerned.

But is he? Is he really?

"You want some water?"

Adele nodded. Fin put a half full bottle in her hand and then helped her to sit up. "Easy does it," he said. "You might feel dizzy."

After drinking the rest of the water Adele rubbed her head and winced. "Ouch."

Fin nodded. "Yeah, I bet. That's gonna leave a mark. I had to carry you out of the cave over my shoulder. You're heavier than you look."

"Gee, thanks."

"Sorry, I didn't mean it like that."

Adele felt herself getting stronger. "I know. It's fine. Say, did you go back into the cave after you put me in here?"

Fin reached into his pocket. "Actually, I did. I found this." He handed Adele her phone. "The screen is cracked, but I think it's still working. Unfortunately, we still can't get a decent cell signal. I've been walking around trying for the last twenty minutes."

"You went in there just to get my phone?"

"It wasn't any trouble. Most the bats had left."

"You sure my phone was the only reason you went back?"

"I didn't say that was the only reason. Why do I suddenly feel like I'm being interrogated?"

"Because you are. Why weren't you trying to get help? I was hurt. What if I had been hurt bad?"

"You were just sleeping. I wanted you to have a chance to get some rest. And like I already said, I couldn't get a signal."

"I'm not going to say you're lying, but I'm also sure you're not telling me the whole truth."

Fin stood, went to the door, and then turned around. "Look, I knew you were going to be fine. I also knew you dropped your phone in the cave. So, I went back and got it. What's the problem?"

"I can't make you tell me everything, Fin. That's up to you. In the meantime, I suggest we get going."

"But it's almost dark."

"I know."

"You sure you feel up to driving the boat back at night?"

"I didn't say we're going back to Roche."

"No?"

When Adele got up, she nearly passed out. Fin caught her before she fell. "You aren't ready to go anywhere," he said.

Adele took several deep breaths and waited for the dizziness to pass. "That's not your decision. You can come with me or stay here. It's up to you."

"But where are we going?"

"It's not far."

"I'm not letting you go there alone."

Adele looked Fin up and down and then nodded. "Okay."

Outside, the early evening air felt good on Adele's face. She ignored her throbbing head. There wasn't time for pain. The sun dipped low on the horizon to the west, covering the islands in a golden hue. She calculated it would take them nearly thirty minutes to reach the old sheriff's abandoned home.

That's not enough time. It'll be fully dark by then. You don't want to go back to that place at night.

With each step Adele took down the hill it felt like a little bomb detonated inside of her head. She would have given a week's earnings for a few aspirin. Instead of moving slower, though, she sped up. Soon she was back on the bike as Fin called out for her to wait.

Adele leaned forward, gritted her teeth, and peddled even harder as an old hell awaited her return.

18.

"This is where it all started for you, isn't it? Your life here on the islands I mean. You found her when everyone else thought she was long dead. You found her and set her free."

Adele didn't feel like talking. She saw the same trees lining the long gravel drive. The same piles of junk that dotted the unkept yard. The same dilapidated porch with the rotted steps. And the same house where a deranged former county sheriff and his son kept a woman prisoner year after year after year.

"You've never been back?"

Adele shook her head as she stopped in front of the porch. The very last of the day's light reflected off the home's dirt-encrusted windows. An old strip of police tape hung down from one of the paint-chipped posts.

"We don't have to go in."

"I do."

Fin frowned. "Why?"

"I just do. You wouldn't understand." Adele walked toward the side of the house.

"Where are you going?"

Adele ignored the question. When she reached the back patio, she again stopped and looked around. It was where

Sheriff Speaks had confronted her as she attempted to escape with Calista. The place still reeked of stale cigarettes.

"Is this the spot where the sheriff shot himself and the boy?"

Adele glared at Fin. "The sheriff's son was a man. His name was Will. He was simple. He didn't understand what he had done. None of this was his fault. Martin Speaks allowed it to happen. He used Calista's presence as a way of pacifying Will. He was the one who kept them all prisoner here."

"For a father to kill his own child . . . I can't imagine. You're so lucky he didn't turn his gun on you and Calista Stone as well."

Adele wanted to tell Fin to shut up for his insistence on stating the obvious but instead opened the back door and went into the home. She had to use her phone to see. Fin followed close behind. The smell of tobacco and mold oozed out of the nicotine-stained walls. Adele didn't stop in the kitchen, the living room, or the hallway. She knew where to go. She knew where she needed to be.

Once inside the former sheriff's bedroom she shined the light on the wall and found the access door to the cellar that had once been hidden behind a freezer. The freezer was gone, but the same scratches in the wood floor that had been the clue that led to her finding Calista were still there.

Adele pulled back the deadbolt and opened the door. A rush of cool, damp air hit her face. She had never been in the cellar. There had been no reason.

Until now.

"It's another damn cave," Fin muttered.

Adele crouched low, held her phone out in front of her, and took the first step down. She didn't wait for Fin. Whether he followed didn't matter. She didn't need anyone with her. Not this time.

"Well, we've had our fill of bats, so I guess it makes sense we get to see some rats now, yeah?"

Adele paused mid-step. "Shut up." She pointed the light of her phone toward the earth floor.

It's just dirt. Nothing down here can hurt me.

Adele kept going until her feet touched the muddy floor. She didn't want to go deeper into the cellar but knew she must.

"Now I know what a grave must feel like," Fin said.

Adele was about to curse Fin out for yet another stupid comment that did nothing but further magnify her fears when she sensed something familiar under her shoes. It was the same vibration she had noticed in the crystal cave. "Feel that?"

Fin nodded. "Yeah, just like before. It's not as strong, and I can't hear it, but it's there." He stood next to Adele and slowly moved his phone's light from one end of the cellar to the other and then bent down and put his hand over the ground. "I think it's a little warmer down here as well."

Adele pressed her palm against the earth. "You're right."

"Might explain how your friend was able to survive in here during the winter months. It's still cold but far from freezing. Not that that makes it any less horrific. I mean it's still a—"

Fin nearly fell backwards as a rat scurried by a few feet in front of him. "Serves you right," Adele said. "All that talk about rats and graves. You had it coming."

"That was no mere rat," Fin exclaimed. "It was the size of a small dog." He looked far more nervous than he had been just seconds before.

Adele moved further into the cellar. "You can stay by the stairs if you like. I'm going over here."

"What the hell for?" Fin asked. "We confirmed the same phenomenon we felt in the cave is also happening here."

"I need to see something."

Fin cursed under his breath as he continued to follow Adele. They both had to stoop even lower as the space between the floor and the ceiling decreased. Fin yelped and then frantically brushed a cobweb off his cap.

"You sure know how to show a fella a good time. Spiders the size of rats and rats the size of dogs. And where there's one you know there's more. I can smell them—the piss and droppings. They're down here in the dark watching us right now with their little rat eyes."

Adele barely heard what Fin said. She was staring at the indentation in the corner of the cellar that reminded her of a shallow grave. To reach it she had to get on her hands and knees and turn onto her side in order to keep hold of her phone so she could direct the light in front of her. She slowly pulled herself over the dank mud until she came to the hole that had been Calista's bed.

The ground was warmest there, though she could no longer feel any vibration.

"I thought you were claustrophobic?" Fin called out right before he reached Adele and then noticed the hole. "How'd you know this was here?"

"I read the police report," Adele replied. "There were photos."

"So, this is where she spent most of her time?"

"Yeah—decades."

Fin scooped up some dirt and rubbed it between his fingers. "It's warm."

"I know."

"I have a theory. Care to hear it?"

Adele turned her head. "Sure."

Fin dropped the dirt and sat cross-legged facing Adele with his phone in his lap so that the light illuminated the area around them. "The vibration, the sound we heard before, the heat or energy or whatever you want to call it, I think it represents the island's beating heart and that heart has arteries that extend all over the island to places like this one. And maybe, as crazy as it sounds, the energy traveling in these arteries is some kind of preternatural life force that helps to make people stronger, healthier, and live longer. I'm starting to wonder if there really could be something to what the woman at the museum told us. How the cave, the crystals, the rumors about Bloodbone and Robert Moran, it could all be connected. Here, give me your hand."

Adele felt Fin put something in her palm. It was a small crystal. "Did you take this from the cave?" she asked.

"I did. Look at it closer. Notice how it's glowing? It started doing that when we came down here. It's faint, you can hardly tell, but it's definitely glowing. I'm sure of it."

The crystal did seem brighter. Adele closed her fingers around it and then looked up at Fin. "This is why you went back into the cave. It wasn't to find my phone. It was to steal this."

Fin held out his hand. "Give it back."

"This wasn't yours to take."

"I'm not asking, Adele. It's mine. Now give it to me."

"Why did you take it? You left me alone in that shack and went back into the cave so you could come out with this. Why?"

"Why wouldn't I? Whatever this is, the cave, the crystals, the humming in the ground, lifeforce, energy, call it what you want, it's something extraordinary, Adele, and it should be shared with the world."

"Shared with the world? What do you mean?"

"I don't need to explain a damn thing to anyone. Now give it back or I'll take it back."

"Is that a threat?"

The anger in Fin's eyes softened as his head dropped. "No, of course not. I didn't mean it like that. Can we get out of here?"

Adele opened her hand.

Fin snatched the crystal with the speed of a striking cobra. He dropped it into a pocket. "Thank you."

Something, or someone, was moving through the house. Adele and Fin both looked up at the same time.

"Glad to know I wasn't the only one who heard it," Fin said.

Adele began to crawl toward the stairs, fearful that something was about to go very wrong. Fin caught up to her. "Hold on," he whispered. "It could just be an animal."

A footstep. A creak in the floor. Adele couldn't help but imagine herself as Calista, trapped in the dark and listening to the movements of her captors above her.

The door to the cellar slammed shut followed by the sound of the deadbolt sliding into place. Adele found the stairs and bounded up them two at a time until she reached the door. "Who's there?" she yelled.

Nobody answered. Adele pushed against the door. It wouldn't open. She pushed harder. "It's locked. We're trapped."

"Let me try," Fin said. He put his phone away and shoved at the door with both hands. "Who could have possibly known we were down here?" He shoved again, hard enough it made the middle of the door bend out and crack.

"Wait." Adele put a hand on his arm and pulled him toward her. "What's that?"

Fin took a step back and then looked up as Adele shined her light on the inside of the door.

The words were the same.

Be a slave to the truth or know freedom from the lie.

Fin kept staring at the door. "What the hell is going on?"

Adele told him to move. Once she was past him and facing the door, she ordered him to push against her so she wouldn't fall backwards.

"I don't understand."

"Just do it," Adele snapped. "Don't be afraid to push hard if you have to. Just make sure we don't end up tumbling down the stairs."

She steadied herself, took a fighting stance, breathed deep, and then kicked at the door as hard as she could. Fin grunted from the effort of keeping them both upright.

Another kick followed. The door buckled and the frame cracked. Adele kicked at it again and then shouted triumphantly when the door gave way. She prepared to launch herself into the room, but Fin grabbed her shoulder and held her back. "Wait," he said. "Whoever locked it might still be in the house."

Adele's eyes were fire as she pushed Fin off. "That's what I'm hoping for." She stepped through the opening with her phone lighting the way, ran out of the room and into the adjoining hallway, and then paused to listen.

A floorboard creaked. Adele took off, ignoring the warning from Fin that if she didn't slow down, she would hurt herself again. She found the back door hanging open. It was night but the skies were clear and lit up by the moon and stars. Adele heard Fin crashing through the house until he emerged next to her with his fists clenched looking ready for a fight. "Where are they?" he asked.

Adele scanned the tree line for any sign of movement. "I don't know."

"They can't have just disappeared. Maybe they ran to the front of the house."

"Go ahead and have a look and yell if you see something."

"Where are you going?"

"I'm staying—" Adele stopped midsentence as she noticed the dark outline of a man standing a hundred yards away beneath the branches of a large evergreen. He was tall and lean, with long, white hair and unusually sharp cheekbones. A large crystal hung around his neck.

It was him—the same man on the cover of Delroy's book.

Adele locked eyes with Karl Bloodbone.

"Do you see him?"

"I do now," Fin whispered.

Adele stepped forward as Bloodbone stood as still as the trees while staring back at her. She continued walking toward him. A cloud crept toward the moon, slowly eclipsing its light. Adele stopped. She was still too far away to know for certain, but Bloodbone appeared to smile at her. The cloud covered the moon fully and the area went dark. When the moonlight returned a few seconds later, Bloodbone was gone.

"Dammit," Adele muttered right before she sprinted through the grass toward the trees.

Fin ran by her. "It's really him," he exclaimed. "I'm not letting him get away."

When Adele reached the trees, Fin was already scurrying around looking for Bloodbone's hiding spot. "I don't understand. He was right here. We both saw him. There's no way someone that old could move that fast."

From somewhere in the tree directly above them a raven called out. Both Adele and Fin froze and then looked up. Adele watched the raven hop to a lower branch. Fin walked backwards toward her. "Ah, c'mon," he said. "Enough with the mystical bird crap. I'm not buying it." He turned in a circle. "Where are you, Bloodbone? I know you can hear me. Show yourself. I'm not going to hurt you. I just want to talk and have a look at that crystal of yours. What do you say?"

Adele took her eyes off the raven to look at Fin. "The crystal?"

Fin shrugged. "Yeah. It's the one my father wrote about, right? The Lekwiltok Crystal. Why would I ever pass up a chance to get my hands on that?"

"Get your hands on it? You intend to take it for yourself?"

Fin rolled his eyes. "Stop being so dramatic. You know what I mean."

"No, Fin, I don't. You're not making any sense. None of this is making any sense."

The raven hopped across the branch and croaked loudly while spreading its wings out. Fin reached down and picked up a stone. "Shut up," he said as his arm drew back.

"Don't throw that rock," Adele growled.

"It's just a stupid bird," Fin replied.

Adele walked over and clamped her fingers around Fin's wrist. "I mean it. Put it down."

Fin dropped the rock. "Fine. You happy now?"

The raven raised its head, cackled, and then took off into the night sky.

"Nice," Fin said. "Now you have the birds laughing at me."

"I'm sure you'll get over it."

"Where to now?"

Though Adele couldn't see water she knew where it was. No matter how far away it always tugged at her. She looked west. "I'm returning the bikes and then I'm going home. You can come with me or stay here. It's up to you."

Fin scuffed the ground with the heel of his shoe. "Guess the stress of the day turned us sour. I apologize if I said or did anything you feel was out of line."

"I told you I'm waiting for the whole story of why you're really here. As of right now I'm tired of waiting. I think your time here is reaching its expiration date. We can go back to Roche together, but after that . . ."

Fin nodded. "I get it. By that I mean I understand where you're coming from. Our being here has dug up a lot of unpleasant history for you, not least of which is your memory of my father. You knew Delroy. I didn't. So the pain of remembering him is yours more than it is mine."

"I don't have a problem with remembering Delroy. He was an amazing man. At least the version of him that I was blessed to know. My problem is with *you*, Fin. There's something you're not telling me. I intend to find out what that is."

"So you said."

"And I'm saying it again in the hopes that this time you'll hear me."

"Hey, I'm just a poor little Irish boy without a daddy looking for a friend in a big, scary old world."

"Okay, fine, if that's how you want to play it. Don't ever say I didn't give you the chance to come clean."

Fin tipped his cap and winked. "I've been making my own chances my whole life, darling. I don't require any more from you."

"I meant it as a gesture of kindness."

"And I sincerely thank you for that."

Adele gave up. She was too tired to argue any longer. She started walking. An hour later, she was behind the wheel as the Chris Craft skipped across the nighttime waters. Fin sat at the back of the boat with his arms folded across his chest.

It was an especially cold ride home in more ways than one.

19.

A dele took an extra-long shower the following morning, hoping to clear her head so she might better focus on what had happened the previous day. Either Karl Bloodbone was alive or someone who bore a remarkable resemblance to him was running around Orcas pretending to be him. Then there was the question of the same words being written on the inside of both the shack door and the cellar door that had been Calista's prison. Delroy had written in his book that Bloodbone had left the message in the shack. Was Bloodbone also responsible for the message in the cellar, and if so, why?

Strong coffee followed the shower. Adele sat in her robe inside the warm cocoon of the sailboat sipping from her cup as her mind raced with various possibilities of what it all could mean.

And what about Fin? He had been so determined to leave the cave with a crystal and so willing to go down into a muddy, rat-infested cellar to seek out more information about what alleged powers those crystals might hold. It didn't make sense and that in turn frustrated Adele even more.

After getting back to Roche they had separated last night without saying anything to each other. Adele went to the sailboat and Fin returned to his room inside Tilda's hotel. Now it was a new day with new questions and Adele intended to get some answers. She dressed quickly, went outside, and walked to the hotel where she knew Tilda would already be waiting.

"He isn't here," Tilda replied after Adele inquired about Fin.

"Did he check out?"

"No, I don't think so. What happened yesterday? Did you two argue?"

Adele summarized the events of the previous day as Tilda sat at the table in her room and listened. When Adele was finished, Tilda got up and went to one of the windows that overlooked the marina below. "That's a remarkable story," she said. "I've wondered myself about how quickly Calista was able to recover from that terrible ordeal. I assumed it was her love of Decklan. Perhaps it was that but also something more." She turned around and looked at Adele. "As I've said before, these are the islands where all things are possible. What do you intend to do now?"

"I'm not sure. I could return to Orcas and try to find Bloodbone or whoever that was that looks so much like him, but I should probably check in with Lucas first."

"Good idea. Having the help of the sheriff would be wise. And what about Mr. Kearns?"

"Heck if I know. He's hiding something. I'm sure of it."

Tilda pursed her lips. "Who doesn't have things they wish to keep to themselves? That doesn't automatically make him unworthy of your support."

Adele's eyes narrowed. "Are you talking about Fin or someone else?"

Tilda looked out the window again. "I haven't seen Roland around. You would think with the house being built on the hill and the yacht tied up at the dock he'd be here."

Adele decided to share what she knew about the pending sale of Roland's bank. Hearing that it was more than just a rumor clearly rattled Tilda.

"I really didn't want to believe it was true. The Soros family bank has been a fixture of our community's independence for as long as I can remember. I never really considered the possibility it could be swallowed up by some New York conglomerate. I know now that was foolish of me. Roland has always displayed an appetite for more—family legacy be damned."

"After you first told me what you'd heard from your financial adviser in Bellingham, I said something very similar to Roland. He didn't like hearing it."

Tilda furrowed her brow as she bit her lip. "No, I imagine he didn't. And no one else knows about the sale? Not even the sheriff?"

"You're the only one I've told so far. Roland said I was free to write about it in the paper, which does seem to suggest it's very close to a done deal."

Tilda sat down and scratched at the white tablecloth. "Roland's bank likely holds the mortgages on at least half the residences and businesses on these islands. Thank goodness I own the hotel free and clear. The thought of making payments to some faceless big bank sickens me and I'm far from the only one around here who feels like that. If Roland goes through with the sale, he is going to be very unpopular among his neighbors."

"I know. That's what I tried to tell him. He wasn't interested in listening then and now he won't accept my texts."

"Shame on the little brat. His grandfather will be rolling in his grave. Even for Roland it's a decision that stuns me. He's always been so vocal regarding the need to maintain local control of our community. There must be more to this. It doesn't make sense."

"It does if the reason is greed. You've said it yourself—Roland wants the money."

Tilda got up. "You find Roland and bring him here. I need to speak with him."

"I have no idea where he is or how to get a hold of him."

"You'll manage. When it comes to finding things, you most often do."

"What do you want to say to him?"

"Honestly, I'm not really sure. I just want the chance to say it."

"I'll try, but if Roland doesn't want to be found I can't guarantee I can get him here."

"That's fine," Tilda said. "Until then where are you off to?"

"I'm going to Friday Harbor to meet with Lucas."

"And will you be telling the sheriff the news regarding Roland's bank?"

Adele shook her head. "Not yet. I want to discuss it with Roland first."

"Very well. Let me know how everything goes."

Adele promised she would and then left the hotel. Despite the swirling troubles with Roland and Fin, she made sure to take a moment to appreciate the beauty on display during the drive to Friday Harbor. Wildflowers growing alongside the road promised of the warmer spring days to come. The sky was again clear, the sun bright, and the tall grass fields a vibrant green. When she reached the sheriff station, she looked to her right and saw Lucas parking alongside her.

"Good timing," he said, smiling as he got out of his SUV. "You look like you want to talk."

"I do. And you're looking a whole lot better."

Lucas pulled his uniform tight over his muscular chest. "I'm definitely feeling better."

"Can we go inside?"

Lucas opened the front door and then stepped aside. "After you."

There was something about his tone that made Adele pause. Lucas was almost always considerate, but he seemed especially so this morning. "Is everything okay?"

The smile on Lucas's face fell away. He looked around and then lowered his voice. "C'mon. I'll tell you in my office."

Adele sat and waited. Lucas shut the door, closed the blinds, and then plopped down behind his desk. "It's about Mr. Kearns," he said.

"Okay."

Lucas stuck his elbows on the desk, folded his hands together, and propped his chin on them. "I heard back from my Interpol contact. It seems there's more to Mr. Kearns than he was letting on."

"Such as?"

"Did you know about his connection to Irish travelers? They're a semi-nomadic group sometimes referred to as gypsies."

"I did. Fin told me his mother did business with them— horses mainly."

"Ah, I see. And that's it?"

"Pretty much. He said she sold horses to the travelers. Why?"

"Well, it's more than that. A *lot* more actually."

"Go ahead."

"Fin's mother is a woman by the name of Ava Kearns. She's kind of a big deal among the travelers of southern Ireland and enjoys a lot of influence primarily in the counties of Cork and Waterford. Being her son, Fin benefits from that status as well. He doesn't have a criminal record himself, but he undoubtedly associates with those who do."

Adele sat up straight. "Fin's mother is dead."

"No, she's not. Ava Kearns is very much alive."

"Why would Fin lie to me about that?"

Lucas shrugged. "Petty crime is a way of life for travelers, so I imagine lying comes easily to them. Fin may not have a criminal record, but his mother does, and they're both well acquainted with the Irish authorities."

"Is he dangerous?"

"Nothing in the Interpol report I was given indicated anything violent. I'm sure he's been around it plenty though."

"And his mother? Why does she have a record?"

"Selling stolen property. Horses were taken from farms in the north and then transported for sale to travelers in the south. The authorities believed Fin was involved as well, but his mother agreed to a plea that exempted him from any prosecution. She was to serve a year in the Limerick prison—not an easy place to do time."

"Is she still there?"

"No," Lucas answered. "She was granted an early release about six months ago. The report didn't say why."

"And now you want me to help you bring Fin in."

"I do but just to speak with him. As far as I know he's done nothing wrong. That said, he did lie to you about his mother. That suggests he's willing to lie about other things as well including his reason for coming here. Did anything odd happen while you two were at Orcas?"

"That's one of the reasons I came here to talk to you. It was beyond odd."

Lucas leaned back in his chair as Adele recounted the trip to Mother Mary Ophelia's on Shaw, their visit with Prunella Brown at the Historical Society Museum in Eastsound, and the discovery of the clearing with the shed and the cave that led into the hillside. Then she described what happened at the abandoned house where Calista had been kept prisoner.

Lucas's mouth dropped open. "You went to the Speaks house *alone*?"

"No, I went there with Fin."

"You know what I mean."

"Yeah, you seem to think if I do something like that without you, regardless of who's with me, then I'm doing it alone."

Lucas held up his hand. "I'm done getting mad at you for taking those kinds of risks, Adele. You are who you are. I understand it and I've even learned to respect it. Still, I can't say it doesn't make me worry. And you really believe you saw Karl Bloodbone there?"

"It was either him or someone wanting to look like him."

"Huh. Well, it's the second option of course. Karl Bloodbone had to have died a long time ago. By the way, I know the book you mentioned—the one Delroy wrote. My father had it in his office at home. I remember him telling me a little about the big conflict between Bloodbone and some of the Orcas locals back in the 1970s. That was what—more than 40 years ago? That's before you or I were even born. There's just no way Bloodbone could still be alive. And even if he was, a man that old running around Orcas locking people in cellars? Nope. It's someone playing a game and we need to figure out why."

"I feel the same way. I also think it could somehow be connected to Fin."

"Maybe. Who knows? It definitely makes me want to sit down and speak with him even more now."

"And is there anything new regarding Sandra Penny?"

Lucas shook his head. "No, nothing to suggest she had anything to do with what happened to you in the parking lot at Roche. I've asked that she bring her vehicle by so I can have it looked at to see if there's any evidence it was broken into. She said she'd have to get back to me on that. Apparently, things are unusually busy at the bank."

Adele nearly told Lucas about the pending bank sale but decided against it. She would stick to her plan of talking more about it with Roland first.

If I can find him.

"Were you going to say something?" Lucas asked.

"No, my mind was wandering. Sorry. Have you seen or heard anything from Roland?"

"You two still not talking?"

"We aren't anything. Nobody knows where he is. I try to message him, but they just get kicked back. I'm actually starting to worry a bit."

"I'm sure he'll show up. You know how Roland can be."

"I thought I did, but now I'm not so sure."

"You want me to add him to my 'looking for' list?"

"I would. Thanks."

Lucas leaned back again and jammed his thumbs into his gun belt. "All part of the job, ma'am. Now don't you go worrying your pretty little head. I'll locate our little banker friend in no time."

They both laughed.

It felt good.

The moment passed quickly, though, leaving Adele to again contemplate questions she had no answers to. Fin had lied, Roland was missing, either Sandra Penny or someone using her car had tried to intimidate her, and someone else who looked exactly like Karl Bloodbone was out there doing things for reasons that made no sense.

So many mysteries. So little time.

It was almost enough to make Adele smile.

20.

"**Y**ou lied to me. Don't deny it. I know the truth about your mother. If you want us to remain friends, you need to come clean. No more lies."

Fin stared into his teacup as he sat with Adele inside her sailboat. "You say the sheriff had me investigated?"

"Not an investigation. He just made an inquiry. Don't take it personal. It's what he does."

Fin looked up. "And I'm sure the damn Garda were only too happy to share their opinions on my mother. The authorities are the same everywhere. Poking and prodding without thought to how it might impact others. I *do* take it personal, Adele. It's my life and the lives of my people."

Adele knew to proceed carefully. Whatever emotional wound Fin had been nursing in secret remained very raw. "I've experienced loss as well, Fin. I know something of that kind of pain. What I don't understand is your reason for wanting me to think your mother was dead when she isn't."

"She *is* dead. The doctor pointed to her and said as much. He might as well have stamped an expiration date right onto her forehead."

Fin went quiet. Adele waited. When he was ready, he'd start talking again. It didn't take long.

"It's her heart. It's failing, and due to her age, she's low priority on the transplant list. So, she told the doctors no more. Said she wasn't going to waste what little time she had left sitting inside a hospital. That's her pride. Her refusal to give up control. If she is to die it'll be on her terms. I was so angry when she told me there'd be no more attempts at treatment, no more pretending that the inevitable could somehow be changed. It feels too much like giving up even though down deep I know she's right. My mother's dying."

"But why come all the way here to the islands? Why not be with her during whatever time she has left?"

"She's not the only one who's stubborn. I refuse to sit back and accept her death sentence. No, I intend to find a miracle, the same miracle my father was researching. It's destiny, Adele. Don't you see that? Delroy explored the legend of remarkably good health and long life associated with Orcas Island and now here I am following through on his work. I am going to put that legend to good use and try to save the life of my mother."

"But Delroy concluded that Karl Bloodbone was a fraud."

"According to the nun that was a lie. I'm certain she implied Bloodbone intimidated him into publishing that conclusion. Delroy was an academic, a man of science. His reputation would never survive going public with the truth of what he saw. I told you I came here to learn more about my father because I knew you would accept that. You'd feel obligated to help. Sharing that I'm here to find a cure for my dying mother? That makes me nothing more than a desperate man chasing a hoax—one that you would quickly reject being a part of. You know I'm right about that."

Adele nodded. "You are. It doesn't excuse the lie though. It just means you manipulated me into doing what you wanted."

"Yeah? And what of it? Is *your* mother still alive?"

"Yes. She lives in Arizona now."

"Okay, put yourself in my shoes. She's dying and you think there might be a way to save her. Or let's say it's Tilda who has just a few months left and there is a rumored remedy on a nearby island that could change that. Would you waste precious time trying to convince others or would you get right to it?"

"I'm not going to engage in hypotheticals with you, Fin. We all took you in on a false premise, which tells me you're just here to use us. You can't expect me to be okay with that. This is my home and the people you lied to are my friends."

"And a tight-knit bunch you all are. We have far more in common in that regard than you likely realize. Travelers are many things, not all of them good, but in the end, no one can accuse us of not being survivors. I apologize for the deception, Adele. I mean that. I'm also asking for your help. I intend to return to Orcas as soon as possible."

"Why?"

"To find Karl Bloodbone of course. I'm going to purchase the crystal around his neck and take it with me back to Ireland."

"Oh, Fin, that piece of crystal won't save your mother."

Fin's jaw clenched. "Don't do that. Don't you dare dismiss me like I'm some wretched child. I won't have it."

"I don't see you as a wretched child. I see you as someone who deceived me."

"You missed something you know. I all but told you the truth the other night on our way back from Orcas. I suppose that was the part of me that wanted to tell you but wasn't sure how to do it."

Adele cocked her head. "What did I miss?"

"We were arguing. I said I was just a poor little Irish boy without a daddy looking for a friend in a big, scary old world."

"And?"

"If both my parents were dead why would I have excluded my mother from such a statement? I'm surprised you didn't catch that omission."

"This isn't a game, Fin. At least not to me."

"No, it isn't. It's about the life of the only family I have left in this world. My point was to show that I really did want you to know the truth."

"Then you should have started with it."

Fin looked down at his cup again. "You're right. I apologize."

"The sheriff wants me to bring you to the station in Friday Harbor."

"Why? I've done nothing wrong."

"You lied."

"I didn't break any law. He can request to speak with me all he wants. I don't have to comply."

"You don't want to make an enemy of Lucas."

"I'm not intimidated by a man with a gun and a badge. I know my rights. If he wishes to come here to speak with me that's one thing. Taking me in to see him as if I have no choice? No, that won't do."

"Okay, but he won't be happy about it."

Fin smiled. "I've read your articles, remember? I know for a fact you don't follow every order Sheriff Pine gives to you."

"Where were you this morning?"

"Ah, back to the interrogation, is it? I thought perhaps the ice between us had thawed."

"Just answer the question."

"I took a long walk to the Roche Harbor cemetery. I had to see it for myself. Your stories, as good as they are, still don't do it justice. What a remarkable thing that marble mausoleum, how it rises from the earth surrounded by all those ancient trees. And the one intentionally broken pillar, did you know it allows both the morning and evening sun to shine into the center of the tomb and that the structure has the exact same dimensions as the interior of King Solomon's Temple in Jerusalem?"

"I knew some of that, yes."

"When the sun comes up, the mausoleum is illuminated by this golden glow that to me signifies the bond between the earthly realm and the spiritual one, like your insistence on science and my belief in something beyond that science. And like the cave and the cellar we visited on Orcas, there is power that surrounds it. Remember when I told you how I thought there could be arteries that extend out from the heartbeat of the Turtleback Mountain cave? Having seen and felt the mausoleum this morning I'm now convinced it was built on top of one of those arteries as well. John McMillin, the founder of Roche Harbor, had to have known that."

"If you're right, I imagine he did."

"He was also the original builder of Tilda's hotel. Her family purchased it from his. It remains the oldest continually run hotel in Washington state."

"Really? That I didn't know."

Fin's eyes widened as he nodded. "Yes, your friendship with Tilda is truly a link to Roche Harbor's past. And John McMillin knew Robert Moran. Knew him well in fact. For several years the two vied for most influential status here on the islands. One man dominated Roche Harbor on San Juan Island and the other Rosario on Orcas Island. McMillin died in 1936 and Moran in 1943. Both men lived into their 80s. Do you know what the average life expectancy in the United States for a white male born in the 1850s was?"

Adele dipped her teabag as she struggled not to appear amused by Fin's enthusiasm. "Go ahead."

"It was just 40 years. And for those who managed to live past 40, less than 15% reached the age of 60. Both Moran and McMillin easily exceeded that mark. In fact, San Juan County has by far the highest life expectancy for both men and women of any county in the state and, as I said before, one of the highest life expectancies in all the world. I'm telling you, Adele, there's something very different about this place—something beyond merely being a beautiful destination. There's real magic here."

"I won't say that's impossible, Fin, but I've found the word magic is most often applied to phenomena that actually have more practical-based explanations. Yes, these islands *are* different. Believe me, I know. That's why I feel so blessed to live here. I'll help you to locate Bloodbone, or whoever it is pretending to be him, not because of any kind of belief in the supernatural but because I want answers—real ones. But before we go back to Orcas you do need to speak with the sheriff. I'm not going to help you avoid him. I'm sure if I ask Lucas to come to Roche to see you, he'll make the trip here."

"I tell you what, Adele. If you can help to get this sheriff nonsense wrapped up quickly and then take me to Orcas again, I'll be in your debt. This isn't a casual promise. I give you my word on the life of my mother that should you need my help, however far away I might be, I'll return here to provide it."

"Why would you think I'd need that kind of help?"

Fin sipped from his tea. "The Russians for one. Travelers have done business with them in Ireland over the years. Not often though. We prefer to avoid their kind. We know of Vlad Vasa and his daughter Liya. Those are very powerful enemies you've made, Adele. Ones that will require far more than the kind of protection your friend the sheriff can provide."

Adele had put the Liya problem on the back burner because thinking about it made her want to scream at Roland all over again. "Lucas and I managed Liya before. We'll do it again if we have to."

"That's dangerous thinking. Liya and her brother were two. Liya's father Vlad might very well send a dozen here to carry out their revenge. What then?"

"You really do like seeing me worry, don't you?"

"Not at all. I just want to make it as clear as possible that by helping me now I will be available to help you whenever you need it. Just say the word and I'll be on the first plane from Ireland to here."

"If Vlad Vasa were to send more people how would your being here change anything?"

Fin leaned back and folded his arms across his chest. "When my father helped you to find Calista Stone did that make a difference?"

"You already know the answer to that."

"That's right and if needed I *will* be a significant help to you and your friends. Despite my previous deceptions please trust me when I tell you this. Earning that trust back means a great deal to me."

Adele stuck out her hand. "Fine. Shake on it?"

Fin's hand was as warm as his smile. "Bless you," he said. "Our reaching an understanding pleases me greatly."

Adele squeezed Fin's hand a little more tightly. "No more lies."

Fin nodded. "No more lies. I promise. What now?"

"I call Lucas and tell him you're here and available to talk."

"You don't waste any time, do you?"

"No, I don't."

This time it was Fin who squeezed Adele's hand and held it in place as he stared into her eyes. "Good. Neither do I."

21.

Adele leaned against the side of her sailboat nibbling on a cheese bagel and watching Lucas question Fin. They stood at the end of the dock next to Roland's yacht. Despite Lucas putting on his best "I'm the sheriff around here" intimidation face, Fin appeared at ease and smiling. The conversation lasted about ten minutes. After they were done Fin was the first to walk up to Adele.

"He seems to be a nice enough fella. All business like most who wear a badge but fair. Seems he wants to talk to you alone now so I'm going back up to the hotel. Can I get you anything?"

"No, I'm good."

Fin kept walking and then turned around. "When do you think we might get back to Orcas?"

"We'll see. Won't be today. Maybe tomorrow."

Fin tipped his cap. "Until then."

Adele heard Lucas come up behind her. "Your new friend is smooth under fire," he said. "I'm guessing he's had plenty of practice dealing with the authorities. I think I might actually have been more nervous than he was."

"So, are you going to let him stick around?"

"Sure. Like I said, he's done nothing wrong. Lying to you about his mother doesn't sit right with me, but if lying alone was a crime we'd have to build a bunch of new prisons just for all the politicians and reporters."

"Hey, watch it."

Lucas grinned as he took a chunk of Adele's bagel and plopped it into his mouth. "Not *all* reporters of course. There are still a few good ones out there. At least that's what I hear. I'm still waiting to actually meet one."

Adele nodded. "Uh-huh. Keep digging that hole, bagel thief."

"Innocent until proven guilty."

"I just watched you steal a piece."

Lucas swallowed and then shook his head. "Sorry, no evidence."

They both turned toward the sound of a great blue heron beating its wings as it landed on the radar arch of Roland's yacht. The nearly four-foot-tall bird shook its head, adjusted its wings, and then let out a deep, dinosaur-like squawk.

Lucas looked down at Adele. "Have you checked his yacht lately?"

"No."

"Maybe he snuck back on when you weren't around."

"What about the bank? Has he been there?"

"According to Penny not in the last week or so, but apparently that's not unusual. Roland is a man who can afford to live by his own calendar. His name might be on the building, but she runs that bank, not him."

"And no other leads regarding who would have been using Penny's car to try to scare me the other day?"

"No, and she still hasn't got back to me about bringing the car by for us to inspect."

"You think she's hiding something?"

Lucas shrugged. "Don't know. There wasn't an actual crime committed. Someone revved their engine at you. I'm limited in what I can do beyond talking to her. I'm not saying it's not on my radar, especially after the warning from Yuri about Liya Vasa. It's just that beyond watching and waiting there's not much else I can do right now."

"I understand. So, what about Roland?"

"Give me another bite of that bagel and I'll tell you my plan."

Adele ripped what was left of the bagel in two and gave half to Lucas. "Really?" she said. "That's all it takes to bribe a sheriff? I'll bring donuts next time. Then you'll do whatever I want."

"That's a hurtful cliché, Ms. Plank."

"How about a nice Bismarck? All that dark chocolate on top with the cream-filled center—warm and fresh right from the oven."

Lucas licked his lips. "You're right. That would probably work."

After they finished the bagel Lucas pointed to the yacht. "Ma'am, do you believe Mr. Soros might be in some kind of danger?"

Adele scowled. "Huh?"

"In order to enter the yacht, I'll need an exigent circumstance. So, let me ask you again. Do you believe Mr. Soros might be in danger?"

"Oh. Uh, yeah, I do think it's possible."

"And have you seen or heard any suspicious activity around the vessel within the last 24 hours?"

"As a matter of fact, I have. Just a second ago, a very strange croaking noise came from over there, like someone inside the yacht might be choking."

Lucas nodded. "That sounds like a possible emergency brought to my attention by a concerned neighbor. Would you agree?"

"Absolutely, Sheriff."

"Okay, we better go check it out."

Adele had to hustle to keep up with Lucas's long-legged stride. They walked up the boarding ramp together and then Lucas knocked on the yacht's portside entrance. "Sheriff's department. Anyone in there?"

The heron flew away. The yacht was silent. Lucas opened the door. "Who keeps a ship like this unlocked?"

"Someone who doesn't have to worry about money."

"Sheriff's department," Lucas cried out again. He paused, listened, and then stepped inside as Adele shut the door behind them. No lights were on and most of the window blinds were closed. It took a moment for her eyes to adjust.

"It's almost exactly like the other one his family owned," Lucas said. "Right down to all the dark wood trim. The furniture, the artwork, Roland must have spent more on this one item than I could earn in three or four years as sheriff."

Adele knew the amount was actually more than that, but she didn't care how much money Roland spent on the yacht. She just wanted to know where he was. "Can we look around?"

Lucas nodded. "Sure. Officially that's what this is—a safety check."

Adele didn't have to look far. A note was stuck to the stainless fridge in the galley. "Found something," she called out.

"What is it?"

Adele took the note down and read it out loud. "Off to see my cat for a few days. P.S. Don't forget to lock up on your way out."

Lucas frowned as he scratched the stubble on his chin. "Roland has a cat?"

Adele didn't realize she was smiling until Lucas asked her what was so funny. "I know where he is," she said.

"Yeah?"

Adele stuffed the note into her pocket and went outside. "Got to go, Sheriff."

"Where to?"

"Can't say. I'm not sure Roland wants people knowing about his hideout. Do me a favor and tell Fin that I'll talk with him first thing tomorrow about Orcas."

"Now I'm your message boy? C'mon, Adele, tell me where you think Roland is."

Adele started walking backwards while staring at the top of the yacht. The space where the dinghy was kept was empty.

I should have known he might go back there. We must have just missed each other.

Lucas came down the ramp. "Hey, I mean it. Don't leave me hanging. I just bent the rules so we could have a look inside."

"And I appreciate that. Now I have to go." Adele jogged to her Chris Craft.

"You're going on the water? There are white caps forming. It's going to be blowing hard soon."

"All the more reason I need to go now." Adele jumped behind the wheel, turned the key and then looked up at Lucas. "Can you untie me?"

"Not unless you let me come with you."

"Don't be silly. You have a job to do. Now stop worrying. I'll be fine." Adele reached out and untied the boat from the dock. "See you soon. I promise."

Lucas watched stern-faced as Adele backed out of the slip. "Don't you dare make me come looking for you," he said, sounding more worried than annoyed.

Adele turned the wheel hard and pointed the bow toward the increasingly churlish surface of Spieden Channel. Both the sky and water were a swirling mass of heavy gray. She crept along slowly until she reached the western corner of Davidson head. The white caps Lucas had warned about were already getting worse.

It was approximately ten nautical miles to her destination.

Ten miles in a car was nothing, but ten miles on waters made worse by a fast-approaching storm was something very different. In those conditions such a distance could feel like forever.

The Lancer's bow lurched to the side as a series of large waves crashed against the hull. Adele spun the wheel, turned on the wipers, huddled underneath the hardtop, and accelerated. More speed meant more pounding, but it also meant she'd be back on land before the approaching storm's full fury hit the islands.

Adele knew the Chris Craft could take far more than she could. It was a small but heavy fiberglass beast made to withstand such waters. With more power to the prop it tracked true, its diesel growl sounding a challenge at anything Mother Nature might throw at it.

The wiper blades clacked against the windshield frame, their tempo accompanying the rise and fall of the bow as it climbed one wave before crashing into the next, bathing the entire front of the boat in salt spray.

Adele waved as a fishing vessel crossed in front of her on its way to Friday Harbor. She could see its captain turn his head to look at her, likely wondering why she was heading out when everyone else was going in. The conditions reminded her of the night she crossed the same channel with Delroy behind the wheel of Decklan's little runabout. They had eventually made it to Decklan's house and the protected waters of Deer Harbor—but just barely.

The wind and waves were quickly getting worse. Adele had to grip the wheel tighter in order to keep the bow pointed straight and estimated a window of no more than ten or fifteen minutes before the weather turned the water into a dangerous washing machine. At her current speed she knew it wasn't enough time, so she went faster.

The Lancer felt like it might roll over as a rogue wave lifted it high and then dropped it down hard. Adele gritted her teeth, turned into the next wave just like Delroy had first taught her, and straightened the boat out. This was repeated over and over as the Chris Craft shrugged off the worsening conditions and plowed forward.

There.

The small community dock adjacent to the ferry terminal finally came into view. Only one other boat was tied to it—a center console inflatable dinghy.

Roland's dinghy.

Once she was tied up and had turned off the key Adele felt her body release the tension that had built up during the ride over and was grateful to be looking back at the roiling seas from the safety of the shore. The storm continued to gain power as layer after layer of ominous clouds collected over the islands, courtesy of a thirty-knot wind. The downpour would start soon. She had a long and wet walk ahead of her.

With one last check to make sure the Chris Craft was secured to the dock Adele made her way up to the road she hoped would take her to Roland.

22.

"**W**hat in the world are you doing out in this mess? Get on in here before you catch your death."

Ophelia opened the door wider and stepped aside so that Adele could enter the convent. "My goodness you're soaked," she said. "Come sit by the fire."

"It's not so bad," Adele replied. "I'm used to it." Despite her words Adele was grateful for the fire's warmth. Ophelia handed her a cup of hot cider and then sat down beside her.

"Drink that. The apples come from our own orchard. It'll warm your belly."

Adele sipped from the cup and smiled. "It's good. Thank you."

Ophelia leaned forward and put her hand on Adele's knee. "I recall you coming here last year looking for him. I suppose that means he wants to be found."

"I guess so. I *hope* so. Is he here?"

"Yes, in the same guest cabin as before—the one his grandfather stayed in a lifetime ago when he had his own troubles."

"How's he doing?"

"Oh, he's fine. Him and that cat are inseparable. At the end of the day, despite all his superficial faults, Roland really is a good boy. Of course, you know that already. That's why you're here."

"Did he seem especially upset or stressed when he arrived?"

Ophelia shook her head. "No, not at all. He gave me a big hug and asked if it was okay if he stayed for a few days to unwind."

"And you don't mind him showing up unannounced like that?"

"Just the opposite. It is a blessing having him here. This is a place of physical and spiritual restoration open to all no matter how great or small who require such things."

Adele finished her cider and stood. "Can I go see him?"

Ophelia took the cup. "Of course. He's likely expecting you. Perhaps you can try to convince him to shave that mess off his face."

"You don't care for the beard?"

"No, not really. His grandfather was clean-shaved. It's a look that suits Soros men the best."

Adele again glanced at the photo of Roland as a boy standing with his grandfather and a much younger Ophelia. For the first time she noted a resemblance that had escaped her before—a discovery that made her eyes widen and her mouth fall open. "Was it your decision to hang that photo?"

Ophelia appeared slightly annoyed by the question. "I suppose so. It's been there a very long time. Why do you ask?"

"Well, I know it was Roland's grandfather who hung the same photo inside the entrance to the bank. It just seems like the picture sort of connects that place to this one . . . or Charles Soros to you."

When Ophelia didn't reply Adele turned to face her. "Is something wrong?"

"No, I'm fine. Are you ready to see Roland?"

She isn't denying it, Adele thought as her heart started to beat a little faster.

"I said are you ready to see Roland?"

Adele nodded. "Yes. Thank you."

Ophelia's smile wasn't quite cold but hardly better than lukewarm. "Good. One mystery at a time and this one happens to be mine to tell, not yours." Her eyes locked onto Adele's. "Understood?"

"Of course."

Ophelia reached out and held Adele's hands. The old nun's grip was strong and her skin rough and calloused from countless hours working outside. "Go ahead then. You know your way around this place."

Adele went outside and walked the narrow stone path to the convent's guest cabin. The earlier downpour had lessened to a drizzle and the early afternoon air was warming. Rows of emerging multi-colored tulip bulbs lined the way. Adele knocked on the door. When no one answered, she knocked again.

"Roland? Are you in there?"

The cabin was unlocked. Adele pushed the door open and stepped inside. It felt even smaller than she remembered it with space for just a single bed, a chair, and a lamp. A little space heater sat on the floor humming quietly. The bed was unmade, and a book was on the pillow. Adele picked it up and looked at the cover. It was a copy of *Don Quixote*. There was a dog-eared page near the back, indicating Roland had almost finished it. She returned it to the pillow, sat in the chair next to the bed, and waited.

After ten minutes, Adele got up and returned outside. The rain had stopped, and the sun peeked out from behind fast-moving clouds. She thought she heard Roland's voice carried on the breeze and attempted to follow it. She found a dirt trail that wound through the trees and appeared to lead northeast in the direction of Blind Bay. When Roland's voice became louder, Adele quickened her pace and followed the trail further into the woods.

When she spotted him, Adele hid behind one of the larger trees and then poked her head out to watch as Roland walked through a grass clearing with the monastery cat trotting alongside him. He was both shirtless and shoeless, wearing only a pair of mud-splattered jeans, his face nearly covered by his rain-soaked hair and beard, but even from fifty yards Adele could see him smiling as he stopped and looked down at the cat.

"See? I was right, Mr. Cash. The sun has returned to our little secret corner of the world." The large, black cat snuggled Roland's shin and then stood on its hind legs and reached up with its front paws toward his thigh. "I'm not a scratching post. We talked about this, remember? If you want up, you have to ask nice."

The cat let out a wailing meow. Roland's smile grew even bigger as he nodded. "That's better," he said as he reached down, picked the cat up, and put it on the back of his neck so that the cat fell across his shoulders. "You like the view from up there, don't you?"

Adele decided to step out from behind the tree. "Hey."

Roland didn't appear the least bit surprised to see her. "Hey yourself. It looks like you got the note I left on the yacht. I bet Lucas was with you when you did. Am I right?"

"He was."

Roland chuckled. "Good old Lucas. Predictable as ever. You get a chance to talk with Ophelia?"

"I did. She said you were doing well."

"That's because I am, Adele. I really am. Something about this place always seems to set me right." The cat's tail started to twitch. Roland turned his head toward his shoulder, so they were eye to eye. "Mr. Cash, this is my friend Adele. I don't believe you two have been formally introduced. Ms. Adele Plank, this is Mr. Cash, otherwise known around here as the cat in black."

"Nice to see you again, Mr. Cash." The cat looked at Adele briefly and then closed its eyes. "I'm afraid I didn't make much of an impression."

"Don't take it personal. Mr. Cash plays it close to the vest. He thinks you're okay."

"That's a relief."

Roland snapped his fingers. "You want to see something cool? I was on my way back from there, but I'd love to show you. It's always nice to be able to share these kinds of discoveries with someone else. What do you say? You have time?"

"Sure." Adele didn't know what to make of Roland's good mood given it wasn't so long ago that he was refusing to even accept a message from her.

Seemingly thinking the same thing, Roland reached down as he was walking, plucked a blade of tall grass, and stuck it between his teeth. "If it's alright with you I'd rather not waste time or energy fighting."

"I feel the same way. You were the one who put a block on your phone, though, not me."

"Oh, *that*. It wasn't just you, Adele. I blocked everybody. I needed some time alone. I know we left off on a negative note and I apologize for getting so mad. The whole bad Russians thing is a sore point with me because I know I'm to blame for a lot of it and it just makes me sick thinking it might not be over yet."

"Apology accepted. Will you accept mine?"

"What do *you* have to apologize for?"

"I didn't have to bring up the problem with the Russians. I put that in your face because I wanted you to feel bad. I use it as a weapon against you when you're doing something I don't like. That's not right and it's not fair. We need to both move past it."

Roland nudged Adele with his elbow. "I'm not as good with the words as you are so I don't think I can adequately express how much that means to me. I'll just say thanks. You telling me that means a hell of a lot."

"Speaking of which, are there any new developments on the bank sale?"

"I really don't want to talk business. Not here. Is that okay?"

Adele shrugged. "Sure. Say, aren't you cold? Not that I'm complaining. You look pretty good in a wild man of the woods sort of way."

Roland tilted his head back and rubbed against the cat that remained sprawled across his shoulders. "Cold? Heck no. Not with Mr. Cash to help keep me warm."

"It's nice to know you're proving the crazy cat lady cliché wrong. Clearly men are just as susceptible to losing their minds to their feline companions."

"You hear that? He's purring. He really does like you."

Adele reached up and scratched behind Mr. Cash's ear. "He does seem to be a pretty cool cat."

Roland smiled. "Yeah, he's pretty much the best cat in the world."

"Are you going to bring him back to Roche?"

"No, this is his home. It's part of why he's so special. I'll just keep visiting him from time to time. That's how cats like it. If we were around each other too much he'd start to take me for granted and get into the habit of bringing up the Russians or bank business whenever I annoyed him. We both need our space."

Adele didn't know how to respond. Likely sensing her uncertainty, Roland nudged her again. "That was a failed attempt at a joke."

"Ha. Very funny."

Roland suddenly stopped and pointed straight ahead. "There. Check it out."

Adele looked up. "Wow," she whispered.

A wide gap in the trees allowed them to see out over Blind Bay and miles and miles beyond to the purple-tinted Canadian Coastal Mountains that appeared to be looming directly over nearby Orcas Island.

"Isn't it something? It's like an optical illusion. I don't know if it's a combination of the water magnifying the sunlight or what, but it seems like you could almost reach out and touch the snowcaps. I was standing here last night, and the moon looked huge."

Adele remained stunned by the combination of the sea and snow peaks and all the magnificent colors illuminated within the space between. Then her eyes focused on something else that was much closer—Turtleback Mountain on Orcas. The area appeared darker and more ominous than everything else around it.

"See something?" Roland asked.

"Turtleback Mountain—I was over there the other day with Fin."

"That's right, your new Irish friend. How did *that* go?"

Adele detected a hint of jealousy in Roland's tone. "It was different. Did Ophelia say anything about it?"

"She mentioned you two had stopped by on your way over there, but that was pretty much it."

Adele wondered why Ophelia hadn't already asked her about the trip to Orcas with Fin. For something that had so clearly worried her it seemed a bit strange that now she wouldn't even bring it up.

"I should talk to her."

"Who? Ophelia?"

Adele nodded. "Yeah. Thanks for showing me this lookout. It's pretty awesome, but now I have something I need to do."

"Sure, no problem. I should get back and clean up anyways. I don't think Ophelia will allow me to sit at the dinner table like this."

"You two seem to get along well."

When Roland went to scratch his beard, Mr. Cash playfully swatted at his fingers. "Yeah, she's great. Ever since I came to the islands after my parents died, she's been a part of my life. My grandfather never spoke a bad word about her."

"What about your grandmother?"

Roland glanced up at the sky and squinted. "Huh, I never thought about that before, but you know what? Grandmother never mentioned Ophelia. I don't recall the two of them ever being in the same room together."

"Does that seem odd to you?"

Roland shrugged. "I don't know. Both my grandparents were people of few words. They were from a very different time. These days they'd be called cold or rude. Nobody seems to have the ability to just shut up and think about stuff from time to time."

Not wanting to break her promise to Ophelia, Adele stopped pushing Roland about his longtime relationship with the nun. Instead she made sure to enjoy what was left of the walk and the sun on her face while listening to the satisfied purrs coming from Mr. Cash as they made their way back to the convent.

23.

"Please pass the salt and pepper." Adele pushed the shakers toward Roland who told her thank you and then lightly seasoned the steamed vegetables on his plate. He had cleaned up nicely in a crisp white dress shirt with the sleeves rolled up and a pair of loose-fitting tan slacks. Adele kept sneaking glances his way, wondering if she should reconsider her earlier opinion of the beard. Like the hair on Roland's face, it was growing on her.

"I'm so happy you two decided to stay the night," Ophelia said. "Is everything to your liking?"

"It's wonderful," Adele replied. She held up a yellow cherry tomato that was stuck to the end of her fork. "These pickled tomatoes are to die for."

Ophelia gave her a grateful smile. "Yes, we had quite a harvest of those last fall, nearly 100 jars worth. The secret is a touch of garlic. I find it really complements the natural sweetness of the tomato."

Roland bit into an ear of corn and then used a napkin to wipe the buttery juice off his chin. "Hard to beat corn on the cob. I haven't had any for so long. When I was a kid, it was one of my favorite things to eat. It's weird how I had forgotten that."

"For years I sent your grandfather some ears of corn from here at the end of every summer," Ophelia said. "Charles was like you. He absolutely loved it. Despite being a man of means he never forgot how to appreciate the simple things. I always admired him for that. A lot of people on the islands did."

Roland put his corn down slowly while staring at his plate. "Yeah, I remember that corn. It came in a crate. Grandfather would bring it into the house and we'd schuck it together before dropping it into the pot of boiling water. Sinatra would be playing in the kitchen and there'd be another pot cooking up some crab. Corn and crab, Grandfather loved eating them together. We always had all kinds of fancy food in the house, Kobe beef, foie gras, caviar, but I never saw him so excited for a meal as when there was corn and crab cooking. We'd sit outside at the picnic table looking out over Friday Harbor and he'd be cracking open crab shells, biting into the corn, drinking a beer, and say how it doesn't get any better than that. I had no idea it was *your* corn though. Isn't that something? It's like coming full circle by way of a vegetable."

"The greenhouse allows us to grow corn year-round. I could send you some from time to time, just like I did for Charles. Would you like that?"

"Sure, but you don't need to go to the trouble of having it delivered. I could just stop by and pick it up myself. It'll give me another excuse to come here and spend a few days unwinding. Unless my being around more is a problem with the other nuns."

"It's not problem at all, Roland." Ophelia reached across the table and put her hand on top of his. "You come by whenever you like. This door is always open to you— *always.*"

"And you're welcome to see my new place in Roche Harbor. I'd love to show it to you."

"It's shaping up to be quite a home," Adele added.

"Oh," Ophelia said. "You two will be neighbors. How wonderful."

Roland grinned. "Yeah, I figure we'll get along great when we're not trying to kill each other." He looked over at Adele. "Isn't that right?"

Ophelia plopped a single pea into her mouth. "Relationships are complicated things, but the right ones are always worth the effort. What good is life without someone to share it with?"

"Amen to that," Roland declared while raising his empty wine glass. "To friends and a life worth sharing."

Ophelia got up from the table. "I can't believe I forgot the wine. I'll be right back." She returned with an open bottle and filled the glasses. "This was produced right here at the convent some years ago. I've been saving it for a special occasion." She held the bottle up and turned it slowly in her hands. "Yes, there's the date—1987."

Roland stopped swirling the wine in his glass and looked up. "Really? That's the year I was born. I guess that qualifies it as a particularly good year."

Ophelia sipped from her glass and then gave Roland a thin smile. "Yes, it was."

Roland had a sip and then nodded. "Mm, this *is* good wine. Have you and the other nuns ever thought of commercializing your little operation here? With the farm-to-table movement going on I'm certain it would generate a nice bit of revenue for you. I'd be happy to help with seed money, logistics, a promotional campaign, whatever."

Ophelia wagged her finger. "No talking business at the dinner table, Mr. Soros."

"Fair enough," Roland said after emptying his glass. "As long as you keep that wine coming."

Ophelia pushed the bottle across the table. "Help yourself."

"Don't mind if I do." Roland refilled his glass and then held the bottle over Adele's. "Ready for more?"

Adele nodded. "Sure, fill me up."

Roland arched a brow and smirked as he poured the wine. Then he set the bottle down and raised his glass. "Okay, let's have a proper toast." He looked at Adele and Ophelia. "To our gracious host, Mother Mary Ophelia. One could not ask for a finer meal and better company. And to the bravest, most intelligent, and yes, sometimes most aggravating young woman I know, Adele Plank. It is my honor to be sharing this table with the two of you this evening."

"You forgot one thing, Roland," Ophelia said.

"I did?"

"You forgot beautiful."

"You're right. To the *beautiful*, Mother Mary Ophelia."

Ophelia shook her head and pointed at Adele. "Not me, *her*!"

"What?" Roland stroked his beard. "Adele? *Beautiful*? C'mon . . ."

Adele elbowed him in the ribs. "You're such a twerp."

Roland nearly spit out his wine as he started laughing. "You've called me a lot of things since we met, but I do believe this to be the very first time you've used twerp." He finished his wine and then raised his glass again. "To first times. May they come again and again and again." After a brief pause, he continued. "Oh, and to the *very* beautiful Adele Plank."

Adele opened her mouth to say something but quickly closed it again as Roland leaned over and kissed her lightly on the lips. "Never before," he whispered, "has anyone made a bad boy want to be so good."

It could have been the wine, the words, or maybe even the beard that made Adele do what she did next. She didn't know and she didn't care. All she wanted then was to repay Roland with the exact same kindness he had just shown her. When he went to pull away, she put her hand behind his head, ran her fingers through his hair, and pulled him close. Instead of kissing him she gently bit down on his earlobe. "Never before," she whispered, "has a good girl wanted to be so bad."

Roland sat up and blinked a few times with his mouth hanging partly open while Adele looked over at Ophelia, hoping the dinner table display hadn't offended the nun. "My goodness," Ophelia said. "Aren't you two something?"

"I'm so sorry," Roland stammered. "That wasn't appropriate. I fear the wine got the better of my manners."

Ophelia scowled. "Not appropriate? Don't be such a prude. There's nothing wrong with two people being attracted to one another—nothing at all. I'm happy for the chance to play matchmaker. As for the wine, there's still some left. If there is one hard rule to this place it's never to allow a good bottle to go to waste so drink up or shut up."

After the wine was finished the three sat by the fire. Not long after, Ophelia's eyes closed, and she began to snore. Roland quietly placed a few more logs into the hearth and then turned around. "I can sleep in a chair out here and you can have the bed in the cabin," he said. "Or vice versa. Whatever you want."

Ophelia's eyes opened. "Don't be silly. Share the cabin. I trust you both not to do anything that would disrespect my hospitality."

Roland shrugged. "You can still have the bed and I'll take the floor."

"Sure," Adele replied. "That'll work."

Ophelia closed her eyes and smiled. "See?" she mumbled. "That wasn't so hard. Don't worry about me. I'll put myself to bed in a bit." Within seconds she was snoring again.

Roland had Adele use the convent's first floor bathroom first to take care of her toiletries. When she returned to the cabin, he left to do the same, which also allowed her some privacy while getting ready for bed. She stripped down to her underwear and T-shirt, got under the covers, and waited. It wasn't long before she heard a knock at the door and Roland asked if it was okay to come in. She said yes, he entered, and then closed the door behind him.

"You sure you'll be okay sleeping on the floor?"

"Sure," Roland said. "Throw me down a pillow and I'll be good. No worries. Fact is that mattress is pretty firm. I doubt it's much better."

Adele pulled the covers up to her neck and stretched her legs. "It's comfy, like the bed on my sailboat."

Roland took his shirt off, adjusted his pillow, lay back, and looked up at Adele. "I'll have to take your word for it. I wouldn't know."

"Maybe someday."

Roland put his hands behind his head and grinned. "That's a verbal contract, young lady. And don't think I won't hold you to it. I have a whole team of liars, I mean *lawyers*, to argue the dispute."

"I said *maybe*. It's not contractually binding."

"It implies intent. There's really no need to waste time and resources on a messy legal battle though. We'd both be much better off coming to a mutually acceptable agreement.

"Oh? And what might *that* be?"

Roland sat up. "Something along the lines of a proper goodnight kiss would probably work."

Adele struggled to keep the serious facade going. "I don't know. That might just complicate the case."

"No, it would make it all go away. It's a win-win. It really is the only option that makes any sense."

"I've kissed you once tonight already."

"And once is enough?"

"Sure—more than enough."

"Ah," Roland said, grinning. "It was that good, huh?"

Adele shrugged. "What I meant is that when something's not all that great to begin with then having it once is all you want to bother with. Sort of like fast food. You have too much of it and it just makes you feel awful."

Watching the concern spread across Roland's face made Adele want to break out laughing. "Are you still messing with me or are you being serious?" he said.

Adele reached over and turned out the light before Roland could see her smiling. "Goodnight, Roland." She heard him lie back down and felt his eyes on her. "Roland?"

"Yeah?"

"I'll confess. I was messing with you."

Roland sat back up. Adele couldn't see his face but could make out the outline of his head and shoulders. "You change your mind about that goodnight kiss?"

Adele propped herself up sideways onto her elbow. "Sure. Why not?" She still couldn't see Roland's face but felt his breath on her skin as he inched closer until the tips of their noses touched. He breathed deep as she enjoyed the sensation of his lips brushing her cheek, and then the kiss arrived with a speed and urgency that took Adele by surprise. For a second the rational part of her thought to push him away, but another part of her, one that was at that moment much stronger, welcomed the intrusion, embraced it, and demanded more. They had been together once before years ago, but that time had been an alcohol-fueled moment of desire and naivete mixed with equal parts insecurity. This time felt much different.

It felt better.

A lot better.

So, when Roland suddenly lay back down again, leaving Adele struggling to catch her breath, she was again surprised by how much she had wanted him to continue. It had been a long time since she had wanted something that bad.

Roland let out a long, satisfied sigh. Though Adele couldn't see him she knew he was smiling.

"Goodnight, Adele."

24.

Adele sat inside her sailboat in front of her laptop staring at a blank screen. She had promised Jose a story by the end of the day. It was already late afternoon, and nothing had come to her yet. Her mind kept wandering back to last night and the intense yet much too brief kiss with Roland.

Focus, Adele. Stop acting like a love-struck schoolgirl. You have work to do.

Fin had stopped by earlier asking how the trip went and when they'd be back to Orcas. Adele talked with him for a few minutes but then sent him away with an apology that she was up against a deadline. He took it well with a grin and a tip of his cap and a promise to be by later to see if she was hungry, in need of a drink, or both.

Jose suggested she write about the cave on Orcas. She hadn't told him the backstory to that discovery and her motivation for going there, especially the part about Karl Bloodbone, but now she was rethinking that omission.

She took her phone out and scrolled through the pictures of the cave and the clearing she had taken and then decided the one showing the odd inscription on the inside of the shack door would strike just the right tone for the article.

Be a slave to the truth or know freedom from the lie.

Adele repeated the phrase to herself several times as her fingers hovered over the keyboard. She typed the words, deleted them, then typed them again as thoughts led to possible destinations and the article's potential began to finally take shape.

The door, the inscription, and a shared adventure with the son of the man who had first helped her to make the islands her home. Adele nodded. The next edition of the paper was going to be a good one.

She began to write.

The Island Gazette

"Be a slave to the truth or know freedom from the lie."

by Adele Plank

Orcas has long held a special place in our island community as a destination of secrets, adventure, and spiritual awakening. Its rocky, weather-worn shores and dense evergreen forests whisper of rumors that continue to hide truths and a future that remains bound to a far less serene and sometimes violent past marked by names like Skull Island, Victim Island, and Massacre Bay, as well as the ecological abuses of the powerful Hudson's Bay Company.

It was in search of some of that past that took me to Orcas recently with a man who is himself tied to our little watery oasis by way of simple genetics. Many of you reading this are familiar with the name Delroy Hicks. I was very blessed to know more than just the name. Delroy was my friend and one-time mentor. And like Orcas Island, Delroy, too, was a thing of secrets that hid behind layers of seeming indifference and good intent.

His name is Fin Hicks and he is Delroy's son. He shares a lot in common with his father—both good and bad. There is the lopsided grin, cordial warmth, and easy charm, as well as the inclination to sometimes jump first without checking to see what might be below while taking others with them. A longtime Roche Harbor resident, while watching Fin moving about the docks, remarked how he looked like a bit of a rogue.

Indeed.

I journeyed with this rogue to Orcas Island to follow up on research originally begun by his father during a conflict that took place more than forty years earlier between a man named Karl Bloodbone and other island residents who didn't appreciate his particular version of spirituality. Some called Bloodbone and his followers a cult and a lie that fed off the desperations of the sick and dying. His supporters knew him as a Native American healer uniquely in sync with the primordial heartbeat of the island.

The dispute between both sides burned hot for a while but then, as most often happens with such things, it dissipated and was largely forgotten, including the book Delroy wrote about the people and events of that time. It was titled *The Mystery of the Lekwiltok Crystal,* a reference to the stone that was often seen hanging around Mr. Bloodbone's neck. Delroy's final published assessment of Bloodbone was not kind and clearly sided with his many detractors.

But was that final assessment the truth or the lie?

Fin and I went in search of the answer. What we found was both less and more than we expected.

The photograph that accompanies this story is of a shack in a clearing that was the one-time home of Bloodbone and his followers. The inscription inside the door remains some forty years after it was put there, though its true meaning remains a mystery.

Be a slave to the truth or know freedom from the lie.

Could Delroy Hicks have been the slave who won his freedom by publishing a lie?

I don't have that answer—yet.

There are those who believe Karl Bloodbone remains very much alive despite multiple accounts of his presence on the islands dating back to the time of Robert Moran's arrival to Orcas in 1906—113 years earlier. Surely such a lifespan isn't actually possible.

Is it?

Years earlier, I arrived at these islands a guest and then returned wanting to remain here forever. Perhaps what happened between then and now could in a way be called magic, how a place and a person seem destined to be a part of each other. Some of you readers likely consider that to be overly sentimental nonsense. I'm a sensible sort except when it comes to the San Juan Islands. There really is something different about this place. It can be difficult to pinpoint that difference, but you know it's there, like gravity or the air we breathe—invisible yet so very essential to our existence.

Fin Hicks traveled here from Ireland hoping to learn more about a father he never met. I came here hoping to find myself. Similar stories of self-discovery are legion in this place of rock and sea where we are all allowed the time and space to be islands unto ourselves. Is that magic? I like to think so.

Following the publication of this article I intend to continue trying to solve the mystery of Karl Bloodbone. I look forward to sharing the outcome of that work with you all in an upcoming issue of the paper.

Wish me luck.

25.

"Hold up. I was just on my way to see you."
Adele turned around to see Lucas jogging
toward her. The early evening wind was
blowing cold across the Roche Harbor docks. It would be
dark soon.

"Is everything okay?"

"You have a minute?" Lucas replied.

Uh-oh, Adele thought right before telling Lucas she was
on her way to see Roland on his yacht.

"Good, then you already know he's back. I had
messaged him a few times and he finally replied earlier
today saying he was back in Roche."

"Yeah, I found him at the convent on Shaw again. We
stayed overnight there. Apparently, he just needed some
time to unwind or whatever. You know how Roland can
be."

Lucas pursed his lips as he shrugged. "Sure. You two
spent the night together?"

"It was innocent. I was just there to make sure he was
okay."

"And?"

"And he's okay. That's it."

"But now you're on your way to see him again."

"No, I'm actually standing here waiting to hear what it is you needed to talk to me about."

Lucas sighed. "Sorry, I'm being a bit of a dick. It's none of my business where you spent the night."

"Your choice of words not mine."

"Anyways, it's about Sandra Penny."

"Uh-huh."

"Did you know Roland has been in talks to sell the bank?" When Adele didn't answer, Lucas grunted. "Of course, you knew. He probably told you himself."

"No, he didn't. Someone else did."

"Who?"

"Lucas, that's not important. You're here about Sandra Penny, remember?"

"If you knew about the sale why hasn't there been anything in the paper about it?"

"Do I tell you how to run the sheriff's department? No, I don't. So, don't tell me how to run my newspaper."

"Fair enough."

Adele glanced behind her wondering if Roland was watching. When she looked up at Lucas, he was pouting. "What?" she said.

"Nothing."

"Are you going to tell me about Sandra Penny or not?"

"Sure. That's why I'm here."

Adele raised her brows. "*Well?*"

"It's about the sale. I thought that could have been Sandra's motivation for trying to scare you. That is if she was actually the one driving the car that morning."

"I don't understand what one has to do with the other."

"I was thinking—this is all hypothetical of course—that she wanted to scare you into believing she was one of the Russians, get you to blame Roland and make him have second thoughts about the sale so that she doesn't lose her position there. I'm not saying it's a perfect explanation, I know it has a lot of holes, but I also wanted you to know that I believe you. Someone *was* looking to intimidate you and whoever it was used Sandra Penny's car to do it."

"Are you more willing to think it could be her because she didn't want to bring the car in to be looked at?"

"That's certainly part of it, but then you add that with the pending bank sale and she's looking more and more like the only likely suspect. She's been running Roland's bank for years. If he sells it, she might not be running anything."

"I appreciate the input, I really do, but you already said it yourself; revving an engine isn't a crime."

"That's true, but if she lied to me that could be. And then there's the question of why she would do it in the first place and if she's willing to do something more. I thought it best to make you aware for your own protection. Be on the lookout for her, Adele—and don't tell Roland. Let me handle that part."

"Why don't we go tell him right now?"

"No, now isn't the time. I'm still putting some things together. Can I count on you not to say anything to him yet?"

"I don't want to lie to him if that's what you mean."

"I didn't say anything about lying. Just don't bring the subject of Sandra Penny up to him."

"What if Roland brings it up?"

Lucas looked up at the darkening sky and sighed. "You're a smart girl. I'm sure you can figure it out."

"You're right you know."

"About what?"

"You're being a bit of a dick."

"I'm not going to let you bait me into an argument. That said, if you staying with Roland last night is a sign you two are getting close, you know he's going to find a way to disappoint you again. He always does. And I'll be there like I always am to help you pick up the pieces of that mess because that's what friends do and that's who I am."

"I agree. I owe you and you owe me and that's never going to change, Lucas."

"Around and around we go and yet it seems like we always end up in the same spot—*this* spot."

Adele shook her head. "No, we don't. This spot is different because we're different. There's been so much change in both our lives. I've finally learned to stop trying to figure out what the future holds because I don't have a damn clue. I just know I want people like you with me and I hope you feel the same."

"You know I do, but I have to ask you again about why you haven't reported the potential bank sale in the paper. It's a huge story."

"Because Roland asked that I hold off and then, when he's ready, he'll give me an exclusive interview."

"So, I'm not supposed to suggest how you should run your business, but Roland is? Do I have that about right?"

Adele's eyes flared as she pointed at Lucas. "How did *you* hear about the sale?"

"You remember a man by the name of Randall Eaton? He was here last summer during the Liya and Visili Vasa trouble."

"The FBI agent? Of course I remember. What about him?"

"The feds haven't stop watching Roland. They likely knew about the sale almost as soon as he did. Eaton was the one who told me."

"And why would he do that?"

"He wanted me to know as a way of making sure everything was on the up-and-up. Look, Roland has a history with some very shady business partners. You can't expect the authorities to just forget that."

"Including you?"

"Least of all me. My job is to protect this community, remember?"

"Oh, that must be why you broke into Roland's yacht the other day—*to protect the community.* Or was it actually because Eaton told you to and then you used my concern for Roland to justify it?"

Lucas glared at Adele. "I did that because you were worried about him and don't you dare make it out as anything different."

"Or what? You'll arrest me?"

"Is everything alright with you two?"

Adele and Lucas both turned to look at Fin. "We're good," Lucas growled.

"No offense, Sheriff," Fin said, "but I was talking more to the young lady who you're looming over. Some might even mistake it for intimidation."

When Adele tried to move in front of Lucas, he pushed her back and stepped toward Fin. "I wasn't looming over anyone. We were having a conversation. Now mind your own business, shut up, and be on your way."

Fin held his hands out at his sides and smiled. "I believe America is still a free country, Sheriff. At least that's what they've been telling the rest of us. I have as much right to be standing on this dock as you."

"I'm warning you, Fin. I'm in no mood."

"Mood for *what*? Are you going to come over here and try to intimidate me like you were just doing to Adele? You're a big fella I'll give you that, but I've tangled with bigger than you and have come to learn that big doesn't always mean tough."

"Fin," Adele said. "I'm fine."

"See?" Lucas added. "Now do like I asked and get out of here."

Fin's eyes narrowed. "You asking, Sheriff, or are you ordering? Where I come from, my people, we don't respond well to things like threats and orders."

Adele saw the vein throbbing on Lucas's forehead and knew she needed to act fast before the situation devolved into something that could get Fin hurt. "I said I'm fine. Everyone needs to take it down a notch, okay?"

If either of them heard a word Adele said they didn't show it. Lucas took another step toward Fin with his hand resting on the butt of his gun.

"Ah, just like an American to reach for a weapon," Fin said. He held his fists upside down in front of him like a bare-knuckle boxer from the Victorian age and nodded. "How about we keep this civilized, Sheriff? Just a bit of good old fashioned knockin' about, yeah?"

"You're threatening an officer of the law. I can arrest you for that."

Fin clicked his tongue. "Hiding behind that badge, are you? What a pity. Here I thought you at least resembled a real man. Guess I was wrong."

"I don't need a badge to kick your ass." Lucas took off his gun belt and badge and set them down on the dock. "You sure you really want to do this?"

Fin skipped from side to side as he made little circles with his fists. "C'mon then, Sheriff. Less talk and more walk."

Lucas rolled up his sleeves and shook his head. "Okay, don't say I didn't warn you."

"Stop it," Adele yelled while putting both hands against Lucas's chest. It felt like trying to push against a slab of granite. "You're both acting like idiots."

When Fin put his hands down, Lucas pointed at him. "I knew you wouldn't go through with it."

Fin raised his fists again. "Step out of the way, Adele. No worries. This won't take long."

Adele stared up at Lucas. "I mean it," she said as she pushed against him even harder. "Don't do it."

Lucas gently moved Adele out of the way and then faced Fin. "Last chance."

"Don't waste time worrying about me, Sheriff. You don't know it yet, but you've really stepped in it. You'll know soon enough though."

Fin didn't swing first and neither did Lucas.

To the shock of both men it was Adele who struck the first blow.

26.

"That almost hurt," Lucas said while rubbing the spot on his lower chest where he'd been hit. "What do you think you're doing?"

Adele remained in her fighting stance as she stood between Lucas and Fin. "I'm trying to get your attention before you do something really stupid. Now put your badge back on. You're the sheriff. Act like it."

"That's right I *am* the sheriff and you just assaulted me. But you want it both ways, don't you? I'm only supposed to bend the rules when it's something *you* want."

"I could have hit you a lot harder, Lucas."

"Hey," Fin called out from behind Adele. "I don't need anyone to do my fighting for me. I'd have dropped the dumb goon quick like a wet sack of grain falling off the back of a truck."

"Not likely," Lucas seethed as he clenched his fists.

Adele heard footsteps and leaned to the side to see past Lucas. It was Roland walking toward them. He stopped and pointed at Lucas's gun belt and badge. "You drop something, Sheriff?"

Lucas turned around and glared at Roland. "What do *you* want?"

Roland stuffed his hands into his pockets and shrugged. "Just wondering what's going on out here is all. I heard some yelling and saw two men puffing out their chests and looking like they were about to either kiss or throw down and then Adele trying her best to knock some sense into them. Do I have that about right?"

"Point of clarification, Mr. Soros," Fin said. "I didn't need Adele's help. I don't want folks around here thinking I'd allow a woman to do my fighting for me."

"Point taken, Fin. We all know Adele is no ordinary woman though, don't we Sheriff?" Roland stared at Lucas. "And I'm guessing that's what this is *really* about. Look, nothing happened. We were both on Shaw, it got late, we stayed over, and then we came home. Not that it's any of your business. You should know by now there's no caging a woman like her. What I don't understand is why you'd ever want to."

Lucas grabbed his gun belt and badge and put them on. "A lecture from you is the last thing I need to waste my time listening to."

"You're right, Sheriff. That said, if I ever see you looking like you might hurt Adele again that'll be it for you on these islands. You'll be done. I'll see to it personally."

Lucas looked at Adele and then Roland. "*What*? I wasn't going to hurt her. I'd never—"

"He's right," Adele said as she put her hand on Lucas's arm. "I was just trying to stop him from hurting Fin."

"Ah, c'mon now," Fin whined. "How many times do I have to say it? The good sheriff was about to get properly thumped."

The marina's automatic night lights kicked on, illuminating the docks in their florescent buzz. Adele folded her arms across her chest. "It's getting cold."

Roland nodded. "That it is. You were on your way to see me, right?"

"Actually, I think I'm going to head up to the hotel instead."

"Why? I already opened a bottle of red for us."

"I didn't ask you to do that."

Lucas stuck his thumbs into his gun belt. "Wasn't it you who said not to try to cage her? I should haul your ass in right now just for being such a spoiled hypocrite. How about it, Roland? You want to spend the night behind bars?"

Now it was Roland whose eyes flared, and his fists clenched. "Take your best shot, Sheriff. Everyone knows that the only thing big on you is your mouth."

Lucas took two long strides, grabbed Roland by the shirt, and nearly yanked him off his feet. "This has been a long time coming so keep talking. Go ahead. I dare you."

"Boys. You turn around and look at me right now."

Tilda emerged from the darkness and was clearly in no mood for further nonsense. She tapped Lucas on the shoulder. "I mean it, young man. You let him go this instant. We have guests at this marina who shouldn't have to witness this embarrassment. I won't tell you again. Let Roland go."

Lucas took a deep breath, sighed, and then stepped back. "All due respect, Tilda, but this isn't your concern."

"Everything that goes on here is my concern, Sheriff. Now all of you follow me back to the hotel and not another word from any of you until we get there. And then we're going to sit down and have a talk—a *real* talk."

"Will there be food and drink?" Fin asked. Everyone turned at the same time to look at him.

"*What*?" Tilda replied.

"Well, I'm getting pretty hungry and I wouldn't say no to a pint either. Talking and listening can be hard work. I need proper sustenance if I'm to contribute to the intended conversation. We all do. Isn't that right?"

Whatever anger Roland had toward Lucas appeared to melt away as he smiled and pointed at Fin. "I don't know our Irish guest well, but I know him well enough to say I like him. I'll grab the wine from the yacht and bring it with me. It's already open and it'd be a shame to waste it."

Tilda straightened her dress and arched a brow. "What's the wine?"

"Just a little Syrah from Paso Robles. It's good stuff. You'll like it."

"I'm sure I will. Then it's settled. Shall we go?"

Adele could feel the heat of Lucas's aggression still coming off him. She reached out, took his hand, and tilted her head toward the hotel. "C'mon. It'll do us all some good to clear the air."

"I don't know, Adele. What's more talk going to do?"

"A lot more than trying to pick a fight with everyone."

Lucas squeezed Adele's hand hard enough it almost hurt. "I don't have anything to say to these people."

"That's because you're still angry. Let it go. Come with us to the hotel. We'll sit, we'll have something to eat and drink, and we'll talk."

Fin put up his fists and winked. "It's a better plan than staying here and getting your ass kicked, Sheriff."

As soon as Fin said "Sheriff" he looked up at a low-flying seagull and then cried out after a slimy white glob splattered across the bridge of his nose. "Ah, I've been hit," he wailed. "Oh, it smells so bad." He leaned forward and reached out to Tilda. "Wipe it off. For the love of God wipe it off me."

Tilda shuffled backwards. "Absolutely not, Mr. Kearns. You're on your own."

Fin went around in circles flailing his arms. "It's in my eyes. I can't see. Oh, the smell—it's awful. I've been done in by a damn bird. Help me. Tell me what to do."

"Get down and put your head in the water," Roland offered. "Hurry, before it burns your eyes out."

Fin shut his eyes tight and suddenly became very still. "It can really do that?"

"Oh yeah," Roland replied. "I've read all about it. Seagull crap can burn the paint off a car. Imagine what's it's doing to your eyes right now. You better get that head under the water pronto."

Fin dropped down onto his hands and knees and crawled toward the edge of the dock. "That's it," Roland said. "You're almost there. Just lean over and make sure to dunk your whole head in and give it a few good shakes while you're down there. Hopefully it's not too late."

The threat of being too late seemed to motivate Fin even more. He removed his cap, hung over the dock, and dropped down into the water all the way up to his shoulders.

Tilda pointed at a dark mass speeding through the water toward Fin. "What's that?"

Before Adele could yell a warning, a harbor seal was already floating no more than a few inches from Fin's submerged head. When Fin came up gasping for air the two were nose-to-nose. The seal's dark eyes widened as it barked a warning for Fin to get back right before unleashing a grunting wet sneeze that sprayed Fin's face.

Fin launched himself away from the water, fell backwards, and then screamed again. "The beast tried to make a meal of me."

Roland bent down and gripped Fin by the shoulders and shook him. He appeared very concerned and sounded just as serious. "But can you see, man? Tell us if you can still see."

"Yeah," Fin said as his eyes went blink-blink-blink. "I can. I'm okay."

Roland whistled. "Whew, thank goodness. That was close. You acted quick and most likely saved your life. I've seen the seals around here rip through men twice your size. Their appetite for blood is insatiable. Just last summer, an entire flotilla of confused and careless tourists fell in and they were lost forever. Fortunately, it was just a bunch of retired Canadians, so it didn't even make the news. A harbor seal feeding frenzy is truly something to behold. If there's one standing rule about Roche Harbor, it's this—*never* go into the water."

"But *you* were the one who told me to dunk my head."

Roland stood, put the back of his hand against his mouth, and snickered. Fin's eyes narrowed. "Wait a damn minute. Were you putting me on? Having a laugh at my expense eh, Mr. Soros? Well, to hell with you then."

When Tilda and Lucas started to laugh, Adele soon joined them. Everyone but Fin doubled over with tears streaming down their cheeks. Roland held his side and said he couldn't breathe. Lucas leaned against a piling and appeared to have regained control but then looked at Fin and lost it again.

Fin got up and nodded. "That's it. Make fun of the new guy with the funny accent. Get it out. Laugh it up. Ha-ha. Oh, yes, it's all so very amusing."

"I'm sorry," Adele managed to say between giggles. "But the seagull, you sticking your head in the water, and then the seal, I've never heard anyone scream like that. I really thought I might pee my pants."

The seal barked at them again as it swam by. When Fin gave it a one-finger salute it took another five minutes for the others to compose themselves.

"And on *that* note," Tilda said while dabbing away her tears, "I ask that everyone follow me to the hotel."

Fin reached down, snatched up his cap, and put it back on his head. "I'll be sitting right in front of the fire with a proper whiskey in my hand. You all owe me that much for the entertainment value alone."

Lucas clapped Fin on the back hard enough it made the Irishman grunt. "You got it. At least now I don't feel like kicking your ass anymore."

"Now, Sheriff," Fin said, "we're just getting past all that but if you really want me to bloody you up, I'll be happy to oblige. Just say the word."

"Nah," Lucas replied. "Maybe next time."

Tilda led the way along the dock. Behind her were Lucas and Fin, then Roland, and last to follow was Adele. The soft breeze that caressed her face was almost warm, a reminder that the long winter was finally giving way to spring.

When Roland slowed, looked back at her, and then held his hand out, Adele took it.

A new season was fast approaching.

Change was coming.

27.

Roland was tired of the question. Everyone else was tired of his refusal to answer. They had spent the last hour sitting around Tilda's table enjoying wine and a large platter of finger foods that she had prepared for them. The bottle Roland brought was quickly emptied. Tilda had opened a second and now they were well on their way to finishing a third.

"Does it have anything to do with Eaton?" Lucas said.

Roland didn't look up from the wine that he was slowly swirling in his glass. "What about him?"

"He contacted me recently and told me about the pending sale."

"The feds can go to hell. I'm sick of their meddling, the intimidation, and all their damn rules. It's ridiculous how some empty-headed bureaucrats and their staffs on the take in Washington D.C. can pass equally empty-headed regulations that reach out all the way to our islands and force more and more costly compliance. Do you know how impossible it's getting to do business in this country anymore?"

It was the first time that night that Roland had been willing to open up, even if it was just a little, about his reasons for selling the bank. He put his wine down but continued to stare at it. "I don't like being told what to do."

"Who does?" Lucas replied.

Roland looked up. "You want to know what I *do* like, Sheriff?"

"Sure."

"Eighty-seven million reasons to *not* have to listen to anyone telling me what to do anymore. That's the offer that's on the table right now—$87 million for my little bank. Eighty-seven million ways for me to tell all the Randall Eatons of the world to kiss my ass and leave me alone. That's what I *really* want. For my days to be my own. I know you can understand that. I know there was a part of you that not so long ago thought of quitting being a cop because you felt the same as me. You were tired of people telling you to do things *their* way when you knew it wasn't the *right* way."

"But I didn't quit. I'm still the sheriff."

Roland grabbed his glass and raised it high. "Indeed, you are."

Adele noticed Fin fidgeting with his napkin. She watched him drop it and then he cleared his throat. "Uh, just to be clear, Mr. Soros, am I to understand you're soon to be an $87-million-dollar man?"

"It won't be that much after taxes but in the end it's still a very nice pile of cash, yes. More than enough to allow me to do all the things I could possibly want."

"And what exactly is *that*?" Tilda said.

"I already told you—whatever I want. Would you like to know some of the things I have in mind?"

After the others nodded Roland wiped the corners of his mouth and leaned back in his chair. "I had no idea my plans were of such interest to so many."

Now it was Tilda who swirled her wine. "It's not that you're so interesting, Roland, but rather that your plans so often impact others and not always in a positive way."

"Oh, now I get it. You're worried."

Tilda's response was immediate. "Exactly."

"Well, don't bother. I intend to use the money for good to help protect places like Roche Harbor, make it self-sufficient so it will never need to succumb to outside influence. Did you know there are nearly twenty acres of undeveloped property between here and the main road? That's like an unlocked back door where anybody could get in. I'm going to prevent that from happening."

Adele detected a hint of slurring in Roland's words. The wine was getting to him, lowering his inhibitions, and making him feel more willing to talk. When Tilda reached across the table and refilled his glass, she realized that had been Tilda's plan all along, which also meant Tilda had already suspected Roland was up to something.

"And how do you intend to do that?" Tilda asked.

Roland had a bite of cheese followed by more wine. "I'm locking up that back door to help keep people like you and places like this hotel safe. The property on the hill where my new house is being built was just one part of a much larger acquisition. Those twenty acres I just told you about? I'm buying all of it. It's going to be subdivided and then made into rows of historically-accurate, Victorian-themed vacation rental homes. The revenue stream during the summer months alone will be hundreds of thousands of dollars and I estimate in another ten years it will be worth more than my bank is now but without all the regulatory obligations that come with owning a financial institution. It's a win-win."

"A win-win?" Tilda seethed. "For you perhaps, but you said it yourself, Roland, I own a hotel and you now intend to put vacation rentals in *my* backyard? How in the world could you possibly see that as a win for me and my business? And while we're on the subject, when exactly did you plan to notify me of your plans? Or was your *real* plan to use some of that $87 million to grease the wheels of county government and get this proposed monstrosity approved without any public input from impacted property owners?"

"You haven't let me finish, Tilda. I assure you this *will* be a good thing for Roche. The vacation home rentals will be high-dollar, well above what you charge for a room at your hotel. There won't be any direct competition to you but rather just the opposite. It'll further elevate the appeal of the resort and make access to your hotel even more valuable—all without you having to spend a single penny yourself to make that happen. And I promise, in nearly all my own marketing materials, and I intend to spend a *lot* of money on getting the word out about the vacation home rentals, your business will be prominently featured—with your permission of course. This hotel is the most iconic fixture of the Roche Harbor resort. I want to help make sure that doesn't ever change."

To Adele it felt like the room was holding its breath while everyone waited to see how Tilda would respond. Tilda slowly tapped the table with the tip of her fingernail. "It appears you've thought of nearly everything," she said. "Why the sudden keen interest in Roche Harbor?"

"My interest in Roche is hardly sudden," Roland answered. "I spent more days growing up here than anywhere else. You know that. How many times did you stand on your balcony and watch me lower the little Boston Whaler dinghy from my grandparents' yacht and take off from the marina as happy and content as any boy could possibly be?"

Tilda's eyes twinkled as she smiled. "Many times. You were such a precocious, confident little thing. And just as often the other boat owners would shake their fists and tell you to slow down, but you never did."

Roland smiled back. "And I never will. I have a new Whaler dinghy on order right now due to be delivered in a few weeks. Some say you can never go back but you know what? Eighty-seven million dollars says different." He turned to Lucas. "And it's not just Roche. You've been forced to operate with a skeleton crew of a department since you took the job of sheriff. I'm certain the county thought you'd fail working under those conditions, but you haven't. I haven't yet told you how much I respect that, Lucas, and I apologize for not doing so sooner. You work long hours, complain little, and get the job done. Imagine how much more you could accomplish with some new equipment and more staff. I'll be in a position to help make that happen. Keeping law enforcement local has always been a top priority of mine."

"But keeping our bank locally controlled isn't?" Lucas said.

"It's only a matter of time before an outside financial institution sets up shop here. When that happens, the value of the bank goes down. This is the last best opportunity to sell. Nearly everything is being done online these days. There's less and less practical viability for a small brick-and-mortar community bank like mine. I've fought against that fact for a long time just as my grandfather did. At some point you have to put your fists down and accept reality. It's a good offer. No, it's a *great* offer, the kind of offer that won't come around again. I'd be crazy not to take it. Besides, I'll retain ownership of the building and property both in Friday Harbor and the branch office in Eastsound. The new owners will be required to sign a 99-year lease for both locations above and beyond the $87 million purchase price, guaranteeing yet another revenue stream. And despite new ownership the look of the bank will remain the same. The transition for the community will be minimal."

Lucas shook his head. "How much is enough, Roland? All this money, property, rental income, and lease agreements, will it *ever* be enough for you?"

"Don't be jealous, Lucas, just because I'm in a position to find out."

"I'm *not* jealous. I wouldn't trade places with you for all the money in the world."

Roland glanced at Adele before his eyes settled back on Lucas. "I'm not so sure about that."

When she saw his mouth tighten and his jaw clench, Adele acted quickly to intervene before Lucas lost his temper again. "What about your employees, Roland? Will they keep their jobs?"

"That won't be my decision to make. Regardless of whether they do or don't, I'm setting aside funds to give them each a generous severance payment after the deal closes—enough to make them all very happy."

Lucas grunted. "Must be nice to be able to pay for a clean conscience."

"Will the both of you just shut up already?" Fin took off his cap and ran his fingers through his hair. "Right now, I don't understand what Adele sees in either of you. It's bitch and moan about this and bitch and moan about that. Look around. You're among friends sitting at a table with good food and drink in a place most people can only dream of calling home. If some big bank wants to give Roland $87 million for his little bank, where I come from that's a blessing not a curse. You sure as hell wouldn't have to ask me a second time. Stop trying to beat the man down for doing nothing more than being a success." Fin raised his glass. "Good on you, Roland. I say well played."

Tilda raised her glass as well. "To Roland's success. May none of us be harmed by it."

Adele lifted her glass and then looked at Lucas. "To Roland's success."

"C'mon you grumpy turd," Fin said as he leaned over and bumped up against Lucas with his shoulder. "Toast your friend with us. Make it unanimous."

"You're lucky annoying isn't against the law," Lucas grumbled. "You'd all be facing a life sentence." He stared at Roland, shook his head, and sighed. "Don't blow this, Roland. Do some real good with all that money. These islands need it."

Lucas raised his glass. Roland smiled. Lucas didn't.

The toast was unanimous.

28.

"I had no idea how much you enjoyed going fast," Roland said as another wave crashed over the Lancer's bow.

"Oh, she's a speed addict for sure," Fin added. Both he and Roland shared the passenger seat while Adele sped them all toward Orcas Island. Roland had walked out of his yacht that morning just as Adele and Fin were preparing to leave and asked if he could tag along. They both said sure and a trip for two turned into three.

Adele pointed up at the heavy gray clouds that hung over the islands. "Rain's coming," she said. "Trying to get us there before it does." She hugged the shoreline at Diamond Point that marked the entrance into the long and wide body of water that was East Sound, casually avoiding the large rocks even as she increased the boat's speed.

A long, crooked finger of blue-white lightning hissed across the sky followed quickly by the rumble of nearby thunder. Adele turned on the wipers. The sound of rain hitting the boat's hardtop mixed with that of sea spray striking the hull. The Lancer's bow would lift, settle into the trough, and lift again as it carried over and into the next wave. They sped past Rosario and headed toward Madrona Point until the town of Eastsound came into view.

Adele only slowed a little as she spun the wheel hard, put the Chris Craft into reverse, bumped the throttle a few times, and then came to a smooth stop alongside the visitor dock. "Wow," Roland said. "I'm impressed."

"Thanks," Adele replied as she jumped onto the dock and helped Fin to tie the boat up.

The rain dripped off the brim of his cap. "Where to now?" he asked her.

"There's a restaurant overlooking the water just up the road. We'll hunker down there until the weather passes and then head to the museum to see if Prunella is there. How's that sound?"

Fin shrugged. "Anything is better than standing in this mess getting soaked."

Adele asked Roland if he was ready to go. He smiled and nodded. "After you, Captain Plank."

They found the restaurant, went inside, and sat themselves at a table overlooking the water. The place was a mix of dark wood and nautical themes with fish nets and crab pots hanging from the ceiling. The rain was coming down even harder than before. "I think we're gonna be here for a while," Fin said.

"How you folks doing today?" The waitress looked to be no more than a few years out of high school. She was dressed in jeans and an oversized sweatshirt. The tips of her short hair were dyed pink and a small crystal hung around her neck. Fin pointed at it. "That from around here?"

The waitress fingered the crystal. "It was a graduation gift from my mom. She probably picked it up from the shop down the street about a block from here. They sell a ton of them to the tourists, but I'm pretty sure this is one of the good ones."

Adele looked up. "Good ones?"

"Sure," the waitress replied. "You know, one of the real ones. I heard a lot of the rocks they sell to people are actually shipped here from Mexico or something. But some of them, especially the ones they sell to the locals, those are the *real* crystals."

"Besides location," Adele said, "what's the difference between real and fake?"

"I don't know. They're from the island. The old Indian gets them from a cave or something."

"Indian or Native American?" Fin asked.

The waitress rolled her eyes. "Indian, Native American, whatever. His name is Karl and he's like a thousand years old. I mean, not really, but he's supposed to be super old. Like, even before cell phones and computers and stuff."

Roland cocked his head and smiled. The waitress smiled back. "And this old man named Karl goes into a cave somewhere around here and then comes out with these crystals to sell like the beautiful one you're wearing?"

The girl's smile got even bigger as she rubbed the crystal. "You like it?"

Roland nodded. "I do."

"Are you three like crystal hunters or something?"

"Sort of," Roland answered. "So, can you tell us what's the difference between a real crystal like that and the fake ones you say they sell to the tourists?"

"They're supposed to have some kind of power. Like, they keep you from getting sick and stuff."

"Well," Roland said, "you do look pretty darn healthy."

The girl blushed. "Really? Thanks. I used to come down with these terrible sinus infection headaches all the time, but since my mom gave me this crystal, I hardly get them. And she says when she was not much older than me and living in Bellingham, she developed bad arthritis in both knees from all the house cleaning work she did, but now they hardly bother her at all so who knows? Maybe there really is something to it. You probably think I'm really stupid for saying that."

"Not at all," Roland cooed. "If there's one thing I know it's that I don't know much but I'm learning more every day."

"Wow," the girl said. "That's like *really* smart. You kind of got it going on for an older guy."

The smile fell from Roland's face. "Older?"

The girl nodded. "Yeah, like older than me so that's not necessarily old but it's older. That's okay. I'm down for some."

Adele scowled. "Down for *what*?"

"Oh," the girl said. "Are you with him? I'm sorry. I didn't think . . ."

Fin put his arm around Roland. "She's not with Roland. *I am*. And yes, I don't appreciate you flirting with him right in front of me. It's humiliating. I suffer from a terminally fragile ego and you're certainly not helping."

"I wasn't the one flirting. He was."

Fin turned his head, so his nose was nearly touching Roland's "Is she right about that, my love? Was it really you who was doing all the flirting?"

"You know I only have eyes for you," Roland replied.

With his bluff called, Adele expected Fin to pull away. He didn't.

"Ah," Fin said. "That's my lovely Roland. Let me have a taste of those lips."

Now it was Roland who Adele was certain would end the joke. She was wrong again.

Roland stroked the stubble on the side of Fin's face, closed his eyes, and opened his mouth.

Fin pulled away. "God, man, you were actually gonna do it."

The waitress pouted. "You two were pretending?" Then she snapped her fingers. "Wait, he called you Roland. As in the rich guy from Friday Harbor? The one the reporter said was selling the bank. You're him?"

Adele and Roland shared a glance and then Roland looked up at the waitress. "What reporter?"

"She was in here yesterday asking me and the customers what we thought about the bank being sold and how we felt about you."

"Was her name Marianne Rocha?" Adele said.

"Yeah," the waitress replied. "I think that was it. Pretty lady with a real banging bod. Said she did the news for one of the Seattle stations. I don't remember which one. I don't follow the news much except when I catch it on Comedy Central. Anyways, are you going to order something? I'm supposed to ask because if not then you'll have to leave— paying customers only."

Fin held up three fingers. "Three Guinness. I know you have it on tap. I saw the sign."

The waitress nodded. "Guinness? Sure. I'll get that for you. Be right back."

"It's not even noon yet and we're drinking beer?" Roland said.

"A Guinness is alright morning, noon, or night," Fin replied. "It's far more than just a beer. It's breakfast, lunch, and dinner in a glass. Besides, the way that rain is dropping outside we're gonna be here for a spell. Might as well get comfortable."

The drinks arrived. Fin held his up, sipped from the layer of creamy foam at the top of the glass, and grinned. "Well poured, young lady. It's almost like I'm back home at the pub."

"I thought you sounded British," the waitress said.

Fin put his glass down. "Beg your pardon?"

"The accent. You're from England, right?"

"No, dear girl. I'm from Pittsburg."

"Really? I've never been to that state. I had no idea people from Pittsburg talked so funny."

"Pittsburg isn't a—" Fin shook his head. "Never mind. Off with you then so we can do our drinking in peace."

"Hold on," Adele said.

The waitress turned around. "Yeah?"

"Do you know Prunella Brown?"

"Sure. Everybody knows Prune. Why?"

"We're on our way to see her at the museum as soon as the rain starts to let up. Will she be there?"

"I don't know her daily schedule, but she comes in here for lunch all the time. Like, almost every day. She gets a small salad with the dressing on the side and a glass of water—no ice. Never anything different. Not even once. Old people usually creep me out, but she's pretty cute."

"And what time does she normally come in?"

"Same time every time—noon on the dot."

"Does she eat alone?"

The waitress nodded. "Most times, yeah."

Adele held up two twenties. "This is for the beer and the information. It was a big help."

The waitress's eyes locked onto the bills. She snatched them from Adele and then glanced at Roland. "Mr. Banker should be the one paying."

"I try and I try," Roland said, "but she stubbornly refuses my charity."

The waitress twirled her hair as she looked Roland up and down. "I wouldn't refuse you anything. Nothing wrong with being rich. Nothing at all."

Roland sipped from his beer. "I'd rather be good looking like my friend Fin here."

The waitress looked at Fin then went back to Roland. "You're better looking than him for sure."

"Thank you," Roland replied. "It sounds so much better when you say it. You've restored my confidence. I'm a new man now."

"Uh, okay. Can I get you anything else?"

"Actually," Fin said. "How are the chips?"

"Chips? You mean fries?"

"Sure. Are they any good?"

"I guess. I get complaints about other things but never the fries. You want me to bring you a plate?"

Fin winked. "That would be lovely, my dear."

"Did you just wink at me?"

"I suppose I did. Is that a problem?"

"Well, do you want the fries or not? You winking like that makes it seem like a joke or something."

"Ah, my apologies. Yes, I would like a plate of chips to share with my friends."

"Fries."

"I'm sorry?"

The waitress looked at Fin like he'd suddenly grown a second head. "You keep saying chips, but you mean fries, right?"

Fin nodded slowly. "Riiight."

"Okay. I'll have them out in a bit."

After the waitress left Adele put her face between her hands. "There's ten minutes of my life I'll never get back." She checked the time on her phone. "It's more than an hour until noon. I guess we stay here and wait until then and hope Prune actually shows up."

"Fine by me," Roland said.

"More time to enjoy the Guinness and chips," Fin added.

Adele looked outside. The storm was still getting worse. The wind bent the trees along the shore nearly in half. While they waited, they talked of Marianne Rocha. Roland was convinced it was the FBI agent Randal Eaton who had tipped her off to the pending bank deal.

"It doesn't really matter who it was at this point," Adele told him. "You need to get in front of her report. An interview in my paper like I suggested before will help you do that. I recommend we get it ready for the next issue."

"Not that either of you care, but I'll tell you what *I* think," Fin said. "This big city reporter, she's just trying to rattle your cage a bit, Roland. Get you to reach out to her and ask what's going on and to delay the story. She'll say you two need to talk—likely during dinner. That'll be her way back in. She wants to see you again is all. And can you blame her? You're just so darn cute."

"I'm not too worried," Roland replied. "I'll just have Adele beat her up again."

The fries arrived. Fin sampled the first one after dabbing it in ketchup. "Not bad," he said. "Not bad at all. You Yanks seem to know your way around a potato. I'll give you that."

Soon the fries were gone. Fin ordered everyone a second Guinness. Adele nursed hers slowly, checking the time every few minutes and trying not to grow impatient. She looked up when the restaurant's front door crashed open and Prunella walked in behind a gust of wind, shaking the rain off her coat. Looming over her was a tall, silver-haired shadow with raven-like dark orbs that immediately stared across the room at Adele.

"You see what I'm seeing?" Fin whispered.

"Yeah," Adele said.

"Didn't the waitress tell us that Prune eats her lunch alone?"

Adele couldn't take her eyes off Bloodbone. "I guess today is different."

Indeed, it was.

29.

Prune motioned for Adele and the others to follow her. "Let's take my usual table in the back so we can talk in private. And make it quick. I need to get some food in me."

Bloodbone extended his arm in the direction Prune was going. Everything he wore except for the crystal was black: black jeans, black denim shirt, and black hiking boots. He looked at Adele and nodded. "After you." His voice was a low, smooth baritone that was somehow both soft and loud at the same time. His deeply lined face was a similar contradiction. When he turned his head and the light caught it a certain way, he appeared impossibly ancient. Then the light would shift, and the face suddenly gave off a more youthful and vibrant glow. Whatever Bloodbone's true age, though, the body remained undeniably strong. His posture was straight, the shoulders broad, and the long-fingered hands powerful.

"No, after you," Adele said. "I insist." She didn't want Bloodbone walking behind her. He nodded again and in two long strides caught up to Prune.

"So that's what a 100-something-year-old Native American witch doctor looks like, yeah?" Fin whispered.

Adele felt something on her shoulder. It was Roland's hand. He asked her if everything was okay. She said yes while moving to the table where Prune and Bloodbone sat waiting.

Prune looked up, smiled, and then pointed at Roland. "I've met the other one with Adele, but who are you?"

"I'm Roland Soros."

Adele caught Bloodbone looking Roland up and down. "I knew your grandfather," he said.

"You did?" Roland replied. "Really?"

"Yes. It was another time and a very different world than this one."

Roland took the chair directly across from Bloodbone.

"Go on," Prune told Adele and Fin. "Join us at the table. I promise we won't bite."

Prune's salad and water arrived. Fin had another beer. Bloodbone didn't order anything. He sat quietly with his hands folded in front of him while staring at the others with his unusually dark eyes.

Adele cleared her throat. "Uh, Ms. Brown, were you expecting us?"

Prune put down the cup of dressing she was pouring over her salad and shrugged. "Does it matter? We're all here now, right?"

"It does matter," Adele said. "If you knew we'd be here I'd like to know how."

Prune plopped some lettuce into her mouth. "Karl knew."

If that was true Bloodbone wasn't saying. He continued to just sit and stare.

Adele decided to stare back. "Mr. Bloodbone?"

"Yes?"

"You knew we were coming?"

"I knew you were on the island. I saw you pull up in your boat earlier."

Prune had a sip of water. "And that's when he came and told me."

Adele kept her eyes on Bloodbone. "This isn't the first time we've seen each other, though, is it? You were at the Speaks property the other day. I saw you standing under the trees. How did you know to find us there? We didn't tell anyone where we were going. Not even Prune."

"I saw you there as well," Fin added while staring at Bloodbone's crystal.

"I told him where you two were," Prune said. "First you were up at the clearing and then you were down at the Speaks place. Why you'd ever want to go there I'll never understand, but that's how Karl knew. It was me. I told him. See? No big mystery."

"Right," Adele replied. "Which brings me back to how anyone, including you, would know Fin and I were at the Speaks property."

Prune waved her hand. "Oh, *that*. It's simple. The bikes you borrowed from me? They're equipped with GPS tracking. The tourists are losing them all the time so I stuck trackers on them a few summers back so they could be more easily located."

Fin propped his elbows on the table and leaned forward. "Fine, you were told we were at the old abandoned house, but then where'd you go? It was like you were there and then you were gone—poof."

"That's right," Bloodbone said.

Fin scowled. "Eh?"

Bloodbone looked at Fin with narrowed eyes. "You've traveled far to be here."

"The accent pretty much gives that away."

Bloodbone shook his head. "No, it's your pain and not the accent that speaks loudest and most clearly—the fear of loss. Your father shared that in common with you. As you likely already know, I knew him as well. We're all orphans of the past, Mr. Kearns. Don't allow it to define your present and future."

"I'm no orphan. I have a mother who needs my help and that's why I'm here." Fin leaned forward again. "Say, how'd you know my last name?"

"I told him," Prune bellowed. "Geez, enough with the third degree."

Fin had a long swig of beer and then wiped the foam off his upper lip with the back of his hand. "How much for the crystal around your neck, Mr. Bloodbone?"

"It's not for sale. Besides, it wouldn't help."

"Help with what?"

"With what motivated you to come here from Ireland."

"And what would you know about any of that?"

Bloodbone's soft, confident tone remained unchanged. "It's all but done, Mr. Kearns. I'm very sorry."

Fin's eyes flared. "You messing with, me old man? Because if you are, I don't appreciate it. Not one bit."

"That's enough," Prune warned. "Be respectful or be gone."

Fin emptied his glass and stood. "Fine. Gone it is then." He nodded to Adele. "I'll be outside waiting. Take your time. No worries."

"But it's still raining," Adele said.

"A little rain isn't going to hurt me any, but staying here and listening to the stink coming out of his mouth just might make me do something I'll later regret—namely cracking his skull open with a chair."

Bloodbone looked up at Fin. "That's your fear talking. All things pass, Mr. Kearns. When the darkness comes, don't lose hope. Be patient and keep her memory close to help light the way forward. That's what she would most want."

"Don't tell me what she'd want. You don't have the right. And you damn well better stop talking about her like she's dead."

Adele watched Fin wrap his hand around the empty beer glass and worried he was very close to making good on his promise to smash Bloodbone's skull in. Thankfully Roland intervened. "Get you another beer, Fin?" he said. "My treat."

Fin shook his head. "Nah. I'll be outside like I said."

"That's too bad," Prune said with a sigh. "I'm sorry to see him upset."

"He's so very much like his father," Bloodbone added. "When he was a younger man, Delroy could be quick to anger as well. He always said it was the Irish in him."

"And what can you tell me about *my* grandfather?" Roland asked.

Bloodbone began to rub the crystal between his gnarled fingers. "Charles Soros was a complicated man."

"Ah, everyone says that."

"Likely because it's true."

"Tell me something about him I don't know."

"Is that why you came here? To hear stories of your grandfather?"

"Go ahead," Adele said. "Tell him something."

When Bloodbone's dark eyes fixed on Adele, it made her want to run away and hide. "And that is why you're here as well?" he asked. "To learn more about Charles Soros?"

"No, I'm here to learn more about *you*. We have time, though, so answer Roland first."

Bloodbone pursed his lips. "Mr. Soros should speak to the nun about such things. It is her story to tell not mine."

Roland and Adele shared a quick glance. "Ophelia?" Roland said. "What story does she have to tell me that she hasn't already?"

Bloodbone's face remained unreadable as he leaned back in his chair. "The truth."

Like Fin before him, it was now Roland who appeared annoyed by Bloodbone's penchant for secrets. "What truth?"

"Your truth, Mr. Soros."

Roland clapped his hands together and got up. "Okay, I've had enough of this. And I'll tell you another thing." He pointed at Bloodbone. "I think you're a fraud. I'll be outside waiting with Fin." He squeezed Adele's shoulder. "Holler if you need me."

Prune chuckled while she jabbed at the last bits of salad on her plate. "Boys can be so sensitive." She finished her water and then looked at Adele. "I'll have your friends go with me back to the museum. That'll give you and Karl a chance to talk alone."

"That's fine if that's what Mr. Bloodbone wants."

"Please, call me Karl. And yes, speaking with you alone is my reason for being here."

"You make it sound like your plan all along was to get both Fin and Roland angry enough that they'd want to leave."

Karl's eyes warmed and he looked like he might smile. "Our being alone will help me to feel more comfortable about giving you some of the answers you seek."

Prune put a ten-dollar bill on the table and then stood. "That's my cue to get going. Just stop by the museum when you're done. Your friends will be there waiting. Karl, as always, it's been a pleasure. Don't be a stranger."

Karl finally smiled as he reached up and gently squeezed Prune's hand. "I'll make sure to do a better job of stopping in to visit. Oh, I almost forgot to ask how the hip is doing."

Prune slapped her thigh. "It still pains me a bit. That chaga mushroom tea you gave me last summer did help some. I'm an old woman, Karl. If a wonky hip is my biggest problem, I'll count myself blessed. Now, get back to your conversation with Adele and stop worrying about me."

Adele felt a stab of apprehension as she watched Prune leave. Karl was rubbing his crystal again. She wondered if he was nervous being alone with her as she was with him. "Might we take a walk?" he said.

"In the rain?"

"It's about to stop."

Adele shrugged. "Sure. As long as you're not taking me into the woods to bury me."

"Why would I want to do that?"

"It was meant as a joke."

Karl smiled. "I know." When he stood, his upper body was hidden in shadow making him appear to have lost his head.

Adele pushed the image out of her mind, looked away, and got up. "Where do you want to walk to?"

"The water. I know a path few take. We can speak freely there."

"And nobody will be able to hear my screams, right?"

Karl stepped forward, cocked his head and nodded. "That's true."

"Very funny."

Again, Karl smiled. "I know."

As soon as she was outside Adele looked up. "Just like you said. The rain stopped."

"It always does . . . eventually."

"Hold on," Roland called out. Adele turned around as he was walking toward her. "Prune said you were okay with being alone with him. I just wanted to confirm that with you."

"Yeah," Adele said. "I'm good."

"You sure?"

"Roland, it's fine. Really. Mr. Bloodbone and I are going to have a little walk and talk and then I'll meet you and Fin back at the museum."

"Is your phone charged?"

"It is."

"Okay, you call me for anything, and I'll come running."

"I know. There's no need to worry. Isn't that right, Mr. Bloodbone?"

Karl straightened to his full height and looked down at Adele and Roland. "I may be the one calling you for help, Mr. Soros. I have a knack for telling when a person knows how to take care of themselves and Adele is clearly one of those."

"Yeah," Roland said. "That may be true, but you make sure she gets back without a hair on her head out of place. Understood?" He turned to Adele. "You have an hour to show up at the museum before Fin and I start turning this island upside down looking for you. And don't make me have to call in the big guns to help us."

"You mean Lucas?"

Roland shook his head. "Not Lucas—Tilda."

"Oh," Adele said. "Nobody wants *that*."

"Exactly. So, get back safe and good luck with getting whatever information it is you think he has for you."

"That's the plan."

After Roland left Adele was ready to go, but Karl remained looking in the direction of the museum. "That young man cares for you a great deal," he said.

"And I care for him."

"He loves you."

"I'm not here to talk about that with you, Mr. Bloodbone."

"Very well. Are you ready?"

"For what?"

Karl started walking. "For the truth."

The clouds parted. Adele welcomed the sun's return. She moved to catch up, anxious to know Bloodbone's version of the truth.

From somewhere down near the water a raven called out. The sound reminded Adele of laughter.

I just hope the joke isn't on me.

30.

"You have questions?"

"I have a *lot* of questions," Adele replied.

Bloodbone slowly lowered himself onto the sand and pebble beach that was partly hidden by tall grass and a row of madrone trees. He sat with his arms folded over his knees. "I might need your help getting back up," he said with a smile. "These old legs aren't what they used to be."

"For a man some believe is well over 100 years old I'd say you're doing fine."

"Age is a concept I pay little attention to. I just wish my body would do the same."

"Exactly how old are you, Mr. Bloodbone?"

A warm breeze licked the surface of Fishing Bay. It carried the familiar San Juan Islands scent of salt and pine.

"How old do you want me to be?"

"Please don't answer a question with a question."

Bloodbone picked up a pebble and threw it into the water. "You see the ripples?"

"Sure."

"There are also ripples you can't see—energy that is transferred but invisible to the human eye. Those ripples continue to travel, to expand, far beyond this time and place. That's how old I am."

Adele sighed. "That's not an answer. It's a riddle. I would really appreciate it if you spoke in more direct terms."

"For your newspaper?"

"It doesn't have to be. This conversation can be off the record."

"Then why have the conversation at all?"

"Because I'm curious. I like knowing things and you're an important part of the history of this place."

"Am I?"

"Some people seem to think so. Delroy wrote a book about it."

Bloodbone breathed deep. "Ah, Mr. Hicks. Yes, he did write a book, didn't he?"

"I was told the book was a lie—a lie you demanded be published."

"Was it the nun who told you that?"

"Does it matter?"

Bloodbone skipped another rock into the water. "No, I suppose not. Mr. Hicks is dead and those few who remain from that time will soon join him in that place."

"Including you?"

"All things die eventually. Even me."

"And what about Delroy's book? Was the conclusion in it that you were a fraud in fact a lie?"

"That's not an easy answer to give. What Mr. Hicks published was an opinion."

"Can you heal people, Mr. Bloodbone?"

"Most have that ability to some degree."

Adele decided to continue asking question after question hoping she could eventually crack Bloodbone's circular way of deflection so that he might start giving her some real answers. "I'm talking specifically about *your* ability. Do you believe you have the power to heal?"

"Your friend Mr. Kearns seems to think that power is to be found in certain crystals."

"Is it?"

"My intent in talking with you wasn't to tell you what to believe."

"No? You *do* sell crystals to people, though, right?"

Bloodbone took off the crystal necklace and then dropped it into Adele's hand. "Some I sell. Some I give as gifts. Whether or not the crystal possesses power has nothing to do with me and everything to do with the person who receives it. Please close your hand and tell me what you feel."

"It's warm."

Karl nodded. "Good. What else?"

"I can feel my own heartbeat passing through it, like a vibration."

"That's *very* good. Now shut your eyes and focus on just that heartbeat. Push everything else out of your mind."

Adele played along, hoping to make Bloodbone more comfortable so he would continue talking. "What now?" she said.

"I am going to place my hand over yours. Is that okay with you?"

"Sure."

Bloodbone's skin was sandpaper-rough. His long fingers encircled Adele's like a spider smothering its prey. She felt his pulse joining with hers and then realized their hearts were also beating in time with the water as it advanced and retreated from the shore.

"Many things are one," Bloodbone whispered. "Everything is connected, one part to the next. Past, present, future, it's all a universal thread being pulled from the same ball of string."

Adele opened her eyes and found Bloodbone staring at her with his face inches from hers. "You and I are the same. Delroy Hicks, Charles Soros, Mother Mary Ophelia, Sheriff Lucas Pine, his father Dr. Edmund Pine, Decklan and Calista Stone, Tilda Ashland—they were and are the same as well. All connected. All part of a greater whole."

"The same how?" Adele's lips felt unusually heavy as her mouth struggled to form the words. She was falling into the dark abyss of Bloodbone's gaze.

"Protectors of the islands. The keepers of their secrets. We heal that which was broken and fight to protect this place from injury."

"*Me*? What have I protected?"

"What haven't you protected since you came here? From saving Calista Stone physically and Decklan Stone spiritually, to exposing the dark deeds of a corrupted sheriff and helping Lucas to replace him, guiding Roland Soros toward a better version of himself, and doing battle with the Russian criminals who would see our blue-green waters turned red. Need I go on? It's why Delroy knew you were for this place and this place was for you."

"What do you mean?"

"He chose to spend what little remained of his life helping you to solve the mystery of Calista Stone's disappearance. He gifted you his sailboat to allow you a home unencumbered by debt and gave you a character reference for a job at the newspaper that you now partly own. And from those few things came great opportunity. Roland, Lucas, Tilda, Decklan and Calista, your relationships with them and so many others here began with Delroy's instinctive desire to help you when you first arrived at our islands. He already knew then what I now believe as well."

Adele leaned away from Bloodbone's face. "And what would that be?"

"That of those I mentioned, the protectors of the islands, you are the most important and the most powerful of them all."

"Powerful? Hardly."

"Help me up," Bloodbone said. "I want to show you something."

Adele stood, took Bloodbone's hand, and pulled him up. He took his crystal necklace back from her and then turned and pointed at the largest of the madrone trees behind them. "Follow me."

Bloodbone touched the tree's peeling cinnamon-red bark. "This madrone is among the oldest living things on the island. It was witness to the atrocities committed by my own tribal warriors who came down from the north to murder and enslave their Lummi brothers and sisters. It was here when I was but a boy staring up at the night sky stars and dreaming of worlds far beyond my own knowing. It watched as Robert Moran arrived from Seattle to live out the remaining months he had been told he had left. It knew your friend Delroy Hicks. And judging by its continued good health, this beautiful tree will be here after the both of us are long gone. Please stand under it and look out at the water so you might see the world as it has seen it for so long."

"You want me to pretend to be a tree?"

"Something like that, yes."

Adele stood under the madrone, looked down at her feet, and then slowly lifted her head. The waters of East Sound stretched out before her. The warm air was filled with the light floral scent of the madrone's emerging clusters of early spring blooms.

Bloodbone's long arm stretched out in front of them. "That forested hump to the south is Shaw Island, home of the nun. If you look to the west there is the side of Turtleback Mountain beneath which is Deer Harbor and the private island residence of Decklan and Calista Stone. And if you go further west beyond Turtleback Mountain, and allow your eyes a moment to adjust, you can spy the tops of evergreen trees growing from the rich soil of your beloved Roche Harbor.

"It's certainly quite a view."

"Yes, it's that and more. From here one can observe so much. If you turn to the east, you can make out the road leading to the Speaks property that you rescued Calista from. Roche Harbor, Shaw Island, Orcas Island, the people, places, and events that have been so important to your own experiences and destiny, Adele, are all connected by the view here from underneath this ancient tree."

Adele and Bloodbone looked up at a squawking raven that was resting on one of the madrone's branches. Chasm-deep wrinkles cracked across Bloodbone's face when he smiled.

"There you are, friend. Come down and say hello." Adele watched Bloodbone stick his arm out and then she gasped when the raven landed on his wrist. "This is George," he said. "We've known each other for a very long time."

"I've met him before. The first time was outside the book store in Friday Harbor. He also showed up at the monastery on Shaw Island and then at the Speaks place with you."

Bloodbone gently stroked the top of the bird's head. They both had the same midnight-dark eyes. "Yes, George told me all about it. Ravens are among the most intelligent of the Creator's creatures. Did you know that? My people have long considered them to be the link between this world and the other—a powerful thing of spiritual transition upon whose wings come messages from the beyond."

"You never did explain why you were at the Speaks house. Were you the one who locked us in the cellar?"

"Yes."

Adele was surprised by the quick answer. There was no riddle, no attempted deflection. "Why'd you do that?"

"Partly to prove a point."

"What point?"

"That you were capable of escaping because you're much stronger than you think. It showed me that you're worthy of the great burden that has been placed upon you."

The raven spread its wings, squawked, and then flew off toward Shaw Island. Bloodbone grinned as he watched it go.

"What burden are you talking about?" Adele said.

"I told you already. You are the protector. Soon, very soon, all that you were, all that you have become, all that you might ever be will be challenged. And in your fate is found the fate of these islands."

"Are you saying I'm in danger?"

"Not just you—everyone and everything here."

"If the risks are that great shouldn't you be telling this to the sheriff?"

Bloodbone nodded. "Lucas Pine will continue to play his part. As will Roland Soros, Tilda Ashland, and others who now all share one critical thing in common—you."

"Me?"

"Look at this tree again. Note how it sheds its skin. Each year it is the same but different—like you. You are still the young woman who first arrived here years earlier to interview a reclusive author, but with each passing season you also became something different: stronger, more determined, more capable."

"And what's the big threat you're warning me to be ready for? Is it the Russians?"

Bloodbone turned and looked out at the water. "Yes, and what they represent—the takers. Like Mr. Kearns, and the crystal I know he now keeps in his pocket. It is that kind of thoughtless, greed-inspired taking that is so dangerous to us. It's also why your ongoing influence with Roland Soros is so important to the well-being of the islands. His grandfather helped build an unseen wall of protection around this place. Without knowing it, Roland has been steadily breaking that wall apart. He unintentionally invited greed, destruction, and evil to our home. Your problem with the Russians is simply the most evident example of that fact. But, as bad as it's been, without your intervention it would have been far worse."

"Fin took that crystal because he's desperate to save his mother. I wouldn't call that greed."

"Desperation and greed are often interchangeable, Adele. His father Delroy came to understand this. Be a slave to the truth or know freedom from the lie. Those are Delroy's words not mine. If the truth of these islands was to become known by all then soon nothing of the islands would remain. The soul of this place would be ripped out by the roots. The conclusion in Delroy's book was an intentional lie meant to help prevent that outcome. I suggested the lie and he agreed to its propagation. We were not enemies. Far from it. Like you I miss his friendship, his wisdom, and his generous humanity. Delroy Hicks was the best of all of us."

When Adele blurted out her next words, she was surprised by the anger and hurt behind them. "You're a healer, right? Then why didn't you heal Delroy's cancer so he could still be with us today?"

"Your question is based on a false premise."

"How so?"

"Delroy did, in fact, live a reasonably long life, one that was far longer than anyone else believed it would be."

"I asked why you didn't heal him."

"You're assuming I didn't. Healing and curing are very different things."

"Fine, I'll drop the Delroy subject for something more recent. Why did you write Delroy's line on the inside of the cellar door at the Speaks home?"

"I didn't."

"Then who did?"

"I don't know."

"But you knew the words were there?"

Bloodbone nodded. "Yes."

"You wanted me to see them."

"Yes."

"Why?"

Bloodbone sat on a rock, stretched his long legs out in front of him, and rubbed his knees. "Arthritis."

"Don't try to change the subject. Why did you want me to see those words on the inside of the cellar door?"

"They are the connective tissue between an earlier time and this one. Between Delroy and you. Between then and now and what will be. It is my hope that regardless the changes that are to come, and there will be many, the intent of those words remains. We must not share some of the unique truths of this place with the world or the world will swallow it whole and we will be made slaves to that new and destructive reality."

"You mean the alleged healing power of the crystals, the unusually long lifespan of island residents, those kinds of things are to be kept secret?"

"Exactly. Protect us and the truth of this place through the telling of a lie."

"The lie being that the healing powers, the long lives, the island's heartbeat you can feel in the earth, none of that is true."

Bloodbone stopped rubbing his knees and started rubbing his crystal. "Yes."

"But I'm not even sure if any of those things are true, which means I'm just as confused as to what might really be the lie."

"So long as you don't report what I know to be the truth in your paper we'll be fine—for now. Do as Delroy did with his book and as his son just did with his mouth. Declare me a fraud. That way those who come here seeking to take will remain small in number, a fringe group ignored by the rest of society. I would gladly be scorned by those living in ignorance than see harm come to our islands."

Adele sat beside Bloodbone. "I'll agree to that so long as you tell me one thing right now."

"Go ahead."

"How old are you really?"

Bloodbone lowered his face into his hands and rubbed his forehead. Adele sensed the indecision roiling within him. His head lifted, he sat up straight, and closed his eyes.

"I have helped to deliver newborns into this world and later held their aged hands as they departed it. Over and over I have done this. I do not measure my life in years but rather experiences. That is how old I am."

While not a perfectly clear answer, Adele was grateful for it because it felt and sounded like an honest one.

Karl Bloodbone wasn't merely old—he was ancient.

Adele decided then that it didn't matter how or why. His age wasn't nearly as important as keeping the islands safe.

He was asking for her help and she intended to give it.

31.

Roland and Fin were unusually quiet on the way back to Roche Harbor. Neither asked Adele much about her talk with Bloodbone. Both seemed preoccupied with thoughts Adele could only guess at. Roland sat in the passenger seat while Fin relaxed on the aft bench with his eyes closed, smiling as the wind buffeted his face.

A strong incoming tide pushed multiple patches of floating wood debris throughout the narrow Wasp Passage that divided Orcas Island from Shaw Island. Adele was quick to spot and then navigate around the watery clutter without the need to slow down. It was a slight turn and then the wheel was straightened as the Chris Craft continued its fast charge toward Roche.

Adele glanced to the side and caught Roland staring at her. "What?"

Roland cocked his head and arched a brow. "Captain Sexy."

When Adele rolled her eyes at him, Roland wagged his finger. "I mean it. Watching you behind the wheel of this boat . . . I can't stop looking at you."

Adele tried to brush the hair off her face, but the wind wasn't having it. "I'm afraid I'm no big city D-cup television news reporter."

Roland winced. "Marianne? Please. Let's not go there."

"You already did. She made that quite clear to me when she showed up asking why I was messing things up between you and her."

"Yeah, and now she's working to break the story on the bank sale. She's no friend of mine, Adele. Trust me."

"I wonder if she's still on the islands."

"I don't care if she is or isn't. You'll report the bank sale in your paper first and she'll be left on the outside looking in. After that I doubt we'll hear from Marianne Rocha again."

"I have to admit I kind of feel sorry for her."

"Why is that?"

Adele turned the wheel and just missed running over a floating log by a few feet. "Clearly she fell for you hard and then you pushed her away. I might not care for the woman, but I wouldn't wish that kind of hurt on anyone."

"It's like I told you. It was just a few dates. I think it has more to do with how a woman like her isn't used to not getting exactly what she wants than it is about me. She's a Seattle TV reporter. I'm just some guy who lives on an island. I'm sure she's already over it."

"You're just some guy who lives on an island, huh? I think there's a little more to you than *that*." Adele spotted a large boat wake coming toward them. She looked behind her at Fin. "Hold on back there."

The Chris Craft hit the wake without slowing. The bow lifted and then dove down as salt spray covered the windshield. Seeing Fin still grinning with his eyes closed and his arms spread out across the bench seat made Adele laugh.

Roland was staring at her again. "You know," Adele said, "there's a fine line between charming and creepy. You keep looking at me like that and I'll have to put you in the creepy category."

A pair of chattering bald eagles flew over the boat, diving and swirling around each other. It was a high-flying courtship dance that took place at the beginning of every spring throughout the islands that attracted bird lovers from all over the world. Sometimes the eagles would lock talons and then drop from the sky before letting go just seconds away from mutual oblivion, something ornithologists believed to be a pre-mating test the birds instinctively used to better determine the health and flying abilities of their potential partner.

Adele craned her head to watch the eagles as the Chris Craft passed underneath them. She detected movement, looked to the side, and found Roland leaning over her. "What are you—" Before she could finish Roland's mouth was on hers. When she started to pull away, his lips followed, and the kiss continued. It was more playful than aggressive, a light touch, a flick of tongue, a touch of noses, and then a slow retreat.

"That had to be done," Roland said. "I had no choice. You just look so good I couldn't hold out any longer."

Adele licked her lips, savoring the lingering remnants of the kiss. Then she remembered Fin was sitting right behind them. She turned her head and found his eyes were still closed but his grin had turned into a wide smile. One eye opened and then winked before closing again.

Something hard struck the boat. Adele's head snapped back as she tried to determine what it was. She pulled back on the throttle, leaned over the side, and looked down. "See anything?" she said to the others.

Fin pointed to a log floating some twenty feet directly behind them. "I'm pretty sure that was it. Any damage to the hull?"

Adele listened for the sound of the automatic bilge pumps turning on which would signal they were taking on water. "Not sure," she answered as she took the boat into and out of gear several times. The transmission still shifted smoothly. She put it into gear again and accelerated slightly while trying to sense any abnormal sounds or vibrations. Everything felt fine.

"One hell of a boat," Roland said. "That was a good-sized floater we hit."

"She's built right," Adele replied. "Probably scuffed the gelcoat up, but this is some seriously heavy fiberglass we're floating on. I bet we did more damage to the log than it did to the boat. It's your fault by the way."

Fin laughed as he pointed at Roland. "She's right about that. You distracted the captain you charming rich bastard. We could have gone the way of the Titanic."

Adele hammered down on the throttle and smiled as both Roland and Fin were thrown back in their seats. She wanted to be safely tied up at Roche before the afternoon winds picked up. With the hint of warmer weather came increased boat traffic. They passed several sailboats on the way into the harbor before slowing down once they were inside the no wake zone. Adele had just turned the corner to head toward her slip when she saw Lucas standing at the end of the dock with his arms crossed staring at them as they approached. A raven perched on the top of a piling directly behind him cried out and then took off toward Orcas.

"Is it just me," Roland said, "or does the good sheriff look all kinds of upset?"

Lucas's face was grim. He locked eyes with Adele, nodded once, and then turned to meet them at the slip. Adele's mind raced with possibilities about what the problem might be. When she pulled into the slip, Lucas was there waiting for them.

"What's going on?" Adele said as she stepped onto the dock after the boat was tied up.

"What *isn't* going on is more like it," Lucas answered.

Roland and Fin stood behind Adele. She looked at Lucas and shrugged. "Well?"

Lucas turned around and then turned back. "I don't want to talk here. We should go somewhere private."

"How about my yacht?" Roland offered.

Lucas nodded. "Yeah, that'll work. Both of these things involve you."

Roland frowned. "Me? What did I do this time?"

"C'mon," Lucas said as he started walking. "I'll get you up to speed once we're inside." He stopped and pointed at Fin. "I'm afraid you're not a part of this, Mr. Kearns."

Fin looked at Adele and then at Lucas. "Official police stuff is it, Sheriff?"

"Yeah," Lucas replied. "Something like that. You're welcome to wait up at the hotel. We won't be long."

Fin tipped his cap. "No worries. I'll keep Tilda company. You know she'll be asking me what's going on though."

Lucas was on the move again. "Of that I have no doubt." Adele could feel the tension coming off him in waves. After they reached Roland's yacht, Lucas stopped and looked up with his hand on his gun. "You have an alarm system?"

"No," Roland answered. "Not yet. Why?"

Lucas walked up the boarding ramp, went to the side door, and knocked. "Sheriff's department."

Adele and Roland both shared a quick "what the hell is going on" look as they watched Lucas draw his weapon before he tried the door.

"It's locked," Roland said. "Do you want me to open it for you?"

Lucas stepped to the side. "Yeah, but wait here with Adele while I make sure it's safe."

"Who do you think might be in there?" Roland asked as he unlocked the door.

Lucas went inside without answering, leaving Roland and Adele to wonder what was going on. "It's all clear," he said a short time later. "Come on in."

After he sat down Lucas asked for something to drink. Roland returned with a bottle of whiskey and three glasses. He poured Lucas and Adele a double and then did the same for himself before sitting next to Adele.

Lucas stared at the whiskey for a few seconds, took a sip, and then looked up. "I'll start with the less bad news." He had another sip before continuing. "Sandra Penny stopped by my office this morning and confessed that she was the one who came to Roche Harbor and frightened Adele with her car. She claims that wasn't her intent. She just wanted to talk but then panicked and drove away and then panicked again when I showed up at the bank asking her questions about it. Apparently, she was upset about the pending bank sale and was hoping Adele could help to convince Roland not to go through with it. Then she wondered if Adele might actually be the reason for the sale."

"Why in the world would she think *that*?" Adele said.

Lucas sighed. "The gist of it was that she believes you're the only one Roland really listens to so if he had decided to sell the bank it must have been because you told him it was a good idea. Look, I'm not going to go into all the specifics of her confession. The fact is no one was hurt and beyond lying to me that morning at the bank, she did nothing illegal. I do think we need to all have a discussion, though, so that this thing doesn't fester. Ms. Penny feels terrible for lying but still harbors some serious resentment regarding the bank sale."

Roland finished his whiskey and set the glass down. "And this is supposed to be the good news?"

"No," Lucas replied. "I said this was less bad than the other news."

Adele leaned forward. "You also said both of those things involve Roland. I saw your face when I came into the harbor. Whatever you have left to tell us is a lot worse than the situation with Sandra Penny."

"Yeah," Lucas murmured. "It is." He looked at Roland's empty glass. "You're going to want to pour yourself another one."

Roland's eyes narrowed. "I'm fine. Tell me what's going on, Lucas."

"It's about Marianne Rocha."

"Huh," Roland said. "We were just talking about her on the way back from Orcas. Apparently, she was there recently asking people questions about the bank sale."

Lucas flinched. "She was here on the islands?"

Roland nodded. "That's what we were told. Why?"

The space between Lucas and Adele suddenly grew very heavy. She kept quiet and braced for the bad news.

Lucas sighed again. His head was down. "They found her this morning."

"Who?" Roland asked.

"Seattle PD."

"I don't understand. Found her where?"

"In her apartment earlier today."

There was a pause. Adele heard a soft thump from above and then the familiar croak of a raven. The yacht shifted slightly as small waves smacked against the hull. The afternoon winds had arrived.

Lucas looked up. "Marianne Rocha is dead."

32.

"I'm a suspect?" Roland got up and paced the floor. "That's ridiculous. I would never do something like that, and I haven't been to Seattle in weeks."

"You're actually just a person of interest," Lucas replied. "Not a suspect."

"There's a difference?"

"Yes. A significant one. For now, the death is being ruled an accidental overdose. I spoke for some time with the lead detective on the case. They just had a few questions about your relationship with Ms. Rocha. For now, that's pretty much it as far as Seattle PD are concerned. But then there's the matter of Agent Eaton. The fact he reached out to me within an hour of my being notified of Ms. Rocha's death confirms that you continue to be under surveillance by the FBI. Eaton had more questions about the bank sale. He also came right out and asked me if I thought you were capable of murder. He said she was about to do a report on the sale and your alleged links to organized crime."

Roland sat back down like his legs had given out, looked up at the ceiling, and let loose an f-bomb under his breath.

Lucas nodded. "Yeah, that's pretty much how I thought you'd take that particular bit of information."

"Do I need to make a call to my attorney?"

"That's up to you, Roland, but at this point there is no criminal investigation. The pills were by her bed and the investigators are now awaiting the autopsy results to confirm the overdose. As you said, you weren't close to being in Seattle at the time of death and have plenty of witnesses who can corroborate that fact. Eaton's tone was different though. I don't believe he has anything as far as evidence but he's suspicious that Ms. Rocha's sudden passing and her investigation into your bank sale could be directly or indirectly related. Though he didn't come right out and say it my sense of the situation is that he's likely to make a call to federal regulators to try to delay or even kill the sale."

Roland's face went pale as he shook his head. "I've already spent a small fortune on legal fees navigating the sale to this point. Now that SOB Eaton is going to nuke it with one phone call. The man won't stop until I'm left with nothing."

"I told Eaton that I've been watching closely for any return of organized crime to the islands and that you have been nothing less than a model citizen around here since the run-in last year with the Vasa family. While I'm one of those who doesn't want to see us lose control of our local bank, I also won't help anyone to unfairly slander your name. Nobody deserves that."

"Thanks for the good word," Roland said. "I'm not sure it'll make a difference, but I appreciate the effort."

Adele put her glass down and waited until Lucas looked at her. "What kind of pills were they?"

"Pain pills," Lucas replied. "Apparently, she had been complaining to some of her newsroom colleagues about a sore hip."

Adele recalled the recent fight she had with Marianne Rocha inside Tilda's hotel and wondered if that had led to Marianne's need for pain pills.

I did strike her hip with my knee. God, what if I'm the reason she's dead?

"Adele," Lucas said, "if you're thinking that this is somehow in any way your fault please don't go there. You can't be responsible for how people choose to medicate. There could have been alcohol involved, depression, who knows? What happened between you and Ms. Rocha in the hotel has nothing to do with her death. You were just defending yourself."

"That's right," Roland added. "She was a troubled woman. Driven, obsessive, manipulative, controlling, you name it; Marianne was fighting some version of all those things and more. The fact she attacked you like she did is clear evidence of that."

"What about the Russians?" Adele said. "Liya Vasa? Marianne came at the Vasa family pretty hard with her reporting last year. Could this have been payback as well as a message from them that we're next?"

Lucas nodded. "Both the Seattle authorities and the feds are looking hard at that possibility. There's no recent confirmation of Liya Vasa's whereabouts and no red flags regarding her family preparing to make a move against us here."

"So—" Adele sighed, "—we're supposed to go on as if everything is normal?"

"No," Lucas said. "That's not what I meant. Nothing has changed regarding the high alert status that's been in play regarding the Russians. I continue to be in regular contact with both U.S. and Canadian law enforcement officials. If Liya Vasa shows up here, we'll be ready for her. Even if I have to pull the trigger myself."

Roland rubbed his eyes. "And should I be expecting a visit from Agent Eaton?"

"No. I don't think so. Not at this point. My sense is Eaton is still in watch-and-wait mode."

Another possibility suddenly came to Adele. "Or he's hoping to use us to draw Liya into the open."

"Like bait?" Roland said.

Adele nodded. "Exactly. And he could be doing that not just by waiting Liya out but also by pushing you into a corner. What if Eaton is using Marianne Rocha's death to halt your bank sale deal in the hopes of making you desperate enough to reach out to the Russians for help? Then he swoops in and gets the both of you behind bars."

"I'd be more than a little offended if Eaton actually thinks I would do something that stupid."

Lucas got up. "He might not hold the same high regard for your intelligence that we do."

If Lucas had meant the comment as a joke Roland didn't take it that way. He locked eyes with his old childhood friend and scowled. "Agent Eaton can kiss my ass, Sheriff."

"I meant no disrespect, Roland. I promise I'll keep my eyes and ears open for anything coming from the feds or the Seattle PD. Until then it's likely a good idea to keep your attorneys updated as well—just in case."

Roland stood and shook Lucas's hand. "Already on it. Thanks again for putting the good word in. Hopefully none of this mess goes any further."

"I feel the same," Lucas replied. He turned toward Adele. "Are you going to see Tilda and Fin at the hotel?"

Adele shook her head. "Not yet."

Lucas's eyes darted from Roland to Adele. "Okay. Well, I'll be going then. I'm finally getting around to organizing my father's old patient files in the attic at home. Been putting it off for months. You two stay safe."

***

"I'm so sick of this crap," Roland said after Lucas was gone. He sat and poured another drink. "Every damn time I try to do something different around here it's like some

341

unseen force pulls me back to the same old same old." He looked up at Adele. "Why do you think that is?"

"I wish I knew."

"Sometimes it just feels like too much. I'm the last of my kind. My parents and grandparents are dead. No siblings. No aunts or uncles. It's just me and I'm tired, Adele. I mean I'm *really* tired of this one step forward two steps back rut I seem to be trapped in lately."

Adele thought of Mother Mary Ophelia as she stared at Roland. "You're not alone. You have friends, a home, people who depend on you. And you have me."

"Do I?" Roland tilted his head back and closed his eyes. "I'm sorry. You're right. I have a lot more than most. It's just that sometimes I would sure like to be able to sit down with my grandfather and get his advice, but that's never going to happen. Like I said, I'm the last of my kind." He sat up. "Say, remember when I told you about the trip up the Inside Passage I was planning to take?"

"Sure."

"Well, I'm still hoping you'll join me."

"What if the bank sale situation turns into a dumpster fire because of Agent Eaton's interference? Won't you be sticking around to prevent that from happening?"

Roland sipped from his glass. "This yacht is set up for conducting business no matter where in the world it is. You could turn the trip into a story for the paper. You won't regret it. I promise."

"I tell you what. Let's get past these next few days of chaos and then I'll give you an answer, okay?"

Roland leaned over and kissed Adele's cheek. "Thank you."

Adele kissed him back. "You're welcome."

"Want to stay the night?"

"No, I should stop in and see Tilda. She'll want to hear about the Orcas trip."

"That's two rain checks you'll owe me then. One for the Inside Passage trip and one for the sleepover."

Adele handed her glass to Roland and then stood. "One thing at a time. Let's see how this other stuff shakes out first."

"Deal," Roland said as he got up. "You want me to walk with you to Tilda's?"

"No, I'm fine. You get some rest. Are you really okay after learning of Marianne's death?"

Roland pinched his bottom lip with his fingers and shrugged. "As much as I'm uncomfortable saying it, the fact is I'm fine. It's like I told you already. It was just a few dates and what little I knew of her I didn't particularly like. I'm sad for her and whatever family she has but beyond that . . . I don't feel much at all. Does that make me a bad person?"

"I don't think so. It makes you an honest one. I guess until you learn more about the status of the sale, we should put the article about it on the backburner."

"Yeah," Roland said. "I suppose we should."

The two hugged briefly and then Adele was walking on the dock looking behind her. Roland stood outside leaning against the yacht's railing with a drink in his hand watching her go. There was a cold bite to the early evening air. Tilda's hotel appeared busy. All the lights were on and Adele saw several guests moving along the second-story balcony. The prime tourist season was fast approaching. Tilda wasn't inside though. She stood at the top of the marina dock. As Adele came closer, she saw the concern on her face.

"What's wrong?"

"It's Fin," Tilda said. "He received a message from Ireland."

Oh no, Adele thought. *What now?*

Tilda put her arm around Adele's shoulders. "I believe it concerns his mother. About what exactly he wouldn't say. He took the call, ended it, and then left. I think he went to the chapel."

The Roche Harbor chapel was a small, white structure built on the side of a hill overlooking the water about a hundred yards from the hotel. Its original construction dated back a century earlier to the time of the harbor's founder, John S. McMillin.

"Do you think I should go see how he's doing?"

"Yes, I do. He looked pretty upset and I fear the worst. As you know his mother is in very poor health. I believe he left the hotel because he didn't want his grief to make the guests uncomfortable. That doesn't mean he should be forced to process such a loss alone though."

"No, of course not," Adele said as Tilda's arm slid off her shoulder. "I'll go see how he's doing."

The partial moon helped to light the way to the chapel. When Adele stood at the bottom of the stairs and looked up, she was reminded of the funeral service for Lucas's father, Dr. Edmund Pine. It was both sad and beautiful as Lucas brought out a guitar and gave a somewhat clumsy yet heartfelt rendition of Warren Zevon's *Don't Let Us Get Sick*. The love and respect for the longtime island doctor by those who filled the little chapel that day was something she would never forget.

As soon as Adele's foot touched the first step a raven landed on the chapel roof and squawked at her. "Hello again, George. Shouldn't you be over on Orcas keeping Mr. Bloodbone company?"

The raven's obsidian eyes swallowed the moonlight and reflected it back at Adele. She continued the climb up the stairs to the chapel door, pushed it open, and found Fin sitting in the middle of the back pew with his head down.

"There's no need to check on me," he said without looking up. "I just needed a moment to process and gather my thoughts."

Adele sat. The darkness inside the chapel made it difficult for her to see Fin's face. She decided to stay quiet and let him decide when he wanted to say something more.

Fin looked up. "It was an infection in her lungs that did it. Not her heart but a damn cold."

"I'm so sorry, Fin. Does this mean you'll be going back to Ireland?"

Fin wiped his eyes and sniffed. "Yeah. I should be there to make the arrangements. Her death will be a big deal in the traveler community. There'll be a thousand or more coming from all over to pay their respects. I'll be leaving on the first ferry out in the morning."

"Is there anything you need until then?"

"Sure," Fin growled. "A cure for dying." He got up and went to the door. "I want to thank you for being such a gracious host during my time here. I won't ever forget it, Adele. I'm forever in your debt."

Adele joined him at the door. "I was just helping a friend. There's no debt to be repaid for doing that."

Once outside Fin held up the crystal he had taken from Orcas Island. "What a stupid thing to go chasing such nonsense. What a waste of time. I should have been at my mother's side. Instead I was here chasing the ghost of a father I never knew and thinking I might somehow bring some magic back to save her with."

He threw the crystal away. "A damn fool is what I am."

"Hope," Adele said, "is never foolish no matter how desperate or unattainable it might seem."

"Maybe so, but in this world hope too often becomes hopeless."

"Not always, Fin. And not here. This place really is different."

Fin looked up at the moon. "I won't argue that. I'd like to return someday."

"You better. The islands have accepted you. You're one of us now."

The raven swooped down from the chapel roof, landed at the bottom of the stairs, took two hops, clicked its tongue, and then grabbed hold of Fin's crystal in its beak.

"Will you look at that?" Fin grinned as he watched the raven fly off toward Orcas. "Old Bloodbone wants his rock back. I suppose it's fitting that all things be returned to their rightful place. That bit of crystal was never mine to take."

"Well put."

"Yeah? Coming from you that's high praise." Fin went to take the first step down and then stopped. He shook his head and sighed. "Damn it hurts knowing she's really gone. The one thing in my life I could always count on isn't there anymore. I don't think I've ever felt so alone as I do right now. It's like one of my limbs has just been ripped away. I don't feel whole. There's something missing from deep inside me and I fear I won't ever get it back. I'm headed for extinction."

Fin's words reminded Adele of Roland's struggle to come to terms with his own familial disconnect. Though they were two men from different sides of the world they now shared a very similar kind of pain.

Fin turned toward Adele and hugged her tight. He put his face into the crook of her shoulder and began to sob. "Please don't let go," he whispered. "Not yet. I think I might just float away into the abyss right now."

"That won't happen. I won't let it."

Fin pulled away and stared into Adele's eyes. "Promise?"

"Yeah. I promise."

"I'm gonna hold you to it."

Adele smiled. "Good."

33.

Fin and Adele stood together and watched the arriving passengers unload from the morning ferry. A light drizzle covered everything in a layer of cold mist. Fin stared up at the heavy, slow-moving clouds.

"Reminds me of home."

"I hope you'll consider the islands your second home," Adele said. "You'll always have a place here."

"That I will. And I wasn't kidding last night. Don't you dare forget. You ever need my help with anything, anything at all, just call."

"I won't forget."

"You're one of the few good ones, Adele Plank. A true friend in a world of mud. And please tell Ms. Ashland thank you again for her hospitality."

"I will."

Fin checked the time. "Well then, I guess this is it."

"I guess so."

The two embraced. Fin stepped back, took a deep breath, and nodded. "You take care, young lady. Until next time."

The drizzle turned to rain as Fin walked onto the ferry platform. Despite the wet and cold Adele didn't move. She waited for Fin to look back and then waved goodbye. He flashed the same mischievous smile as he did the first time they had met. "Until next time," Adele shouted. Fin tipped his cap and then he and the departing ferry were both swallowed up by the mist.

Adele was nearly drenched to the bone. Her phone rang. It was a call from Lucas. He sounded even more tired than she was.

"Is something wrong?"

"No," Lucas replied. "Not really, but there are some things I think you should see."

"What things?"

"It's kind of hard to explain. I'm at home. Can you stop by?"

Adele started to walk back to her car. "Sure. I just got done bringing Fin to the ferry. You want me to come over now?"

"That'd be great. I'll put a pot of coffee on. See you soon."

"Dammit."

"Huh?"

"Sorry. I just stepped in a puddle. I don't know about you, but I say bring on the summer. I've had my fill of cold and wet. Be there in a few."

Adele put her phone away and took out her car keys. The sound of footsteps behind her made her turn around.

"Hello again, Ms. Plank," a familiar voice said. "Do you have a moment?"

It was Randal Eaton, the FBI agent who was causing Roland so much trouble. He looked the same: mid-30s, average height and build, light hair parted to the side, and glasses. The air of bureaucratic superiority was the same as well. His tone made it clear he wasn't asking Adele for her time but demanding it.

"I'm actually on my way to a meeting, Agent Eaton. Are you here about Roland?"

Eaton's thin, arrogant smile made his face appear even more punchable. "Among other things, yes. Who was the man you were standing with at the ferry?"

"Have you been following me?"

"No, I was driving off and noticed the two of you together." Eaton pointed to a black SUV on the other side of the street. "That's my vehicle over there."

"Who I'm with is none of your business. Now, like I said, I have a meeting."

Eaton reached out and grabbed hold of Adele's wrist. "Ms. Plank, I'm not the enemy. I came here to get some more information because I want to prevent trouble."

Adele pulled her arm away. "Are you talking Liya Vasa kind of trouble or something else?"

"Yes, the Russians continue to be a threat to you, your friends, and this community."

"I have faith in our local law enforcement's ability to keep us all safe."

"All due respect, Ms. Plank, but Sheriff Pine and his two deputies are hardly up to the task of taking on the Russian mob."

"We'll manage."

When Adele went to open her car door, Eaton pushed it closed. "How well did you know Marianne Rocha?" he said.

"Just enough to feel sorry about her passing. Why?"

"But not enough to call her a friend?"

"No."

"Did you two ever fight?"

He already knows the answer, Adele thought. *He's testing me to see if I'll lie to him.*

"Ms. Plank?"

Adele shrugged. "We had our disagreements."

"Disagreements? Would you care to elaborate?"

"No." Adele got behind the wheel, started the Mini, and drove away. When she glanced into the rearview mirror, she saw Eaton still standing where she had left him. He was talking into his phone. She arrived at Lucas's home a few minutes later and found him wearing sweats and a T-shirt on the covered front porch sipping from a cup of coffee. By the time she reached the porch he had gone inside and then returned with another cup for her.

"I tried to make it dark enough. I know that's how you like it."

"Thank you," Adele said as she took the coffee. "I ran into Eaton on my way here."

Lucas's coffee halted halfway to his mouth. "He's on the island?"

"As of this morning if what he told me is to be believed. He was asking about Marianne Rocha. Wanted to know if she and I had any problems."

"What did you tell him?"

"Not a damn thing."

"Good. Unless he throws a subpoena at you it's best to ignore him. He should have let me know he was here. Was he alone?"

Adele nodded. "Appeared to be."

"Huh. That's odd. He's acting like a lone field agent, which would be highly unusual." Lucas opened the front door. "Then again that's how he was acting last time he was nosing around here. Whatever. I'll chase him down later today and feel him out on what he's up to. Right now, you need to get inside and dry off and check out what I found."

Adele was grateful for the warmth inside of Lucas's home. He hung her coat up and then motioned toward the stairs. "I left the files in the attic. I can bring them down or you can come up—your choice."

"Up is fine. What files are you talking about?"

"You'll see," Lucas called out as he took the stairs two at a time.

That attic was dry and well lit. Adele spotted a few rather large webs that stretched across some of the rafters. Along with bats, spiders held a prominent place at the top of her avoid-at-all-cost list.

"Sorry for the mess," Lucas said. "You should have seen it before I started cleaning up. When Dad had to retire because of the Alzheimer's he had the clinic staff deliver all his patient files here. For a while he promised to organize it, but that never happened and then I'm pretty sure he forgot all about it. More than thirty years of records. It was a disaster, but it wasn't all his fault. I contributed to the mess as well. Shortly after I first came on as sheriff, the state police dropped off copies of their files on the Speaks investigation. I thought they were just duplicates of what we already had at the station, but actually what they gave me was more—a lot more. I didn't bother to look at them until last night. Here. See for yourself."

Lucas handed Adele a file folder bursting with paperwork. "There are photos in there I've never seen."

Adele held up a picture of Martin Speaks' room. Her eyes were immediately drawn to two books on the nightstand.

"You see the reading material by the bed, don't you?"

"Yeah," Adele said with a nod. "I do." One was a copy of Delroy's *The Mystery of the Lekwiltok Crystal.* The other book was Decklan Stone's *Manitoba.* She continued to thumb through other photos and then stopped when she came to one that showed the writing on the inside of the secret cellar door.

Be a slave to the truth or know freedom from the lie.

"Did you notice the writing on the door when you first found the cellar?"

"No," Adele replied. "I pushed back the freezer, opened the door, and Calista crawled out. Then we both ran outside to escape."

Lucas put his hand on the file folder. "Wait. The next few photos, well, they're pretty gruesome."

"I'm fine." Adele looked down and saw the bodies of Martin and Will Speaks lying next to each other. The gun Martin had used to shoot his son in the head before turning it on himself was still in his hand. A second photo was a close-up of Will. Adele turned it over quickly, sickened by the amount of blood that had pooled out the side of the fractured skull. The next photo was a similarly disturbing close-up of the death wound of Will's father.

Adele was about to turn it over just as quickly when she stopped and looked at the image more closely.

A blood-spattered crystal necklace hung around Martin Speaks' neck. Adele closed the folder and gave it back to Lucas. "Is that it?" she asked.

"No. That wasn't the most interesting find I made last night. What made me call you over here was one of my father's patient files—this one."

The folder smelled as old as it looked. The name written in elegant cursive on the side tab read, *D. Soros*. "The D is for Donatella," Lucas said. "She was Roland's grandmother. Both she and Charles Soros were longtime patients of my father's."

"I don't understand. What am I supposed to do with this?"

"Read the first page."

Adele's eyes widened as she scanned the information. She read it again and then looked at Lucas. "This doesn't make any sense."

"That's exactly what I said when I first saw it. My father's notes are very clear. Donatella Soros never had children."

"But she had Roland's father."

"Not according to the medical records. She was incapable of getting pregnant, which leads me to believe Roland's father was adopted."

Adele considered that possibility. Then she considered another. She handed Lucas the folder.

"Here, I have to go."

"Where?"

"To talk with someone who I'm now certain knows a lot more about this."

Lucas put the file down. "Who?"

Adele paused right before she reached the stairs and turned around. "Roland's biological grandmother."

"Say what now?"

Adele hardly heard the words as her feet scampered down the stairs almost as quickly as her mind raced. She sprinted to the Mini and took off for Roche while silently praying that her hunch was, in fact, true.

Roland Soros wasn't the last of his kind after all.

34.

Mother Mary Ophelia didn't appear too surprised when Adele came right out and asked her if Roland was her grandchild. Instead, she merely stiffened slightly, closed her eyes for a few seconds, and then motioned for Adele to follow her as she walked away from the convent.

"This is *my* business not the church's."

It was the same path to the lookout Roland had taken Adele on. The early afternoon air was warm and the sky clear. The old nun moved through the tall grass quickly. When she reached the lookout, she stopped, turned around, and stared at Adele until Adele looked down.

"How long have you suspected?" Ophelia asked.

"Not long," Adele answered. "So, it's true?"

"Yes, it's true. I'm Roland's grandmother. His father Jack was my son."

"But you're a nun. I didn't think that having children was allowed."

Ophelia's lips pressed tightly together. "I'm also a woman. At the time it happened I was young like you and Charles Soros was, well, a very remarkable and charismatic older man. We were infatuated with each other. It happened. I don't regret a single moment of that time and I certainly don't regret bringing Jack into the world."

"The church didn't excommunicate you?"

"My superiors didn't know about my condition. We're largely on our own out here. I took a leave of absence and had my child in secret. Charles promised to take care of it all and he did. I gave birth on Orcas Island."

Adele felt a sudden jolt of realization run through her. "Karl Bloodbone delivered your baby."

"He did."

"Is that why you despise him so much?"

"Bloodbone? Yes, as odd and unfair as it might sound, I suppose it partly is. There are few things worse than having someone know a secret you've spent your entire life attempting to hide from the world. A part of you always feels as if they're holding it over you even if they're not. I spent a very long time keeping this secret. He was one of the last who could reveal it."

"Was this the reason Roland's parents moved to Florida?"

Ophelia turned her back to Adele and looked out at the calm waters of Blind Bay that stretched out below them. "Charles once told me how there had always been an invisible layer of cold between Donatella and Jack. She wasn't a cruel woman but a fiercely proud one. Jack was a constant reminder of her husband's betrayal. So, yes, I'm certain that unfortunate dynamic had something to do with Jack's leaving the islands. When he and his wife were killed in the car accident, I was devastated. I hadn't raised him, but he was *my* son. The pain of that loss was many times greater than the pain of birth. I still feel it you know. Not as sharp, but it remains—this dull, aching absence. And then Charles brought Roland back here and he and Donatella raised him. She was just as desperate to have Roland around as Charles was. I believe it was her way of trying to make up for her failure to be more supportive of Jack. Roland was very loved. He wanted for nothing. Donatella made certain of that."

"Having to hide the truth couldn't have been easy."

"No," Ophelia said as she watched a pair of eagles land in the branches of a tall evergreen on the outskirts of the clearing, "but I was grateful for the life Charles and Donatella gave to Roland. I only wish they had done the same for Jack. We all get older and hopefully wiser, but unfortunately that also leads to a great deal of regret for past mistakes that we then only fully realize."

"Do you think Roland knows?"

"If he did, he would have asked me about it by now."

"This place is important to him. He feels safe here."

Ophelia smiled. "Good. That's how I want him to feel when he visits. I worry though."

"About what?"

"That if he was to know the truth about us that his disappointment would take him away never to return; that he wouldn't understand or even care to try. The Soros men can be terribly stubborn and quick to build up walls around themselves. I saw that tendency in Charles, and I see the same in Roland."

"But you don't want to keep that secret between you two, do you?"

"No need to avoid the subject. You mean until I'm dead?"

"Well . . . yeah."

The pair of eagles took off chirping at each other. "What would *you* do, Adele? After all this time. After a child has grown into a man and the events that created him are now so long ago. Think before you answer because if you look at it honestly and compassionately, you'll realize the answer isn't nearly so easy as asking the question."

Adele didn't hesitate to give Ophelia her answer. "I would tell Roland the truth. Come with me back to Roche Harbor."

"Today? *Now*?"

"Sure. Why not?"

For the first time since she'd known her, Adele saw Mother Mary Ophelia visibly shaken. "Oh, I don't know. I'll need to think about it."

Adele shook her head. "You've had *years* to think about it. Roland deserves to know the truth—not later but now."

"You're a young woman with far too little experience about such matters. What you're asking me to do is no easy thing."

"Few things this important are."

Ophelia's chin dropped to her chest. "I'm not sure I can tell him. It makes me feel so guilty for having kept it from him this long."

"The only way to relieve yourself of that guilt is to tell your grandson who you really are. Part of Roland feels so isolated because he thinks he has no family left. You can change that for him. It won't be easy at first, but in time I know he'll come to love you for telling him the truth."

"How can you possibly be so sure of that?"

Adele reached out and took hold of Ophelia's hands. "Because I know Roland. Despite his flaws he's a good man and it will mean the world to him to know he has a grandmother."

"I should have told him sooner. What kind of person keeps such a secret from someone for so long?"

"You're human, Ophelia. You were scared, but now that fear, all of that hiding, it can end, and you can go from here with your grandson at your side. Let me bring you to Roche."

Ophelia's hands were trembling. "I'm so afraid Roland will reject me and never return to the convent. I'll lose him."

"That won't happen. I promise."

Ophelia's head lifted, her shoulders straightened, and the old determined spark in her eyes returned. "Fine. I'll do it. Let's go." She began to walk toward the road. Adele kept quiet, not wanting to say anything that might make the old nun change her mind.

"What's *he* doing here?" Ophelia hissed as they approached the ferry dock.

Karl Bloodbone stood leaning against a tree with his arms folded over his chest. "I have no idea," Adele replied.

"Did you tell him you were coming to see me?"

"No. I didn't tell anyone."

Ophelia stopped twenty paces from Bloodbone and put her hands on her hips. "What do you want, Karl?"

Bloodbone stepped away from the tree. When he smiled, deep lines exploded from the corners of his dark eyes. "Hello again, Ophelia."

"I asked you a question."

"Just visiting."

Ophelia's hands clenched. "I doubt that."

Bloodbone looked at Adele. "Going somewhere?"

"Back to Roche," Adele answered.

"Together?"

"That's none of your business," Ophelia said as she stepped in front of Adele.

"Does this business involve your grandson?"

"Don't."

"Don't what?"

Ophelia's eyes narrowed. "Don't bring up Roland. He's not your concern."

"Roland Soros is all our concern. A terrible darkness descends on these islands. I know you feel it too, Ophelia. We need to be ready for the battle at hand and there will be no greater weapon than the truth."

"I'm not interested in playing your games, Karl. I wasn't then and I'm even less inclined to do so now."

"This is no game. Don't deny the trouble you sense coming. Charles Soros, Delroy Hicks, Edmund Pine, they are no longer alive to do the difficult but necessary work of keeping our islands safe. The barbarians are at the gate and so it is the responsibility of another generation to prepare for the war that's coming."

"As usual you're being overly dramatic."

"And you're dangerously unprepared. I have watched our islands weather many storms, but this next one might well be the worst yet. We need to be united—all of us. If Adele is taking you to Roland so that he might finally know the true history that exists between you then well done.

You're doing your part to help make him stronger. So, with that said I'll let you get to it and wish you both a safe trip back to Roche."

Bloodbone turned away and then turned back and pointed at Adele. "I suspect you already know of the Seattle reporter's unexpected demise?"

Adele nodded. "Yes."

"Then please make certain we don't lose our island reporter in the same way. We need her now more than ever."

"I have no intention of letting anything happen to me."

Bloodbone rose up to his full height and then appeared to somehow grow even taller. He reminded Adele of the ancient madrone tree he had shown her on Orcas the other day and when he extended his long, gnarled finger to point at her again, that image was reinforced even more.

"Ready yourself, Adele Plank. We have arrived at the turning of the tide. All that you were and all that you are meant to be is about to tested. Delroy Hicks thought you up to the task. I pray that you prove him right."

"What version of God does a thing like *you* pray to, Karl?" Ophelia said.

Bloodbone's smile was faint and fleeting—a barely there confirmation of an inside joke with someone or something that only he knew. "There is but one version that matters, Ophelia. The one that listens."

"Oh, I see."

Bloodbone cocked his head. "I'm sorry. I didn't hear you."

Ophelia's cheeks burned red. "I forgot how much you annoy me."

"And I forgot how much you amuse me. We really should do this more often."

"Not a chance."

"Never say never." Bloodbone nodded to Adele and then turned and walked down the road to the ferry dock. He got into a little wooden boat that was tied next to Adele's Chris Craft.

"He rowed here?" Adele said.

Ophelia rolled her eyes. "He likely thinks doing so makes him nobler when it actually just means he has more time to waste than most."

Adele watched stunned as Bloodbone made his way into the deep waters that ran between Orcas and Shaw. Each powerful stroke of the oars steadily propelled him across the channel.

Ophelia was on the move again. "Are we going to Roche or not?"

Adele nodded and then jogged to catch up as Bloodbone's words repeated inside her head.

Prepare yourself, Adele Plank. We have arrived at the turning of the tide. All that you were and all that you are meant to be is about to tested. Delroy Hicks thought you up to the task. I pray that you prove him right.

35.

"**M**y goodness, Mother Mary Ophelia, what a wonderful surprise to see you again. It's been far too long." Tilda continued to fuss over Ophelia as the nun walked the docks of Roche Harbor.

"It has been too long," Ophelia replied. "I'm happy to see you doing so well."

"Do you need a place to stay?" Tilda asked. "Something to eat or drink? Anything you need—my treat. It would be an honor."

"No," Ophelia answered with a shake of her head. "I'm fine, but thank you. I'm afraid Adele has me busy doing something else. Now if you don't mind, we need to get to it and would appreciate some privacy."

"Of course." As Tilda slowed her pace to allow Ophelia and Adele to walk ahead, she gave Adele a look that made clear she expected an explanation soon regarding what was going on. "I'll be up at the hotel if you need anything. Please don't hesitate to ask."

Adele pointed to her sailboat. "This is my home here."

Ophelia smiled. "Ah, yes, Delroy's old haunt. You don't find it claustrophobic staying down in there?"

"No, not at all. It's cozy. If you're looking for something larger that would be Roland's accommodations. There it is over there."

"I don't understand. I thought the Soros yacht was lost in a fire?"

"It was. Roland recently purchased another one just like it and had it delivered here. He's living on it while his house on the hill gets built."

"House on a hill?"

"Yes. Look up there."

"Goodness," Ophelia said. "It's a castle."

"Pretty much."

"So, he sold his family's property in Friday Harbor?"

"He did. Knowing Roland, I'm sure he managed to squeeze top dollar out of the sale."

"I can't imagine Tilda is happy about having Roland's new home looming over her hotel like that."

"She definitely has an opinion on the matter. Then again, Tilda has an opinion on just about everything that goes on here and when it comes to Roche Harbor it's her opinion that matters most. I don't think Roland moving in is going to change that much."

Ophelia continued to look around. "I forgot how much I missed coming here. Roche has always been such a unique mix of old charm and modern mystery. Charles loved it here. Don't tell Tilda, but from time to time he spoke of buying the place up—all of it."

"Roland was planning to sort of do the same. He's hoping to develop some of the vacant lots behind the resort into vacation rentals. If he loses the bank deal, though, I'm not sure he'll be able to move forward with the plan. At least not right away."

"Don't you just get a kick out of the Soros men and their perpetual financial schemes?" Ophelia said with a smile.

"I figured you for someone who would dislike that kind of thing. You know, money being the root of all evil and whatnot."

"There's nothing wrong with a good dose of ambition so long as it doesn't devolve into outright greed. And it's no easy thing attempting to change a man's way of thinking. They are what they are—Roland included. Admit it. That ambition is a big part of what makes him so attractive."

"That might be true, but it's also what sometimes makes him nearly intolerable to me and a lot of other people."

"Ah, there's often a fine line between attraction and revulsion, and you'll find they often dance together."

Adele shrugged. "I suppose. Are you ready to talk to Roland?"

Ophelia looked up at the yacht and sighed. "I don't know."

"Sure, you do," Adele said as she took Ophelia's hand. "That's why you're here."

Ophelia pulled away and scowled. "Don't think for a second you can force me to do anything I don't want to, young lady."

"Hey, Mother Mary Ophelia, what are *you* doing here?" Roland stood with his hands pressed against the varnished wood railing of his yacht. The sleeves of his white dress shirt were rolled up to his elbows and the first few buttons were open, partly exposing his smooth tan chest. His hair was tousled by the light breeze blowing across the marina.

Ophelia stiffened and stepped behind Adele. "I'm so sorry, but I'm losing my nerve. Let's just go. This was a mistake."

"It'll be fine. Just tell him the truth. It's the truth I'm certain he's always wanted to hear. Roland isn't without family. He has you and that is going to mean so much to him."

Roland walked down the boarding ramp barefoot and smiling. "Is everything okay?"

"Yes," Adele answered. "Ophelia would like a moment to speak with you in private."

The smile fell from Roland's face. "Oh, okay. Sure. Here, let me help you aboard." He put his arm around Ophelia and guided her toward the yacht.

When Adele didn't follow, Ophelia looked back. "Aren't you coming with us?"

"No. This is a conversation you two should have alone."

Roland appeared confused by the response while Ophelia looked even more nervous. After getting Ophelia inside the yacht Roland reappeared at the top of the boarding ramp. "What's this all about?"

"Just listen and keep an open mind and heart. It took a lot of courage for her to come here."

"You know, I was in a great mood today. Now I'm worried that's all about to change."

"What Ophelia has to tell you is good news, Roland."

"Will I catch you later?"

"Sure. I'm going up to the hotel to see Tilda for a bit and then I'll swing by in an hour or so. That sound good?"

Roland nodded as he scratched his beard. "I'll take it. See you then."

"Okay. And be nice to Ophelia. She's very nervous."

"Of course. I think it's a little weird that you think you need to tell me that."

Adele smiled. "Talk to you soon." She turned and walked away but knew Roland was watching her go. She crossed her fingers and hoped his talk with Ophelia resulted in something grandmother and grandson both needed most at this time—understanding.

Tilda was outside the hotel watering the planter boxes that bookended the main entrance. "What are you up to now, Adele?" she said without turning around.

"Hopefully a long overdue family reunion between an old woman and her grandson."

Tilda dropped the hose. "What?"

"Don't act so surprised. Knowing how observant you are I'm guessing you already suspected something yourself."

"That's an old rumor." Tilda's eyes narrowed as she looked across the marina at Roland's yacht. "One that you now apparently believe to be true."

"People knew about Ophelia and Charles Soros?"

"There were some long ago whispers, but why do *you* think she's Roland's grandmother?"

"I saw the evidence."

"And did this evidence involve information given to you by the son of a beloved island doctor?"

"No comment."

Tilda leaned down to smell a newly bloomed tulip. "I planted a few of these last fall. I was told they would smell like apricot, but I think it's closer to honey."

"It's nice to see you taking the time to smell the flowers these days."

"Actually, I was politely changing the subject. I just hope today's unexpected news doesn't ruin Roland's good mood."

"Do you know something about that?"

"What?"

"Roland's mood."

"I do, but I'll leave it to him to explain it to you."

"Does it involve the bank sale?"

"It does. The buyer backed out."

Adele's face tightened. "Oh, no. Why would he be happy about that?"

"He wasn't, but then a potentially better opportunity presented itself courtesy of yours truly. I started working on it as soon as I heard his intention to sell."

"Okay, no more playing coy. What's going on?"

Tilda smirked. "You have your secrets and I have mine." She cocked her head. "Do you hear something?"

Adele looked back toward the marina. "It's coming from Roland's yacht."

Roland was on the bow laughing and dancing with Ophelia as Sister Sledge's *We Are Family* blared from the yacht's state-of-the-art sound system. The sight made both Adele and Tilda break out into ear-to-ear grins.

"Well, that didn't take long," Adele said.

"Seventies party music for the win," Tilda added.

When Roland took a joyous Ophelia by the hand and carefully twirled her around in circles, Adele covered her mouth and shook her head. It was one of the most beautiful things she had witnessed in quite some time. After Roland started to shout the song's refrain as he clapped and cheered and was then joined by Ophelia doing the same with even more gusto it made Adele so happy she nearly cried.

Tilda was still grinning. "You know, sometimes life really is good."

Yes, it was—especially when living it in the San Juan Islands.

36.

Another meeting of what Fin had earlier jokingly referred to as the Roche Harbor Round Table was underway inside of Tilda's private residence. Roland sat with Ophelia holding her hand. Lucas, Tilda, Sandra Penny, and Adele were there as well.

"If you really think you can get it done, I think it's a great idea," Adele said.

Tilda refilled her wine glass. "We'll get it done. I've already received verbal commitment for the initial $5 million payment to Roland, half of which I'm putting up myself using the hotel as collateral."

Adele looked at Roland. "You're really on board with this? Five million dollars is a far cry from the $87 million you were going to get from the bank sale."

"Thanks to Agent Eaton and his meddling that $87 million is gone," Roland replied. "Yet even though the money coming to me is less it's a better deal for the community. So yes, I'm fine with it."

"Roland will also maintain majority interest and CEO status," Tilda added. "And with people and businesses on the islands now having the ability to personally invest in private equity shares of the bank, they'll remain loyal customers and partners even if a big box bank makes its way here. It's a win-win-win."

Ophelia nudged Roland. "It's good business and that's something your grandfather always approved of."

Sandra cleared her throat. "I just want to say thank you again to everyone here for putting their trust in me. I'm so honored to be given the opportunity to be the president of the new Soros Island Community Bank. I also want to apologize to you, Adele. I didn't mean to scare you like I did. I panicked and acted stupidly."

"Apology already accepted, Sandra," Adele said. "I know you'll do a great job. You've already been the face of the bank for quite some time. Roland is lucky to have you running things. We all are."

Roland raised his whiskey glass. "Here-here."

"How long to finalize the deal?" Lucas asked.

"Not long," Tilda answered. "A few months. We'll start with the initial $5 million in shares and then go from there. The reaction from local investors has been overwhelmingly positive."

"It's a brilliant idea," Roland said. "We keep the Soros name on the building, Sandra continues to run the business like only she knows how, and I continue to pursue my interest in giving back to the islands. Tilda had it right. It's win-win-win." He leaned forward to look at Tilda. "Are you sure you want to leverage your hotel though? You've been debt-free for a very long time."

Tilda tilted her head upward. "It's not debt but an investment —one that includes a joint venture between you and I and your Roche Harbor development plan."

Roland's eyes narrowed. "You're not the boss of me."

Everyone laughed.

A short time later, Adele watched from the hotel's balcony as Roland walked with Ophelia to his yacht. He was going to give her a ride back to Shaw Island on his dinghy.

"Neither of them looks like they want to let the other one go," Lucas said as he came up to Adele and stood beside her. "Quite a thing to find out something like that— a grandmother you never knew you had. He seems to be processing it all well enough. And opening his bank up to local investors? That's really something. I guess there's a lot more to Roland than I gave him credit for."

"Funny," Adele said, smiling. "I bet he'd say the exact same thing about you."

"Yeah, I suppose he would. We're all getting older, aren't we? More responsible, respectful, and understanding."

"Any news on the Vasa situation?"

Lucas grunted. "I didn't want to bring it up during the meeting and spoil all the good news. Agent Eaton shared something with me the other day."

"What is it?"

"Eaton is positive that Liya Vasa is coming for us. He wouldn't tell me how he knows, but I don't think he was lying. He assured me the feds will do all they can to keep her away from here but also admitted there's no way to guarantee our safety. If Liya intends to return to the islands, she'll most likely find a way."

"And did he say anything about Marianne Rocha's death being connected to the Russians?"

"No, but my Interpol contact did. Apparently, there was some chatter about it in Moscow, which means Liya's father Vlad was aware of it. That doesn't necessarily mean he was directly involved."

"And it doesn't mean he wasn't."

Lucas nodded. "Right."

"So, what do we do?"

"We stay vigilant. We wait. And we go on living our lives." Lucas put his hand on Adele's shoulder. "I have to get back to Friday Harbor and start reviewing applications."

"Applications? For what?"

"The county council finally gave me funding for a third deputy. I'm hoping to start interviewing candidates next week."

"That's some good news."

"Got that right. It'll sure be nice to have the help. Anyways, you take care, Adele."

"You too, Sheriff Pine."

After Lucas left Tilda took his place next to Adele and they both watched Roland carefully helping Ophelia to step down into the dinghy. "I don't recall ever seeing Roland as happy as he was today," Tilda said. "You did that you know. You brought them together and in doing so made two fractured people whole again."

Adele knew Tilda was right about Roland's happiness but wasn't comfortable taking all the credit. "I just helped them to know the truth about each other."

"Don't undersell truth. It's a powerfully important thing."

Tilda pointed at Roland and Ophelia as they headed out of Roche Harbor on the dinghy with their arms still around each other. "You see them together like that? Both are far stronger now because of the truth you gave to them."

Adele was reminded of Bloodbone's earlier comments to Ophelia prior to their meeting with Roland:

...Charles Soros, Delroy Hicks, Edmund Pine, they are no longer alive to do the difficult but necessary work of keeping our islands safe. The barbarians are at the gate and so it is the responsibility of another generation to prepare for the war that's coming... I have watched our islands weather many storms, but this next one might well be the worst yet.

We need to be united—all of us. If Adele is taking you to Roland so that he might finally know the true history that exists between you then well done. You're doing your part to help make him stronger.

Adele also felt a pang of yearning watching Roland shower his grandmother with so much affection. It was another side to him she had suspected was there but until now hadn't really seen. He had an obvious devotion to family that made him that much more attractive to her.

"So, are you really ready to be in business with Roland?"

Tilda smiled as she swirled the last bit of wine in her glass. "He was going to try to change Roche regardless. This way I have a say in the matter. His intentions were noble. Now I can provide him the good conscience to go with that intent."

"Still, that's a lot of change coming your way and Roland can be a handful sometimes."

"My life had become far too small, Adele. I was retreating further and further behind the walls of this hotel. I'm done with that. Roche Harbor is my home. I intend to keep this place right for future generations and am now confident Roland is the one to help me to do that. I value your ability to judge good character and don't think I haven't noticed how much you've been judging Roland Soros since you first stepped onto our islands. If he's good enough for you he's good enough for me."

Adele felt her cheeks flush. "See?" Tilda said. "Every year that passes your feelings for him go deeper and deeper. If Roland wasn't a good man that wouldn't be the case. I welcome the chance to work with him. Who knows? Perhaps someday in the not-too-distant future I'll watch your children playing in the resort gardens below or see them learning to drive a boat in the harbor."

"Children? *With Roland*? I think you're getting way ahead of yourself."

Tilda shrugged. "Perhaps. Perhaps not. The winds of time are always at our backs, relentlessly pushing us forward into the waiting beyond. The difference between now and then can feel like the blink of an eye."

"If kids do come along someday, I'll be sure to have them call you Grandma Tilda." Adele thought that would make Tilda bristle, but instead she smiled and nodded.

"Grandma Tilda? You know what? I think I might like that."

The afternoon sun fell across the hotel balcony. Adele closed her eyes and welcomed the warmth on her face. A breeze carried the scent of newborn spring. A few boats from the north were entering the marina. In the coming weeks there would be dozens more arriving until every slip was filled and the docks overflowed with busy summer activity.

"You have plans for the evening?"

Adele nodded. "I have a column to write. I've been so busy I haven't had time yet, so now it's down to the wire. What about you?"

"Oh, I'm feeling a little tired. I'll probably go to bed early but if Roland and you want to stop by later for a nightcap just let me know. I can make a fire. Might be the last one until the fall."

"I'm not sure if he's staying over at the convent on Shaw with Ophelia, but I could come by later if you want."

"Don't worry about it. You focus on your work. I'll likely be asleep by the time you're done anyways. We can get together tomorrow." Tilda looked out at the water. "Did you know Charles Soros, Edmund Pine, and Delroy Hicks used to regularly stand here on this balcony to discuss the news of the day?"

"No, you never told me that before."

"Well, they did. Those three were such impressively interesting men in their own unique ways. Charles could be a bit reticent, sometimes even brooding, until he had his second drink in him and then his mood would lighten, and he'd be laughing at all the jokes Delroy would tell. Edmund was most often the bridge between those two. He was kind, quiet, and thoughtful—every inch of him representative of the family doctor he was so proud to be. As for Delroy, he was the same then as when you knew him at the end of his life. Everything was interesting and new and worthy of being enjoyed to the fullest. They were all so strong, so determined, so full of life.

"Charles was the oldest and the first to pass. Delroy and Edmund continued to come here even as Edmund's dementia took its terrible toll. It seemed no matter how bad a day he was having his old friend Delroy could temporarily lift that burden and help him to recall better days. And then Delroy was gone as well and Edmund was permanently buried under the haze of Alzheimer's until he too left us for good.

"The absence of those three . . . I used to wonder if a place like this could ever recover from such a loss. And then Roland took over his grandfather's business, Lucas returned to the islands to become our new sheriff, and of course there is your arrival as well. I can't help but now feel that the balance has been restored."

"I won't speak for Roland or Lucas, but I don't think I'm comfortable being compared to Charles Soros, Edmund Pine, or Delroy Hicks. I still have a lot more growing to do."

Tilda arched a brow. "Don't we all? What's your column going to be about?"

"So much has happened this week I'm not really sure how to go about putting it all down in a way that'll make sense to the reader. I want to mention the visit from Fin, the time on Orcas, and some of what we learned about Bloodbone while still maintaining his privacy."

"Nothing about the new bank deal?"

"Right, and now there's that as well. It's going to be a long night of work at the keyboard." Adele felt her phone vibrate. It was a text from Roland.

Pulling into Shaw now. Ophelia is going to make us dinner. Wanted you to know how grateful I am for bringing us together in a way we weren't before. I have family! See you tomorrow when I get back to Roche. YOU. ARE. AMAZING. -Roland

"Judging by the smile in your eyes I'm guessing it's good news," Tilda said.

Adele read the message a second time, felt that now familiar yearning to be with Roland again, put the phone away, and looked up. "Yeah."

It was time to get to work.

37.

The Island Gazette

Ravens, and Crystals, and Bank Deals, Oh My!

by Adele Plank

In the last issue I promised readers some answers regarding the legend of Karl Bloodbone and the alleged powers of Orcas Island crystals. So, will I be making good on that promise in this issue of *The Island Gazette?*

Yes and no.

I did meet an older gentleman who goes by the name Karl Bloodbone. I also met Mr. Bloodbone's pet raven, George. If you think that's an odd combination, you'd be right, but then again these are the San Juan Islands where what normally passes for unusual isn't really so unusual at all.

As to how old this current version of Karl Bloodbone may or may not be remains left to speculation. What I am more certain of is his kindness, patience, and consideration. At first glance he's an intimidating sort, all deep edges and rough angles, and there is unquestionably a great deal of wisdom and life experience residing within those dark eyes of his. Like all of us who choose to live here, he has a very deep love for the islands and wants to see them nurtured and protected.

Ah, but what of those Orcas Island crystals? Are they the key to good health and long life? Some think so. Others dismiss such belief as misguided or even desperate. The truth is most likely found somewhere in the middle. There is an undeniable mystical-magical quality to Orcas with its fog-drenched peaks and rocky-green valleys. The earth there does talk, though what the true nature of that conversation is remains a mystery—at least to me. I've held some of those genuine Orcas crystals, felt their odd mix of cool warmth, and watched the light dance upon the hard surface of their multi-colored skin. After doing so did I feel healthier? Stronger? More clear-headed?

Not really.

That's not to say there isn't some truth regarding the power of those crystals, but perhaps that truth originates from a simple act of faith—that if you believe long enough and hard enough, the impossible can be made possible.

Who knows?

I am blessed to have met Karl Bloodbone and doubly blessed that I can now call him friend. If some choose to believe he was somehow around to give advice and guidance to men like Robert Moran and John McMillin more than a century ago, well, that's their prerogative. That isn't nearly so important as having Karl alive and well in the here and now. What is far more certain regarding the health and well-being of people here on the San Juan Islands is that we do, in fact, live longer and healthier lives than those in most any other place in the world. Why that is might not be anything more complicated or extraordinary than it is a place people love to be and that love then requires them to take better care of themselves to help ensure they continue to be a part of this place for as long as possible. I know that's my own plan and I'm certain I'm not the only one.

In other news we have not a pending bank sale but rather a *pending bank transformation*. The Soros Bank has long been a fixture of our island community, established by arguably the single most important architect of the region's modern era, Charles Soros. When Charles passed away, full ownership was transferred to his only grandson and heir, Roland. Now Roland is giving local businesses and residents the opportunity to personally invest in the bank that has already invested so much in them, an effort that will transform the Soros Bank into an even greater community endeavor that will, in turn, further help to maintain local control of our islands.

Longtime Roche Harbor Hotel owner Tilda Ashland is spearheading the effort with the capable assistance of newly promoted Soros Bank president Sandra Penny. Roland Soros will remain on as majority shareholder and CEO. Initial interest from local investors is said to be considerable so if you want to get in on this opportunity you best do so now as the available private equity shares are limited. Please contact Sandra Penny at the Friday Harbor branch for more information.

Finally, as spring arrives at long last to shrug off winter's dark coat, I am reminded of some lines from Dublin poet James Stephens and his ode to the coming season and would like to dedicate it to another new friend who will hopefully read this back in Ireland.

We all miss you, Fin, are hopeful for your return, and very sorry for the loss of your mother.

Go, Winter, now unto your own abode,
Your time is done, and Spring is conqueror
Lift up with all your gear and take your road,
For she is here and brings the sun with her:
Now are we resurrected, now are we,
Who lay so long beneath an icy hand,
New-risen into life and liberty,
Because the Spring is come into our land.

38.

"**Y**ou're dead. It happened the moment you murdered Vlad. You just didn't know it yet. So, tell me. Was it worth it? Or do you wish it was you who died at the bottom of the cliffs of Rosario and not my brother? At least then your friends might still be alive. Roland, Lucas, Tilda . . . they're all gone now. Would you have sacrificed yourself so that they might live? Are you truly as noble as you are pretty? No, you don't fool me, little girl. In the end you're a coward like all the others who stupidly chose to cross my family. Others like the annoying Seattle newswoman who dared poke her nose in places she had no business doing so. Yes, she is gone, too, because it is what I wanted, and I *always* get what I want. And do you know what it is I want right now, Adele Plank? To watch the life leave your eyes. I want to see the blood pumping out of your body. I want to hear that last final death rattle wheezing from your lungs.

"What? Nothing to say? Ah, you're not so tough when you know the knife is about to slice your neck, are you? Human skin is very much like gift wrap. Did you know that? It tears so easily. I am not going to merely cut your neck though. No, I'm going to remove your entire goddamn head from your pathetic little body. You'll feel every bit of that first cut. I'll make sure of that. It will be slow and deliberate. The blood will flow. Oh, so much blood. You will scream and scream until you can scream no more. Not because you are dead but because I will sever the cartilage that is your windpipe. You will feel it. You will hear it. And I will smile as I continue to cut deeper and deeper until there is nothing left.

"Go on. Stop averting your eyes and look at your friends over there. See how they stare at you. Their heads are now vacant rooms—nobody home. The sheriff fought so hard. Even with his hands and feet bound it took two men to hold him down. He raged like a bull, but as his blood poured down his chest even he weakened and then gave in to the inevitable. Roland fought as well, but he also attempted to bargain—not for his life but yours. He offered a great deal of money for me to let you go, but this isn't about money, Adele Plank. No, this is about honor. This is about a code. And this is about respect. One cannot murder a Vasa and have it go unpunished. My family has survived far more powerful enemies than you. The ending of your pathetic life is little more than a bit of brief entertainment and distraction.

"And let me tell you more about Tilda. In many ways she was by far the strongest of the three. There was no fighting. No begging. No bargains coming from her. It was almost enough to make me regret cutting her head off. *Almost*. She stared into my eyes and I into hers as the skin of her throat was parted. Perhaps for just a second there was a hint of panic, but it was quickly replaced by a refusal to show me any fear. Not even a tiny bit. I respect that.

Such a shame it was your actions that led to the ending of her life.

"It is now your turn to feel the blade, Adele. Will you fight like Lucas? Will you bargain like Roland? Or will you attempt to hide your fear like Tilda? I really do hope you scream for me. I have waited so long to hear it."

Adele finally looked up. "Then stop talking and just do it, you crazy bitch." Her hands were tied behind the chair she sat in. The space was lit by a single bulb that hung from the ceiling directly over her head. Beyond the light was impenetrable darkness.

Liya emerged from the gloom, grabbed a fistful of Adele's hair with one hand, yanked her head back, and then pressed an already bloodied 12-inch knife against her throat with the other hand. "Beg," she hissed.

"Go to hell," Adele growled.

"Stupid girl trying to act tough, but I can feel the terror coming off you. C'mon now, beg for your life and I might show you mercy. Perhaps your having to live out your remaining days knowing that you were the cause of your three friends' deaths will be punishment enough." Liya pressed her cheek against Adele's and whispered into her ear. "Tell me how badly you wish to live. Beg for your—"

Adele snapped her head sideways and bit down on Liya's lower lip as hard as she could. Liya cried out, dropped the knife, and fell backwards. She brought her hand to her mouth, looked down, and saw her fingers covered in her own blood. Adele spit out a chunk of Liya's lip and then grinned at her, exposing a row of blood-soaked teeth.

"You bitch." Liya picked up the knife. "Now you die."

"Bring it," Adele snarled back at her.

Liya lunged, digging her nails into Adele's scalp and pulling back her head to again expose her throat. Adele felt the blade pressing against her skin. Liya gasped as she struggled to catch her breath.

The first cut was made.

Adele screamed.

The knife went deeper.

Adele panicked as she felt blood rushing into her mouth and throat. She heard a horrible gurgling squeal and then realized she was the one making the sound. With each mad beat of her heart more blood oozed from the wound. More skin was cut, then tendon, cartilage, and finally bone as the blade worked its way through the front of her throat and into the spinal cord.

Liya withdrew the knife and knelt in front of Adele smiling. "Seeing my face will be your eternity. Your heart is slowing. You have just seconds left. I wonder if you can still hear me."

Only a remnant of brain stem kept Adele's head attached to her body. There was no more pain. There was no more anything. Liya's face retreated into oblivion and soon her voice did the same.

Adele was alone without the power to see, or hear, or feel. It was the absence of everything, and it terrified her far more than the cut from Liya's blade. And then even her terror retreated into horrible nothingness.

It was as if she had never been.

From somewhere beyond the beyond came a sound.

A flutter of wings.

A croak.

The call of a raven.

Adele's remaining consciousness was a flickering candle, barely burning and in danger of going out completely, but the raven's arrival gave her hope. As its call grew stronger, so too, did Adele's flame.

The raven's cry was suddenly more urgent.

"That old bird can't save you," Liya whispered. "It is done."

Adele gasped as she sat up in bed while frantically feeling her throat with both hands. *I'm okay. It was just a nightmare. It wasn't real. None of it was real. I'm in my sailboat. Roland, Lucas, Tilda . . . we're all safe.*

The hammering in Adele's chest subsided. The trembling in her hands lessened. She breathed deep, pushed the images of the nightmare away, shuffled out of bed, and started to make some much-needed morning coffee when something made her stop everything.

A flutter of wings.

A croak.

The call of a raven.

Adele leaned forward and looked out the porthole over the galley sink and came face to face with George. Clamped between his beak was a piece of twine and at the end of that twine was a small crystal. He hopped backwards, dropped the twine, squawked loudly, and then took off.

It was an especially beautiful Roche Harbor morning. Adele stepped onto the dock, reached down, and picked up the necklace. Despite its small size the heart-shaped crystal felt unusually heavy in the palm of her hand. She slowly traced its uneven edges with the tip of her finger and then slipped the crystal over her head and around her neck.

"Hey, you. I'm making eggs. You want some?"

Adele smiled but didn't turn around. "Can you do over easy?"

Roland spoke low and slow, like warm syrup being poured over French toast. "I'll do it however you like it."

"I'll take the eggs. You can keep the perverted innuendo."

Roland laughed. Adele turned around. "How's that George Harrison song go?" he asked. "The one where he says you were perverted too?"

"While My Guitar Gently Weeps?"

"Yeah, that's the one. Good tune. So, should I start cracking those eggs?"

"You get to cracking," Adele answered. "I'll bring over the coffee."

After Adele went back into the sailboat and started to pour the coffee, she heard George Harrison singing of someone being controlled, bought and sold, learning from their mistakes, and unfolding the love that was within them.

Roland was right.

It was a good tune.

39.

Three weeks later.

"C'mon, get off that thing and let's go for a morning swim."

Adele closed her laptop and joined Roland at the back of the yacht. "I had to make sure Jose received the pics for the story so we don't miss our deadline. You know how my public demands they get their island news on time."

Roland rolled his eyes. "*Your public*, huh? Girl, you need to learn to unplug and take it all in. I mean really—just look where we are."

The place was Desolation Sound, a 37-mile stretch of protected fjords bookended by the massive snow-capped peaks of the Coastal Mountains located on the northernmost edge of British Columbia's Sunshine Coast that had long been used as the primary seaway connection between the waters of northern Washington state and untamed Alaska. The Burger yacht took them there at a leisurely 12-knot pace that afforded them ample time to enjoy the remarkable views which, at one point included watching a mother grizzly and her two cubs foraging for food on a remote stretch of beach a few miles north of the mouth of the Powell River.

"You sure about the temperature?"

Roland took off his shirt. "These are some of the warmest waters north of Mexico. I promise." He stepped out onto the swim step, bent his knees, and dove in.

"Well," Adele said. "How is it?"

"Perfect."

Adele undid her robe and let it fall to the floor, revealing the almost-nothing-to-the-imagination white bikini she had bought for the trip. "Well? How is it?"

Roland whistled. "Ms. Plank, I do believe you just managed to make perfect even better."

"I really hope you're not lying to me about the temperature."

Roland grinned while floating on his back. "Only one way to find out."

Adele jumped.

The rest of the morning was spent swimming, grabbing a quick brunch inside the yacht, and then using the dinghy for the rest of the day to poke around the nooks and crannies of the rocky shoreline, which included briefly following a massive humpback whale as it slowly made its way north. By the time they returned to the yacht the light from the setting sun arced across the glasslike water in shimmering slivers of golden amber.

"This," Roland said, "is a 1987 Opus One—a Napa Valley red. It's one of the few bottles of wine left from my grandfather's collection. I've been waiting to open it so I could share it with just the right person." He looked down at his watch. "Actually, she should have been here by now."

"Careful, smartass."

Roland had prepared a light meal of caviar and crackers to go with the wine and laid it out on a table on the bow of the yacht. He pulled out a chair for Adele and filled her glass.

"Mm," Adele said after sitting down and taking a sip. "It's very good."

Roland swirled his wine, had a drink, and nodded. "Made even better by the company I get to keep. And we pretty much have the place to ourselves. The nearest vessel is anchored a half-mile away."

Adele peered over the rim of her glass. "I guess that means we can make all the noise we want."

"Hold that thought." Roland got up, went inside, and then came back.

"Forget something?"

Roland cocked his head. "Wait for it." When the music started to play, he smiled. "There it is."

"You and your music."

"Hey, I paid a lot of money for this sound system and I'm a man who expects a strong return on investment." He stuck his hand out across the table. "Would you do me the honor of a dance?"

"Such a formal proposition."

Roland shrugged. "I thought it might improve my chances of getting you out of those clothes later."

"Is that right?" Adele leaned forward. "Just between you and me, I already like your chances in that department. That said, I'm happy to have that dance first."

Roland stood, took Adele's hand, and led her to the front of the bow. Despite the evening chill he remained shirtless and barefoot. He drew Adele in close and lightly pressed his hand against the small of her back. His skin smelled of soap and saltwater. "This is it," he said.

Adele looked into his eyes. "What?"

"The perfect day. I'm never going to forget this for as long as I live. I have a family again and I have you. Nothing else matters as much as that."

A duet by folk artists Johnny Flynn and Laura Marling began to play. Adele felt Roland's heart beating in time to the guitar chords when she pressed her cheek against his chest as he began to sing the words to her. "The water sustains me without even trying," he whispered. "The water can't drown me. I'm done with my dying . . . where the blue of the sea meets the sky and the big yellow sun leads me home. I'm everywhere now, the way is a vow, to the wind of each breath by and by."

"That's beautiful."

Roland looked out at all the water that surrounded them as the sun's departure revealed a twinkling canopy of stars over their heads. "I first heard it at my grandfather's funeral. Delroy Hicks sang and Lucas's father Dr. Pine played guitar."

"Tilda mentioned those three were pretty tight."

"Yeah, they were. You would never think it looking at them. They were so different, but whenever I saw them together, whatever the chemistry between them was, it seemed to work. Grandmother described them as all trouble and triple the nonsense."

"All trouble and triple the nonsense—kind of like Lucas, you, and me."

Roland chuckled and then spun Adele around. "I don't recall them ever dancing together," he said. "Or doing this." He held Adele's face between his hands and kissed her. When he began to pull away, Adele pulled him closer and kissed him back.

The very last of that day's sun winked and then departed for good. Adele and Roland stood together on the yacht's bow breathing in a future they were more determined than ever to experience together.

When a lone shooting star flashed across the night sky, Roland squeezed Adele's hand and told her to make a wish. She put her arm around his waist and rested her head on his shoulder.

"I don't have to."

Roland looked down at her. "No?"

"No," Adele said with a shake of the head. "It already came true."

Prologue Two

Several years before.

Delroy Hicks raised his whiskey glass high. "To Charles Soros. It's been a while since you left us, but it still feels like it was yesterday. We miss you, friend, but are glad to report your island empire remains intact as your grandson Roland does the family business proud."

"Here-here," Dr. Edmund Pine said as he clinked his glass against Delroy's.

A third glass had been poured in Charles's memory and sat between the two older men on the balcony railing of Tilda Ashland's Roche Harbor Hotel. It was a warm spring afternoon decorated with brilliant blue skies and flowers in bloom.

Edmund set his glass down and turned to Delroy. "Can I admit something to you?"

Delroy refilled his glass. "Better hurry and tell me before you forget."

Edmund had been diagnosed with Alzheimer's the previous year and it seemed with each subsequent month that went by since then a little less of him remained. Joking about it was Delroy's way of coping while also trying to put his longtime friend at ease.

"I never thought you'd have outlived Charles. After your first diagnosis I reviewed your file a hundred times. I saw the blood work, the scans, the final prognosis. Your body was riddled with tumors and yet you refused treatment and then somehow managed to outlive the oncologist who delivered you that original six-to-nine-month death sentence."

Delroy absentmindedly rubbed the heart-shaped crystal that hung around his neck. "What I recall is how angry both you and Charles were when I first refused the chemo."

Edmund scowled. "I was angry?"

"Not as much as Charles. He was *really* upset with me."

"Yes, that's right. I remember now. You two had quite an argument."

Delroy grunted. "That we did. I promised out of spite that I'd outlive him. I don't think either one of us actually believed I'd ever make good on it though. I almost felt guilty that he wasn't still here when I went back to the hospital last year and let them cut out part of my liver and blast me with radiation. They pushed the chemo hard again, but I refuse to allow that poison to be put into me. I may not have much time left but what little there is it'll be my own."

Edmund took a sip of whiskey and stared up at the sun. "As sick as you are, I wonder if you might still outlive me?"

"Stop talking like that. You're the healthiest man I know."

"We both understand that's not really true," Edmund replied. "Physically I'm fine but mentally? It's getting worse—like a door slowly closing right in front of me and there's not a damn thing I can do about it. Just yesterday, I walked out onto my front porch and had no idea why. I stood there for five minutes trying to figure it out and then gave up and went back inside. Things like that are happening to me more and more."

"Lucas is coming back home, right?"

Edmund smiled. "Yes, in a few months. He's hoping to get on with the sheriff's department."

"Well, there you go. And I'll wager he'll be running that department before long."

"Perhaps."

"Perhaps nothing. Mark my words, Edmund. We'll be calling him Sheriff Pine in no time. You'll see." Delroy took off his necklace. "In the meantime, why don't you wear this for a while?"

Edmund shook his head. "You know how I feel about that metaphysical nonsense. I don't require the delusion of hope hanging around my neck. I'm a doctor. A man of science. I have a disease for which there is no cure. Your crystal isn't going to change that."

"*Exactly,*" Delroy said. "So, what do you have to lose? C'mon, just put in on as a favor to me."

Before the Alzheimer's Edmund had been a man who rarely lost his temper, but now that temper showed itself more and more. He angrily swatted Delroy's hand away. "I said no."

The necklace fell and bounced off the red brick walkway below. Edmund's face immediately registered his guilt. "I'm so sorry, Delroy. I'll go right down and get it for you."

Before Edmund had time to turn away from the balcony a large raven landed near the necklace, scooped it up in its beak, and flew off toward Orcas Island. Both men looked at each in shock and then Delroy laughed. "The old bastard took it back."

"What?" Edmund said.

Delroy refilled his glass and shrugged. "That's a story that would take more time to explain than either one of us has." He started to bring the glass to his mouth, stopped, and then pointed at something down by the marina. "Who's that?"

Edmund's eyes followed to where Delroy was pointing. "Do you mean the young woman with the ponytail?"

"Yes, that's the one. She appears to be engaged in some rather serious business."

"Ah, yes. Tilda mentioned something about it to me. Apparently, she's here to conduct an interview with Decklan Stone for her college newspaper."

Delroy's brows lifted. "Since when is Decklan granting interviews? He hardly speaks to me let alone anyone else. What's her name?"

"I'm sorry. I don't recall."

"No matter," Delroy said as he clapped Edmund on the shoulder. "I have a feeling I'll be finding out her story soon enough. Wheels are turning and mysteries await. I just know it. Until then, a final toast?"

Edmund raised his glass. "Toast away, old friend."

"To your son Lucas safely returned. To the continued success of Charles's grandson Roland. To loves past and new loves made. And may we all sneak into heaven a half hour before the devil knows we're dead."

Delroy and Edmund downed their drinks and said their goodbyes, including a promise to see each other again soon.

It was another day in Roche Harbor.

That alone made it a better day than most.

End.

(NOTE: Please take a moment to leave a review for Roche Harbor Rogue on its Amazon book page. Your feedback is very important to the story's success. Thank you!)

The San Juan Islands Mystery series will continue with:

The Turn Point Massacre

Visit ulstermanbooks.com for updates and deals!

About the Author

D.W. ULSTERMAN IS A USA TODAY FEATURED AUTHOR WITH NEARLY HALF-A-MILLION BOOKS SOLD SO FAR.

He is the writer of the Kindle Scout-winning San Juan Islands Mystery & Romance series published by Kindle Press as well as the #1 bestselling family drama, The Irish Cowboy.

He lives with his wife of twenty-five years in the Pacific Northwest. During the summer months you can find him navigating the waters of his beloved San Juan Islands. He is the father of two grown children and is also best friends with Dublin the Dobe.

CPSIA information can be obtained
at www.ICGtesting.com
Printed in the USA
LVHW041652140722
723438LV00001B/115

9 781098 583422